I stepped outside, began calling the dog's name. His path through the dewy grass was clearly visible but ended under the trees between our property and Letty MacNair's.

Letty MacNair. The fragile, stubborn woman who could take care of herself, thank you very much. No. I thought as I ran. Not Letty. Nobody better have hurt Letty.

The weeds along the uneven drive slapped at my arms. I was forced to slow before I fell. Which door? Where *was* a door? At the left rear corner stood a sagging, covered porch. Its door to the kitchen gaped open, and Barney's muddy tracks led inside. I could hear his worried whimpering.

Wiping sweat from my eyes, I inched along in slow motion, finally pushing the door wide enough to enter. The kitchen was indescribably squalid, the roach eggs and mouse droppings lay among the empty Dorito bags. The muscles in my throat went rigid.

Letty MacNair lay facedown in filth, her wispy hair and ragged clothes caked with blood.

Also by Donna Huston Murray

FINAL ARRANGEMENTS
THE MAIN LINE IS MURDER

Dear Mystery Lover:

One of the most exciting aspects of the DEAD LETTER mystery program is our publication of original paperback mysteries. As any mystery aficionado worth his salt will tell you, the original paperback mystery has a distinguished history stretching back to the classic days of Jim Thompson and Robert Bloch.

Those decidedly *noirish* gentleman wrote of a time and place long gone, but you'd be surprised what can turn up where. In Donna Huston Murray's excellent Ginger Barnes mysteries, Donna takes crime out of the back alleys and places it in the most unlikely, well-lit settings; like at the tony Philadelphia Flower Show in *Final Arrangements*, or at the exclusive Bryn Derwyn academy in *School of Hard Knocks*. Still, despite the books' posh settings along Philadelphia's Main Line, crime does not gain respectability. With Ginger Barnes involved, greed and murder are not to be tolerated.

I've no doubt that if you continue turning the pages of this book, you'll enjoy Donna Huston Murray's latest illuminating paperback original mystery.

Yours in crime,

Dana Isaacson

Dana Edwin Isaacson
Senior Editor
St. Martin's DEAD LETTER Paperback Mysteries

Other titles from St. Martin's Dead Letter Mysteries

DYING TO FLY FISH by David Leitz
LIVING PROOF by John Harvey
CONCOURSE by S. J. Rozan
THE NUN'S TALE by Candace M. Robb
CURLY SMOKE by Susan Holtzer
HOOFPRINTS by Laura Crum
THE TWELVE DEATHS OF CHRISTMAS by Marian Babson
THE PRINCE LOST TO TIME by Ann Dukthas
MURDER IN SCORPIO by Martha C. Lawrence
MURDER IN THE CHATEAU by Elliott Roosevelt
CRACKER: TO SAY I LOVE YOU by Molly Brown
BONDED FOR MURDER by Bruce W. Most
WIN, LOSE OR DIE ed. by Cynthia Manson & Constance Scarborough
MORTAL CAUSES by Ian Rankin
A VOW OF DEVOTION by Veronica Black
WOLF, NO WOLF by Peter Bowen
FALCONER'S JUDGEMENT by Ian Morson

School of Hard Knocks

Donna Huston Murray

St. Martin's Paperbacks

This is a work of fiction. Names, characters, places and incidents are either the product of the author's imagination or are used fictitiously. Any similarity to real persons, living or dead, is coincidental and not intended by the author.

SCHOOL OF HARD KNOCKS

ISBN: 0-312-96104-9

Printed in the United States of America

St. Martin's Paperbacks edition/February 1997

10 9 8 7 6 5 4 3 2 1

To Robynne Daine (How do you spell that, Diane?) Murray, daughter extraordinaire

Many thanks to Dr. George Jeittles, Sgt. Peter Gangl, John T. Rogers and Bernard A. Zbrzeznj—all of whom trusted me with their expert information and, therefore, probably shouldn't be held responsible for what I did with it.

—Donna

Chapter 1

"Today, a burglary on the 6000 block of Argonne Avenue in Bryn Mawr went horribly wrong," said the slender woman on my twelve-inch kitchen TV. When she extended her graceful hand, the house, an elaborate collection of driftwood cubes connected by glass, appeared to rest comfortably on her palm.

"At 10:15 this morning Mrs. Corinne Novak returned home early from her Sunday aerobics class. She said she had been feeling a little ill . . ."

The newscaster displayed flawless ivory skin and perfectly bobbed chin-length black hair. Her collarless blouse and sculpted pink suit said, "I refuse to dress like a man just to get paid like one." Very now. Very Main Line. I decided she should be inside somewhere nibbling hors d'oeuvres rather than telling me bad news while I baked ridiculous little cheese balls.

"Dammit," I muttered in between burning two fingertips and wetting them with my tongue. My culinary efforts smelled like cordite and looked like a kindergarten kid's first effort with clay. After I dropped the four-hundred-degree cookie sheet on the stove-top, my tiny taste treats bounced and rolled like so many black-eyed billiards.

The miniature reporter on my TV shelf pressed on. "Caught in the act, the burglar panicked and the unfortunate Mrs. Novak walked into the business end of a blunt instrument.''

Okay, so she favors Mickey Spillane. Nobody's perfect. But maybe that explains why she's still doing Sunday evening news instead of Prime Time.

I held my fingertips under running water while I fed the cheese balls into the sewage system.

''After the intruder delivered a near-fatal blow to the back of Mrs. Novak's head, he got away with furs, jewelry, and a coin collection valued at eighty thousand dollars. Police believe this to be the same man who has burglarized several other homes in Chester and Montgomery counties . . .''

The wealthiest counties in the state, encompassing most of the Main Line. Ever since I heard that Chester had finally pulled ahead of Montgomery in per capita income, I've been hoping the brilliant industrialists out there on their hobby horse farms would cough up enough in real estate taxes to make ours go down.

I surveyed the inside of the refrigerator. Fortunately, tonight's guest was Rip's mentor, Gregory Burack, who was practically family. Ah. Cream cheese and mango chutney. Plunk the former on a plate, slather it with the latter, stick in one of those little cocktail spreaders with a mallard on it, throw a few crackers in a basket. Back in business.

Pink suit had begun to interview a neighbor. ''I just don't feel safe here anymore,'' said the young mother. Due to the four-year-old straddling her hip her white blouse was wrinkled and askew. ''We're putting our house up for sale,'' she told me sadly. I pushed the TV off with the cracker basket and headed around the corner toward the living room.

Our daughter, Chelsea, intercepted me beside the plank table at the kitchen end of the long main room. ''May I have some money for new sneakers?'' she asked quietly enough that her father and our guest couldn't quite hear.

At thirteen Chelsea was four inches shorter than me, five-foot-two, but still wore her cinnamon-colored hair in a short, curly fluff. Coloring alone identified us as mother and daughter, but this year our body shapes strengthened the resemblance—Chelsea seemed to be adding contours while I struggled to keep mine.

"Please?" Chelsea implored. Her eyelashes were thick and dark, the better to beg with.

"Can we talk about this later?"

As soon as I said that, I realized how carefully our daughter's timing had been calculated. Parents are mellower when they have company. Statistically, they do not say "no" as often as when they are, say, taking out the trash. Children instinctively know how to make use of such information.

"How much?" I asked.

"About seventy?" Chelsea related with a wince.

"No way," I replied.

Moving over to the Main Line when Rip became a headmaster had not meant giving up my favorite flea market. I'm pretty sure the word "frugal" was coined by someone living on a private school salary.

"Mom!"

"Nada," I responded with emphasis as I proceeded to deliver my foolproof hors d'oeuvre to the distressed pine coffee table. The distress was accidental, but set between a blue plaid sofa and a walk-in stone fireplace it worked, at least it would have to work until our son and his friends stopped kicking it.

Chelsea sullenly retreated down the long downstairs hall past Rip's minuscule office and the kids' two bedrooms to our added-on family room.

The men had saved space for me on the living room sofa. Rip, who was diagonally across the coffee table in a wing-backed chair, continued with his story. ". . . so when the whole middle school left the lunchroom clucking and flapping their elbows, she came straight to my office and threatened to quit—for the third time this year."

Behind his silver-rimmed glasses Greg's pale gray eyes crinkled into half-moons. "What did you say?" he asked.

"I wanted to tell her I was very sorry to hear she was leaving and I hoped she'd be happier in her new position at McDonald's—hell, I'd eaten her chicken as often as the kids—but I handed her a tissue and patted her on the back."

"Finding a cook in the middle of the school year . . ." Greg wagged his head.

"I know," Rip agreed. "Scarce as hen's teeth."

Naturally, we were having chicken for dinner.

Feigning confidence, I fixed a cracker for Greg and handed it to him. Guests needed encouragement to try chutney and cream cheese. I happened to like the combination, but then I had been raised by Cynthia Struve, the most eccentric cook in Ludwig, Pennsylvania. I once peeked into one of her pots and discovered she was simmering up a nice meal of pigs' feet, which, now that I think of it, probably explained a lot about both of us.

Greg dispatched the cracker with a pleased glance in my direction and a sincerely mumbled "umm." Of course, he'd been widowed from his second wife a few years and had probably learned to eat like a bachelor again. Bachelors have always been my best customers.

"How's my Lisa doing?" he asked Rip.

"Fine, fine," my husband replied, leaning forward on his knees. "She's got a lot of potential as a teacher. I think she's going to be fine."

Last March when Lisa had been out of college nearly a year, she made it clear to Rip that she hated her job in retail sales and was eager and available to replace the Bryn Derwyn science teacher who was moving to Michigan. Although Rip had worried about the wisdom of hiring the daughter of a friend, he reasoned that she had probably learned enough to get by as a teacher at the Burack breakfast table. As head of the school where Rip first taught, hadn't her father nurtured him through his own arduous first year? Not to mention that Greg had also guided him through the private school administrative maze that positioned him to run his own school at the tender age of thirty-three.

True, Bryn Derwyn Academy was a struggling upstart compared to places that had been chartered by William Penn, but it had potential that Rip was working hard to develop. Not unlike the eager young Lisa.

Now that it was already April, I realized I knew as little as Greg about how Rip's decision to hire her had worked out. I scanned my husband's face for negative undertones but detected no hint of hesitation.

"Good, good." The older man nodded his pleasure over Rip's encouraging reply.

The two men proceeded to discuss the horrors of health insurance plans for small businesses, so I allowed myself to contemplate the various lifestyle options. Married as opposed to single. Children as opposed to single. Children and single, my least favorite choice and the one that most resembled what I had recently been living. Work widow, that was me.

The stove timer interrupted my private griping, and I excused myself to put out the food. We were having a chicken/broccoli/cheese casserole that could be held safely for twenty minutes—a swing-time that had preserved many a Barnes dinner party in the few years we'd been at Bryn Derwyn. Of course, I learned that trick the hard way. While I tossed salad and heated rolls, I eavesdropped via the pass-through to the table.

"Faculty's had cabin fever ever since the last snow . . . Don't know how we'll raise the money for the new gym . . . Neighbor complaining that after school the kids collect in front of his house to smoke cigarettes . . . Ran out of lacrosse uniforms . . ."

"Dinner's ready," I chirped to interrupt Rip's complaints. So far Greg, while bobbing his white head with understanding, had offered remarkably little in the way of advice.

After the kids had fixed their plates and retreated to TV tables and we adults had settled down to our civilized chicken and white wine, Greg finally responded to his protégé's laundry list.

''They're fairly common problems, Rip,'' he remarked while rubbing the back of his arthritic wrist. ''Sounds as if you need to develop some coping techniques.''

I choked on a bit of broccoli and stared at the wise man we had invited to dinner. Could it possibly be true—Rip had not completely settled into his job? Maybe that explained why he worked thirteen hours every weekday and most of Sunday while I felt like a single mother with an adult male boarder.

''How about starting a journal? Good way to blow off steam,'' Greg advised with a casual wave of his wine glass.

Rip snorted. When he lowered his greenish brown eyes to his plate, a clump of his straight brown hair slipped onto his forehead. He raked it back with a hand.

''What's wrong with sex and booze?'' he asked with a smirk. ''Isn't that what everybody else uses?''

My chest felt like an empty cavity. Sex and booze? Where on earth had Rip dug up that insulting, sorry-for-himself remark?

Greg carefully avoided my eyes, a sure sign that he also thought Rip was being a jerk. He chose to contain the damage by addressing the real problem.

''That road leads to divorce, buddy,'' Greg laughed. ''And you don't want to throw away your best asset.'' He very deliberately smiled at me.

I acknowledged his gesture with a grateful sigh.

Rip's arms lay crossed on the table in front of him, causing him to look up at the two of us with an expression flavored with disdain. Then he smiled inwardly and addressed his food.

I gazed at the reflections in my wine and changed the

subject. "When I was cooking, I saw a disturbing item on the news."

"Oh?" Greg eagerly prompted.

"A woman surprised a burglar in her home and he . . . he hit her with something."

"Near here?" our guest asked with concern.

"Yes. A few miles away. Bryn Mawr."

"That's terrible. Did they have a security system?"

"I don't know."

"Do you?"

"Just Barney." I referred to our aging Irish setter, who was friendlier than most salesmen, but noisy.

"You think a burglar would bother robbing us?" Rip asked with derision. He refilled his wine glass. Greg and I waved away his offer to refill ours.

"Why not?" I asked.

"Because this isn't exactly Bryn Mawr." My husband meant that our street was attractive enough but in the context of the Main Line would be described as modest. Our house in particular had been a handyman's special purchased out of financial necessity. Another of Rip's many sore subjects—our mortgage. If he actually started a journal to list his accumulated grievances, it would soon be thick as the Philadelphia phone book. Why, I wondered, was he revealing so many of these dissatisfactions to Greg?

Because before he went the consultant route Greg had been there. Of course.

Quite suddenly I felt abashed. Sitting so firmly in my own seat, I had temporarily forgotten the view from Rip's. To outsiders his duties sounded like at least three full-time jobs. Even a place as small as Bryn Derwyn encompassed the same areas of responsibility as a huge university. Maintenance, fundraising, PR, student recruitment, athletics, curriculum, hiring, firing, alumni, community relations, faculty this and that, student problems of every description, around and around and around again. All very human stuff, all potentially stressful.

And then Rip said, "Gin has been a bit of an alarmist ever since she solved that murder."

My ego took a short leap off a long pier.

"That was quite an accomplishment," Greg said soothingly.

"Thank you," I replied while frigid waves sapped my energy.

"Oh, yes. The police couldn't have solved it without her."

Rip had not been there to hear it, but that sentiment actually had been expressed by my old elementary school acquaintance, then a scrawny black kid who was now a brawny inner-city cop. Put in charge of a murder at the prestigious Philadelphia Flower Show, he soon found that he related to the victim's social strata not at all, while I at least knew how to blend in. "Hi. I'm Ginger Struve Barnes. Welcome to Bryn Derwyn Academy." My mantra. My job.

Yet it was pressure from my mother that originally involved me in the investigation of her friend's murder, and Cynthia had asked me because she knew what I had already done for Bryn Derwyn. And *that* happened to be a story I hoped Rip would never hear.

So, believing my behavior back in March to be a one-time aberration, my husband was now clumsily trying to tease me about it—or so I assumed. Unfortunately, he managed to make my deductive accomplishment sound suspect.

"So now she sees sinister plots everywhere she turns." Shiny lips. Slightly goofy smile. Challenging don't-especially-care-what-I'm-saying stare. My husband wasn't teasing—he was deep into about one wine too many.

There was no percentage in defending myself just now, so I became Mrs. Congeniality, a role I could play forever or until the party ended, whichever came first.

"No, I don't," I replied dismissively. Sometime when Rip might actually listen, I would explain how much that flower show experience had rattled me, how if I currently seemed a little preoccupied by crime, it was because I was trying to cram it back into its proper perspective.

Greg sighed heavily. "Nobody's safe anymore. Used to be people left their doors open, looked out for each other's kids, returned wallets . . ."

"Returned wallets?" Rip laughed.

Greg met Rip's eyes. "I got mine back once." He smiled when he said that.

"When?"

Greg grinned. "Nineteen fifty-two," he admitted with a chuckle, and we all relaxed into ourselves again.

We had coffee and pineapple pie with a walnut crust, and Rip and Greg shifted into male conversational neutral—sports—allowing me to retreat almost willingly to my kitchen chores.

I hoped Greg would take the opportunity to share a few more coping techniques with Rip, yet if another exchange of advice occurred, it was murmured in the hall just before Greg departed. Rip nodded soberly, but I couldn't tell if that was because Greg's point reached its target or because my husband was displaying the deliberate good manners of the inebriated.

My opportunity to fine-tune my reading ended abruptly when Garry shouted, "Mom, I think the Browders are fighting again."

I shrugged to Rip then kissed our guest's cheek. "Good night, Greg," I said. "I better see what's up." Actually, I was pleased to give the men one last moment of privacy.

Our eleven-year-old son waited for me in the family room. Already up to his sister's height, he stretched tall in his ski pajamas, his straight brown hair slicked down from his shower. Oversized bare feet extended from his narrow legs like the last pair God gave out—take 'em or leave 'em. I couldn't tell whether he was distressed or titillated by our neighbors' behavior.

"What made you say the Browders are fighting?" I asked.

"Door slammed."

"You playing newspaper reporter or what?"

He folded back down on the floor, elbows on a sofa cushion, legs waving in the air, the Tinkertoy version of a boy.

"I just thought I'd tell you. You're the one always interested in what everybody's doing."

"You must have me confused with Nana."

"Sorr-eee."

I tried to muss his hair, but he pulled away.

Arms folded as if keeping to myself, I glanced uphill out of the slightly opened window at the far right end of our house. The arguing couple's spotlighted drive was about thirty yards away, just past another narrow drive leading back to Letty MacNair's. The trunk of Eunice Browder's black Mercedes sedan gaped open.

Suddenly Ms. Real Estate herself emerged from her kitchen door, flung two suitcases inside the car's spacious cavity then slammed the lid closed. Thirty seconds later she carried out a large cardboard box, which she loaded into the back seat. Slam, slam, good-bye, Sam. The Mercedes hit forty as soon as Eunice aimed it out of Beech Tree Lane.

"Thought you weren't interested," Garry said.

"Wise guy," I told him as lightly as possible. "It's a school night, buckaroo. Head on out." That'll teach you to be so astute.

I wanted to touch my husband, to reassure myself. I wanted to talk about the disturbing scene I had just witnessed and to read in my husband's eyes that, like me, he didn't want that to happen to us.

When I went back down the hall, Rip was gone. Not literally, thank God. He had closeted himself in the cramped room off the vestibule that we call his office. With his back toward the opened door, I could see him sending his troubles off into cyberspace.

He scrolled off the screen before my hands rested on his shoulders.

"What's really wrong?" I asked.

When he swiveled to look up at me, I saw that the wine glow had dimmed, leaving him weary.

"Nothing, babe," he lied. "Just little things."

"Okay," I said, but I was lying, too.

Chapter 2

Monday morning found me in the perfect mood to replace the innards of a toilet tank. I had a Sears kit and my wrench at hand. All systems were go.

I almost succeeded, too. Got down to the last quarter turn on the little stack of washers and nuts underneath the tank. A very tricky call, I discovered. A quarter turn gave me a slow ooze, but a half turn produced a steady drip. A whole turn of the wrench squirted me in the eye. There was no such thing as starting over.

"We have a leak . . . ," I reported to our plumber's wife, withholding the part about it being my fault because the last time I told the whole truth she guffawed right in my ear. ". . . so could Dominick please stop by as soon as he can?" He knew our house offered only one overall shutoff valve, so he would realize the extent of our inconvenience.

"After lunch," his wife informed me with only a hint of smirk in her voice.

The kitchen clock said ten, about time for a coffee break with my horoscope and "Hagar the Horrible." Fortunately, my clothes, a sweatshirt and jeans, were warm enough for a hurried trip outside on an overcast April day.

Just as I picked the newspaper off the driveway, an unfamiliar car stopped beside the Browders' mailbox. A woman wearing high heels and a mauve raincoat emerged from the vehicle, took the red and white FOR SALE sign of Eunice's company out of her trunk, and proceeded to hammer it into the Browders' lawn with a rubber mallet.

"Quick work," was my first thought.

"The house must be in her name," was my second.

Both insights were immediately underscored by Sam bursting through the front door shaking his fist. Still in his bathrobe, he galloped down the front lawn toward the intruding woman like Lawrence of Arabia.

Under his flapping blue velour robe were yellow-and-blue striped pajama bottoms and apparently nothing else. Vertical stripes emphasized the slenderness of his waist, which spawned a little speculation on my part about whether the garment would endure all the sudden activity.

It also spawned some unsettling speculation about other activities involving pajama bottoms, and my hormones gave me such a jolt that my mouth dropped open.

My best friend Didi watched men, even lusted after them, but not me. Ginger Struve Barnes was too oblivious, too married, too busy to bother. So naturally my response to Sam Browder set off all sorts of alarms. The resulting fears doused what remained of my hormonal rush.

Perhaps the most frightening part was that my disloyal impulse made a certain amount of sense. Rip had grown increasingly distant in recent weeks, and last night's final exchange had shown—for whatever reason—that he preferred it that way. I felt neglected, isolated, and just plain lonely.

So this morning I got the hots for the first attractive man I laid eyes on. Naturally. And yes it was pleasant, and yes my mind went through acrobatics until it decided to be scared as all get out.

Sam ranted and raved a while longer, stomping down grass with his bare feet, pounding his right fist into his left hand. I had retreated to my doorway by then; but I heard his intensity, if not his words.

Finally the invading real estate woman wiggled the sign

to check her work and, lips pressed tight, stalked back to her car. Sam abruptly loped into his house, where I imagined he would be on the phone to Eunice's office within seconds, scorching her ear with his indignation. He worked out of their home, after all.

As for me, I resumed breathing and managed to lower the crushed newspaper from my chest. Then I went inside, away from Sam's marital problems to address my own.

Clearly, this situation required the counseling of a level-headed confidante, someone who knew how to survive—and even bloom—on very little rainfall.

My neighbor, Liz Kelman, was just such a cactus. Her husband serviced some huge corporation's copier needs. The main office was local, the needs—mostly elsewhere. In honor of the warming April weather I changed into a clean chambray shirt. Then I took a white bakery bag of cinnamon buns out of the freezer, clipped Barney to his leash, and locked the door behind us. If Liz was busy, at least the dog would get a walk.

A breeze pleasantly cooled my cheeks and ruffled the long auburn feathering on Barney's legs and ears. All around us grass was greening, birds chirped, and the air teased the nose with that earthy, sappy smell that drives everybody to distraction.

Nearby a struggle was going on. I could hear *oofs* and *ouches* and *thumps*. Barney tugged me past some shrubbery into the street where I could see Bonnie Diamond, our new next-door neighbor to the right, wrestling with a large cardboard carton at the back of her Volvo station wagon.

"Hello," I called.

"Aah!" our new neighbor exclaimed. The carton began to slip off the bumper toward her foot. As Barney and I approached, Bonnie eased it onto the macadam.

"Ginger Barnes from next door," I reminded her. "Want help taking that into the house?"

Bonnie's limp brown hair was restrained by a headband, which unkindly overexposed her pasty round face. Smears of dust dirtied her blouse and slacks. Her worn-looking loafers had obviously been chosen for comfort rather than show. She replied, "Thanks, but I'm putting it into the car."

We each took two corners and easily deposited what felt like a television into the back of the Volvo. Two other boxes were already inside.

"Didn't work," she said with a self-conscious blush.

"Workmanship's awful these days," I hastily remarked. Maybe a little curiosity had crossed my face, but only a little—certainly not enough to cause the woman any embarrassment.

She nodded, and a small silence grew.

"Well, I'll see you tomorrow at Margaret's," I said by way of an exit. Margaret Raymond, an older, dyed-in-the-wool Main Liner, had invited the neighborhood women to a welcoming tea in Bonnie's honor, scheduled for 10:00 AM tomorrow morning to accomodate those of us with school-aged children. For some, these infrequent social events were the only times we actually spoke to each other. For others, such as Liz and me, the old-fashioned custom had fostered a genuine friendship.

Judging by Bonnie's pinched smile, she looked forward to the party more with dread than eagerness. I wanted to reassure her with what I had learned, which was that people who lived on Philadelphia's Main Line were roughly as good, bad, or indifferent as anywhere else; but since that wasn't a driveway sort of conversation, I settled for a wave good-bye and a promising smile.

Barney and I proceeded past the houses to our left, past the local eccentric, Letty MacNair, past Sam and Eunice's and then Margaret and Sol Raymond's, until we reached the Kelman's sizeable cedar shake and black trim edifice. I tied Barney under a decorative red maple, and he rolled and stretched in appreciation of the new spring grass.

"Gin!" Liz greeted me with both surprise and alarm, but luckily no displeasure. She was dressed with tasteful perfection—patterned yellow slacks and a white, short-sleeved sweater. Her short, frosted hair curled toward her face in a style that both hid and emphasized the suntan wrinkles she had nurtured throughout her outdoorsy thirty-five years.

"I should have phoned," I remarked in response to her greeting.

"Nonsense," she said without diminishing my guilt by one iota. "What brings you here?" She smiled and moved back from the door.

I stepped inside. The early American living room was shadowy after the midmorning light outside.

I waved the cinnamon bun bag in the air, replying, "Men," to answer her question.

Liz tilted back at the shoulders and tucked her chin into a grin as she shut the door behind me. "Oh boy, have you come to the right place." The sparkle in her smile suggested that we might be converging on the topic from different directions.

"Coffee?" she then offered hesitantly.

"Do you have time?" I asked. "You look as if you're ready to go out."

"A few minutes," she replied without elaboration.

I settled into my side of a cushioned kitchen alcove, acutely aware of the indefinite, but looming, deadline—not ideal confiding conditions, to say the least.

Liz filled flowered mugs from the coffee pot on her pristine white counter, then set the sticky buns, butter, utensils, and plates on the table in front of me.

As I watched, I tried to decide what seemed different about my neighborhood friend. A veil of privacy perhaps. A lack of candor? This Liz Kelman appeared more self-absorbed than the previous version. Phoney courtesies were out, blunt honesty was in.

Dropping in on her had been a mistake, yet I could think of no polite way to escape.

"What does Ringo think of the new do?" she asked. Teasing me about my "early Beatles" haircut was almost a signal between us, a shortcut to our usual easy familiarity. "I heard he's a grandfather now."

"Good one." My laugh was appreciative, although a bit forced. Still, I didn't mind doing my part; I wanted to get to that comfortable place with her, too.

I asked Liz if she planned to go to Margaret's tea.

After sliding into the breakfast nook across from me, she relaxed her elbows on the table and thoughtfully stirred her coffee. "No," she said. "No, I think this time I'll pass."

"Why?" I blurted.

My friend gave me a surprised glance, then shrugged and stirred her coffee again. To my knowledge, she never added sugar.

"What's the point?" she said. "A roomful of women eating pastries and drinking tea! In this day and age?" She wagged her head. "I just don't feel obligated to waste my time on Margaret's old-fashioned . . . sense of duty."

"We met at Margaret's," I reminded her only half jokingly.

Liz lifted her eyes and blushed slightly. "You walk that fleabag of yours so often we would have met anyway."

"Careful," I teased. "He's almost trained to slobber on command."

She made a dismissive "puh" sound and muttered that Barney had been doing that for years. Then she pointed her chin in the direction of the sticky buns. "So what's the complaint this time? Rip leave a wet towel on your side of the bed?"

"Worse," I intoned dramatically. "I think he's doing his job!"

"Isn't that just like a man?"

Yes, it is. Lots of them anyway, not to mention lots of women, too. But whenever did statistics interfere with a good kvetch?

Liz buttered a bun and savored a big, sinful bite. "Butter really cuts the sugar, doesn't it," she remarked. Her silver tennis racket earrings swung forward and backward as she chewed.

"Ummm," I agreed.

"So farm the kids out for a night," Liz told me, leaving the rest of her recommendation to my imagination.

"Yeah, yeah," I replied, recognizing the advice I could have given myself. Sometimes our common sense refuses to activate until someone else expresses it out loud, so we can actually hear it.

I polished off my bun and used my napkin. "Better go," I said. "Dominick's coming soon."

"You been at it again?" Liz teased.

"I almost had it," I swore with my hand up.

"That's what they all say." She was packaging the remaining sticky buns for me to take home. "Save these for the morning after. I want to hear everything."

"Not bloody likely," I told her.

She smirked conspiratorially, and I felt somewhat better about us. I'd just caught her at a bad time, that was all. That she'd invited me in anyway indicated that she valued my friendship.

Still, I thought she breathed a bit easier now that I was ready to go. Next time I would phone for sure. You never know what could be going on—and sometimes it's best to keep it that way.

"Come to Margaret's," I implored as I prepared to step out the front door. "Bonnie's a country mouse. She needs you."

"Not another one," Liz rolled her eyes.

"Yes," I emphasized. "And I haven't come far enough to solo without you. She's from the Midwest!"

"Lend her your map to the grocery store. Unless you still use it."

I did the tight-lipped grin. "Believe me. Bonnie needs the whole orientation spiel—from A to Z. From the master."

"I'll consider it. But no promises." The door latched decisively, and she was gone.

The yards on Beech Tree Lane sloped downward from the east to the west, so turning from Liz's door put me on an eye level with some of the opposite neighbor's squirrels. This pleasant queen-of-the-hill perspective lasted only briefly because as soon as I untied Barney from the tree he pulled me three car lengths down the drive into a tunnel of trees and shrubs. We emerged onto the street at a fairly lively clip—and I nearly collided with Letty MacNair.

I yelped. The frail, older woman groaned and staggered. I grabbed her arm to steady her.

"Letty, ohmigod, are you all right?" The flesh inside her sleeve felt like bone surrounded by sponge cake.

"No, I'm dang well not all right. Ye nearly skeered me ears off." Her eye wrinkles confirmed that she was peeved.

Barney, however, was delighted to see our neighbor to the left. He smiled and pranced and commenced licking her hand. She briefly blinked with surprise, patted his head, then returned to scowling at me.

"I'm really sorry, Letty." I saw now that the sweater was the same droopy brown cardigan of last year and probably a few years before that. The dress—interchangeable with any I'd ever seen her wear. She had smooth, oval cheeks, no visible eyebrows, and a large-pored nose. Her hair amounted to a handful of limp gray strands fastened with a blue rubber band.

Barney positioned his head under her hand so that maybe she would scratch behind his ears. When that did not occur, he alternately licked and hinted.

"Is there anything I can do for you?" I asked the older woman. The set of her small mouth and recessed chin continued to express her opinion of my recklessness.

"What's that?" she asked with a crafty squint.

"Excuse me?"

"The bag. What's in it?"

Oh, I get it. Change of subject.

"Some sticky buns." I had nearly forgotten the leftovers.

"That'll do then." Letty deftly relieved me of the whole package.

Not a change of subject after all. The sticky buns were payment for crossing the troll's bridge. "Fair enough," I said, to complete the apology. I was accustomed to being tricked out of goodies by my children, but I had to smile in admiration of Letty's advanced skill.

After the package changed hands, the mouth and chin lifted and the eye wrinkles relaxed, leaving as tolerant an expression as I was ever likely to receive from this strange woman.

Since this was possibly my one and only chance to learn something about her, naturally I choked and referred to the weather.

"Beautiful day."

"Guess so," Letty conceded. Holding the white bag away from Barney's mouth, she leaned down and tickled him under his chin. He grinned appreciatively, his wet tongue dangling.

"Pretty soon everything'll be growing. Grass, bushes. Buds everywhere."

"Yep." Barney cozied up to Letty's leg, and she rocked back and forth on a pair of black lace-up shoes, worn with white socks possibly to improve the fit. "Me friends'll soon be back." She smiled at the sky.

Was this woman daft? I'd lived next to her for two years and never once saw another human being so much as deliver a package, let alone pay a visit.

"Hey," she said. "What's 'e doin' to that mailbox?"

I followed her glare. Forty yards away Sam Browder had angled himself against his mailbox in order to stretch his left Achilles tendon.

"He's getting ready to run . . . for exercise," I explained, not at all certain of this woman's frame of reference. Meanwhile, I openly stared at Sam's muscular legs and the contour of his shorts. I think I inadvertently sighed, too, because Letty lifted a non-eyebrow.

" 'E live there?" she asked.

I was surprised that Letty hadn't recognized Sam, especially since he did his architectural design work at home; but some people can be amazingly unobservant, and I supposed that Letty could be one of them. Also, this morning Sam wore fewer clothes than usual.

Letty grunted again. "Think I'll be goin'." She began to waddle toward the mouth of Beech Tree Lane, the direction she'd been walking when I startled her.

I wondered if the old woman's avoidance of Sam had anything to do with the loud arguments he and Eunice so frequently held in their kitchen. If our pie-shaped lots allowed Garry to catch a few words and most of the volume from our TV room, Letty probably heard much more from her house, possibly everything, including what precipitated Eunice's dramatic exit last night.

Regardless, Letty's elderly legs were amazingly efficient. By the time Sam finished warming up she was nowhere in sight.

With a steady, fluid gait, Eunice's discarded husband began to jog toward me. When he nodded hello, I thought I perceived an extra tightness to that fatalistic, determined expression runners always wear. Sam Browder was definitely practicing stress control.

After about two steps toward my house, I succumbed to temptation and turned to admire him as he loped around the corner onto Monroe. What could Eunice possibly want that this guy didn't have?

"Dumb question, huh?" I addressed the family pet.

Barney tugged on his leash.

That afternoon, nervous that I would miss the arrival of our impatient plumber, I took advantage of the sixty-degree weather and found something to do in the front yard—trimming and shaping our assorted evergreens. With me I carried a trash can and an air of incompetence I had no reason to hide.

I started with a lopsided hemlock that was part of the thick windbreak between the Diamonds' drive and ours. When I reached out to trim a branch, an anguished scream scared the clippers out of my hand. Breathing hard, I looked all around for its source.

''No, oh no, oh no,'' continued the voice, which I finally realized could only belong to Bonnie Diamond.

I ran around the shrubbery to her side as fast as I could. ''Are you all right?'' I asked, gulping in breath.

Bonnie stood white faced and rigid at the back of her Volvo wagon, staring in horror at its emptiness. The television box I'd helped her load into the car that morning was gone. The two remaining cartons had been shifted as if someone had examined them before taking off with the TV.

Bonnie blinked at me. ''I just got back from the bus stop. The kids are changing clothes, then we were going straight to the mall.'' To return the TV and the other two items, I realized.

''Did you lock the car?''

Taking no offense, Bonnie merely nodded and flicked fearful eyes toward her house. I scarcely knew her husband, had exchanged hi's and good-byes and once turned over some misdirected mail. He had seemed perfectly reasonable to me, not the sort to berate his wife over a theft that was really not her fault.

''Could Richard have taken the TV back into the house for some reason?''

''No. No, he's at a job interview.'' The recollection of her husband's whereabouts visibly relieved her, but not entirely.

''If the car was locked, won't your insurance cover the loss? Won't the police find evidence of forced entry?''

Bonnie's face took on sudden color. ''Police?'' She swayed and placed fingers on the car to steady herself.

I empathized—not even unpacked from moving in and already she needed to call the cops. Unsettling, to say the least. Maybe Bonnie overreacted a little, but maybe she had a touchy temperament. Or maybe some other circumstance contributed to her panic. Maybe their Pennsylvania car insurance wasn't yet in effect.

Just then Dominick's truck rattled into view and thumped into our drive.

"That's our plumber," I told Bonnie, revealing a bit of concern.

Even in her addled state Bonnie immediately recognized my need to hurry. Plumbers require patience of their customers, but they never have any of their own. "Go ahead," she said.

"You okay about this?" I asked. "Do you want me to come back?"

"No. I mean, yes. I'm okay." She smiled for me, which was good, because before the smile I couldn't have left—plumber or no.

Dominick grinned at me through the open truck window. In the shade of his greasy Phillies cap his blue eyes shone with humor, possibly even glee.

"You been at it again," he said fondly.

The next time I glanced out front, a police car was pulling into Bonnie's drive.

Chapter 3

Under ordinary circumstances at a gathering of four or more people I automatically shift into hostess mode, which is to say I try to make other people feel comfortable. Tuesday morning was an exception. I was too cranky to help anybody else.

I parted the sheer white curtain at Margaret's front window and impatiently gazed out at Beech Tree Lane. Would Liz do the right thing and come? Should I have stayed home, too?

Mindful of Margaret's standards, at the expense of my own, I had dressed up for the occasion—I put on a skirt. I even worked up my going-out-in-public face: dark brown mascara for my dark brown eyes, blusher, coral lipstick. Scarcely visible gold earrings and a splash of Victoria's Secret Peach/Hyacinth stuff, and I looked and smelled good enough to greet anybody.

However, I felt like the poster girl for a heavy-duty PMS remedy. Rip had been late for dinner last night—very late. Something about the lacrosse bus breaking down and a kid stranded at the school because of the ruined timing. The boy eventually got picked up—at 7:30 PM—and by that time Rip and the lacrosse coach thought they had earned themselves a beer. When my husband finally came home, he had the nerve to be in a good mood. Lonely and then jealous. Not a particularly forgiving combination.

Although Liz's romantic rendezvous idea still constituted a move in the right direction, I hoped to pry a few more long-term marital endurance techniques out of her.

Even more than that, I wanted to see whether the changes I noticed in her were a passing phase or the beginning of the end of our rapport.

Ten-fifteen. Where was she? Had I failed to talk her into coming after all?

Margaret sidled up to me with a tray of tiny pastries. She was a remarkably fit older woman with perfectly white hair and silver half-glasses dangling on a chain across her pillowy breast. "Beautiful street we have, isn't it?"

For the first time today the panorama of green registered in my eyes. Full-grown oaks, hemlocks, rhododendrons and azaleas, grass struggling in their shade, daffodil spears swelling into buds—we truly did live on a beautiful street, if you didn't care too much about architecture.

Architecture. Sam was an architect. I had been told the inside of the Browder house was a showcase of his creativity, their bedroom a marvel of imagination . . .

Guilt swallowed me in one gulp. I couldn't even fantasize about being unfaithful to Rip without wearing a scarlet letter.

"My son wants us to move to one of those retirement condos," Margaret told me. Her gaze seemed to stroke the view of her lawn the way some people pet a purring cat. "Ever since he got engaged that's all he talks about." Her pale blue eyes hardened around those words, and she turned away.

"Wait," I said. "Johnny's engaged?" The guy was pushing forty-five, a thin, bespectacled clothespin who always wore black slacks and a white shirt. Whenever I noticed him disembarking from his Dodge sedan for the occasional Sunday night dinner with Margaret and Sol, he always struck me as the least interesting man on earth. I was genuinely pleased that he had found a woman who loved him.

"Oh, yes," Margaret turned back cheerily. Her half-glasses slid back to their center position on her chest. A handsome, if sometimes prissy woman, today she wore a short-sleeved dress that already revealed the beginnings of this year's golfer's tan.

"He and Diane are to be married October the eighth." Then, although she tried to sound amused, Margaret's smooth face sagged. "Johnny says it's time we gave up all this work."

What work? I wondered, pretty certain that the Raymonds hired people to mow the lawn and clean.

"What would happen to your house?"

When Margaret raised her left eyebrow, I realized she meant all along that Johnny and his bride expected to move in. "It seems perfectly logical to him," she said, knowing I had guessed the rest of the plan.

"But you aren't . . ." I began and quickly stopped myself. I have this compulsion to fix things, and I'm trying to learn to pick and choose with a little more discretion. Mother Cynthia's admonitions notwithstanding, I cannot do everything she thinks I can. I can't even do everything *I* think I can.

In this case maybe Sol or Margaret had a medical problem and their son really was exhibiting concern. Maybe a lot of things, and none of them would benefit from my opinion.

Meanwhile, Margaret's eyes widened at my blunt half question. "Why, no, dear. Sol isn't ready to retire." She and her pastry tray moved on to the other women seated around her soft blue living room.

I felt sorry that I had inadvertently criticized Johnny's scheme, but at least my first instinct was right—the Raymonds did not want to move, despite their son's pressure.

I refocused my attention onto Bonnie Diamond, the beneficiary of Margaret's neighborly good manners. Ensconced in a huge wing-backed chair, she seemed overwhelmed and concerned, and not just because something had been stolen out of her car yesterday. Whatever her background, it probably had not included teas with carefully dressed-down, intensely I'm-me, Main Line women. I felt like slipping her a card. "If you ever need a friend from the other side of the river, put the coffee on and open your kitchen window."

The doorbell rang, startling everybody, especially me. Since I was already standing, I scurried to answer it. However, it was not Liz. It was Eunice Browder.

My face displayed inordinate surprise before I could temper it. Eunice's extended stare told me she caught on immediately, that she realized I knew about her separation. She waved her head in an almost imperceptible "no."

I acknowledged her warning with a hearty, "Hi, Eunice. How nice to see you," imbuing my voice with superficial indifference, my way of illustrating that I meant to keep my mouth shut about her private life. For a brief instant before the businesswoman launched into her own charade, she fixed me with a dose of distaste.

For the rest of the room Eunice used the minimalist approach. A harried nod to Margaret, a blink at everybody else. She tossed her purse and omnipresent calfskin folder on a chair, smoothed her suit skirt and accepted a cup of coffee.

"Between appointments?" I suggested.

"Yes. Only have a minute or two." She remained wary of me, but not overly so.

When she and Sam moved onto Beech Tree Lane a year and a half ago, I would have described Eunice as a happy, and therefore, attractive woman. Her shoulder-length chestnut hair still gleamed, and her trim yellow-and-black spring suit telegraphed confidence in her business ability; but her beauty had somehow hardened.

I had always tried to like her—I try to like everybody—but on behalf of Bonnie I took offense at this morning's you're-lucky-to-get-me attitude. All of us there had other priorities, but at least we were sincerely interested in making a newcomer feel welcome. Perhaps that was why I said, "Then you'll want to meet Bonnie right away," with all the finesse of a clenched fist. Later I realized that Liz's absence had probably made me a bit edgier than I'd thought.

Eunice took a second to puzzle out my meaning. "Yes," she said. "Yes, of course."

"Excuse me," I told two women who had assaulted the guest of honor's eardrums long enough. "Eunice would like to meet Bonnie before she has to go back to work." Too much, probably. But I didn't care.

Wendy Shannahan, the brunette pixie, and honey-blonde Gail Vickers stopped talking to stare at me. Like pigeons on eggs they nestled on their skirts, making no move to vacate their seats.

I summoned forth my best Emily Post manners and addressed my new next-door neighbor. "Bonnie, this is Eunice Browder. She's in real estate. Eunice this is Bonnie Diamond. You may have noticed her two beautiful children at the bus stop." You probably had to steer around them with your Mercedes.

Eunice set her coffee cup on the saucer in her left hand, reached her right across the knees to pump Bonnie's fingers, then stood waiting for someone else to take the conversational initiative.

Bonnie broke the silence quite effectively by saying, "I've been wondering. Is this street really safe?"

A silence of a different nature elapsed while the rest of us took a visual poll. If any of us were thinking about the burglary in Bryn Mawr, the thought did not reveal itself.

Margaret exerted her seniority. "I've lived here thirty-three years, and I'd say it's quite safe. You have to be vigilant these days no matter where you are, but I feel safe here. What about you?" She turned to me because I was handy.

"It's a cul-de-sac. That helps a lot."

"Yes, but the bus stop's all the way at the other end from me. Do you think I have to stay with the kids every time? Some mornings . . ."

"What are you worried about, honey? Kidnapping?" Patsy Crouthamel asked, flicking crumbs into a napkin. The straightforward, Earth-Mother type, Patsy was also overweight to an unfortunate extent. "I didn't think anybody worried about that unless their husband was a big corporate executive."

To everyone's acute discomfort, Bonnie instantly reddened.

"What?" Patsy said. "What'd I say?" Apparently not everyone had been given Bonnie's background along with their invitation.

"Bonnie's husband works for G.E.," I enlightened Patsy as gently as possible. When we bought it, our house needed a total overhaul; but the one the Diamonds purchased to our right was on a larger lot, and the four-bedroom house had been kept in mint condition. Even considering today's depressed market, in this desirable territory that probably did make Richard some sort of executive. Most likely nowhere near the kidnapping salary range—but who knew?

"Oh, hell. I'm sorry, Bonnie. As usual, I should've kept my mouth shut." Coincidentally, Patsy's eyes rested on Margaret's pastry plate.

Bonnie wiped her cheeks with her palms and straightened her back. "That's all right. Richard doesn't work for G.E. anymore, and . . . and it wasn't kidnapping I was thinking about anyway. Something was stolen out of our car. I was really just asking."

"It's a good question," I said, heading off further conversation about the theft. "There are lots of weird people out there. Luckily they haven't found Beech Tree Lane yet; but if it makes you feel better, my kids are eleven and thirteen. They can keep an eye on Alison and Michael until their bus comes."

"My boys are too old for the bus, but tell your little ones to run for my house if they're scared," Patsy chimed in. "It's right there on the corner. I'm always in the kitchen." And then she blushed.

Rudely, Gail had begun a separate conversation with Wendy. Her house had been on the market over a year, and the topic was never far from her mind. I overheard the words "disgraceful" and "slovenly" being used while I was trying to listen to Bonnie.

In the silence from Patsy's faux pas we all heard Wendy's response to Gail. "Appearances are so important," something she said regularly without opening her mouth. On April Fools' Day her front door sported a colorful cardboard Joker that blended with the dove-gray stucco and apricot shutters. On May Day there would be an artful basket of silk flowers dangling from the doorknob.

The Queen of Calendar Kitsch became aware of her audience. "Which brings us to something I've wanted to talk about for years."

Subtly, the group froze to attention. Any normal family could be accused of appearance negligence from time to time, but nobody wanted their neighbors on the alert for recurrences. I ran a mental check—trash cans forgotten on the curb, leaves molding too long, that patch on the roof that doesn't quite match . . . could my dog have squirted a neighbor's flowers, or worse—could one of our party guests have?

"The old Doland estate," Wendy pronounced heavily. An obvious topic, yet a few of us twitched with relief. I'd forgotten about Letty's place quite deliberately, the only way to deal with an eyesore of such monolithic proportions. Gray stone streaked with rust and grime, crumbling garden walls, weeds the size of trees, trees unwieldy and sick, a potholed stone driveway reduced to a path by overgrowth—the only saving grace being the narrowness of exposure to Beech Tree Lane.

Back when railroad moguls created Philadelphia's first

suburbs by purchasing large estates out along their company's "main line," Letty's house was a mansion. Built by an importer named Doland on a hundred and ten woodsy acres, it was presently a disaster of total neglect subsisting on less than an acre. That it should exist in the midst of obvious middle-class comfort was a sadness and a mystery.

"Oh that place," Patsy Crouthamel sniffed. "Max wonders why it hasn't been condemned."

"Our houses will probably fall down first," Gail speculated. "More's the pity. I sometimes think that mess is why we haven't sold ours. Cars come to check out the neighborhood. They creep all the way down to the turnaround at Ginger's, then they can't speed out of here fast enough."

I opened my mouth to protest, but Eunice beat me to it. "I doubt if Letty's place is the whole reason," she declared. "We've got a lovely street, but it's not what most people expect of a Main Line neighborhood."

"What do you mean?" Margaret asked.

Eunice considered her answer. "Only one two-story colonial," she nodded toward Wendy, "a woodsy impression rather than formal gardens . . ."

"More casual," suggested Camilla Grogan. An older woman, but not of Margaret's white-haired elegance, Camilla and her husband were professors—music history and computer science respectively. The Main Line boasted the highest concentration of colleges and universities in the country, so two professors on one street came as no surprise.

"Oh, come on," Wendy pressed Eunice. "If you wanted to sell your own house, you'd ask Letty to clean up her yard, too."

"What do you mean, want to? Didn't you see the sign?" Gail snapped.

"What sign?"

Eunice had gone pink. "We're just testing the market," she told the room with deliberate finality.

Wendy's olive coloring remained high. "Well, regardless, I think someone should do something about this Letty MacNair woman. She's got eyes. She can see that her place is a wreck."

"But clearly she doesn't have much money," I said. "Old clothes, no car . . ."

"She's got enough to stay in that house," Wendy argued.

Gail nodded. "You never know. She could be filthy rich and just plain nuts. Has anybody ever talked to her?"

I met Eunice's eyes, but she shook me off, apparently unwilling to offer an opinion on our mutual neighbor's sanity.

"I've talked to her," I said.

Seven women turned to stare. "You mean you're friendly?" Patsy asked.

"Not exactly."

"So?" Wendy was undeterred. "How'd she sound?"

About as logical as my mother, but I wasn't prepared to admit that. "She's in her own world," I answered, "but that doesn't mean she's crazy."

"But you get along with her. She doesn't actively dislike you."

Yesterday's encounter replayed itself in my mind—the cinnamon bun heist, the remark about her imaginary friends. It had been a peculiar conversation, but certainly not hostile. "No," I answered reluctantly.

"It doesn't matter," Gail interjected. "If Ginger's the only one who has actually spoken to the woman, then she's the one to tell her."

"Tell her?"

"To clean up her yard. If she can't do it herself, let her hire someone."

I shook my head. "I really don't think she has any money, Gail. I honestly can't imagine how she manages to eat." I looked to Eunice for support but was met with a blank stare. Meanwhile, Gail and Wendy's preference for the rich/crazy theory was written across their tight lips.

"It doesn't cost anything to knock down those weeds, mow the grass in front of the fence," Wendy insisted. "There's plenty she could do."

Eunice glanced at her watch and abruptly stood. "I'm terribly sorry, Margaret, but I've got to go. Nice meeting you, Bonnie."

Bonnie fidgeted from the sudden attention. "Nice meeting you, too."

When Margaret returned from seeing Eunice out, Wendy slapped her knees. "Then that's settled," she said. "Ginger will speak to Letty."

"Me?" I hadn't agreed to anything.

"Just tell her how we feel," Gail patted the air. "She probably has no idea we care what her property looks like. I'm sure she'll be happy to comply once you've talked to her."

A glance around the room swung my sympathy toward Letty. I might not make any headway with her, but I didn't trust anyone else to respect her feelings.

If anything, Rip and I respected them too much. That's why we hadn't interfered in the woman's business before, despite the appearance of need. She seemed healthy and contented with her reclusive lifestyle. With her obvious preference for privacy, offering help would have been presumptuous and rude.

The yard problem was different. If I didn't deliver the message, someone with less regard for her privacy certainly would.

"Okay," I said. "I'll ask about her yard. But that's as far as I go."

"Fine," Wendy agreed.

"Sure," Gail concurred.

Margaret breathed. Camilla moved over to speak with Bonnie. Patsy furtively lifted a pastry to her mouth, and something thumped against the front door.

I immediately thought of Liz, but by now it seemed clear

that she had chosen not to attend the party at all. Plus the sound had been more of a thud than a knock.

''Must be a UPS delivery,'' Margaret concluded. She walked briskly toward the door and opened it.

While the rest of us watched, she scanned the yard through the screen door. Then she looked down at the front step and screamed. I rushed to steady the woman before she toppled over, then I, too, looked out at the doorstep.

Liz lay crumpled in a heap. Blood had dried in a horrible pattern down her cheek. More red oozed from a spot where her frosted hair was black and matted.

Whimpering, trembling, Margaret shrugged herself free from my grasp. There were bright red marks on her forearm where my fingers had bruised her.

Chapter 4

"Call 911," I told Margaret. She blinked and let go of the doorjamb. Behind us the roomful of women stood breathless with fear. "An ambulance," I prompted our hostess.

"Yes," she said as if I had suggested she brew another pot of coffee. "Yes, of course."

Liz's body prevented the front door from opening, so I sprinted around the corner into the kitchen. A few of the other guests gravitated toward me then receded like surf. I passed Margaret as she spoke into the receiver of the wall phone. "Hello?" she told someone while I exited the back door as fast as I could.

Cursing my inhibiting skirt and low beige heels, I hurried to the left around the huge bushes flanking the Raymonds' brick and clapboard house. Emergencies always catch us unprepared.

Yet running to help felt natural and good. I sensed my parents urging me on, especially my father. *Don't just stand there—do something*, the Struve family motto.

As I passed the front window, the faces of the other women blurred past my eyes, a snapshot of various emotions. I ignored them all, and finally I was there.

Hands on my knees, catching my breath, I tried to assess Liz's condition. She must have plunged forward when she fell before rolling back face up against the doorjamb because fresh blood oozed from a gash on the top of her head. What seemed to be an older injury above her left eyebrow—the wound responsible for the ghoulish streaks of blood—had become swollen and encrusted with black scabbing.

"Near fatal," I heard Sunday night's newscaster telling me in my kitchen. *". . . business end of a blunt instrument . . ."* It seemed that the bad guys had discovered Beech Tree Lane after all.

The fresh bleeding told me Liz was still alive. Very little else suggested that. A bit of shallow breathing—very shallow breathing—and nothing else.

"You're okay," I cooed. "Hang in there, kid." Mother talk, universal in any language. She did not look okay. She did not appear capable of lasting more than a couple more minutes.

Yet she had managed to crawl for help, evidence enough that settling her into a more comfortable position would probably not hurt her further. So slowly, gently, I straightened her legs across the cement doorstep.

Earlier this morning she had dressed herself in navy and white linen slacks and, although they were gone, probably flat blue shoes, clothing perfectly appropriate for a morning social event with other women. It may have been petty of me, but I was pleased to think I had convinced her to attend Margaret's party after all.

Except now the shoulders of her white linen shirt were stiff with bloodstains, the elbows brown with dirt. Great streaks of grass and mud were also permanently ingrained down the front of the slacks.

I hauled in a big breath and told Liz, "Take it easy, kid. Help is on the way. You're a brave girl, the bravest . . ."

I kept talking until I had smoothed down my skirt and parked my fanny in the soft shredded mulch beside the step. Seated there, I was able to ease Liz's shoulders and head onto my lap. She sighed and went deathly still again, causing my pulse to hammer painfully until I detected a little warm breath coming from her nose.

My throat constricted as I thought of the timing. While I was selfishly watching for her, she was probably returning home from some errand, opening her door, stepping into an ambush . . .

"Easy," I told her. "You're going to be okay," I crooned. I smoothed her curls away from her fresh wound and stroked her cheek with my hand as I would a troubled child.

Examining another person's face in minute detail was a privilege of intimacy, nothing that friends like Liz and me would ever do. Consequently, it was an unexpected surprise to notice that her eyelashes were a taupe brown darkened with soft brown mascara. Beneath the bloodstains her skin was beautifully clear except for a few light freckles. From so many years of outdoor activities, her eyes were etched with an endearing web of fine lines.

She looked exceptionally fragile and human lying heavily in my lap. I couldn't stop thinking about how easily life can slip away, how many diseases to which we are prey, not to mention accidents and, yes, deliberate acts of violence. We hear about eightieth birthdays and golden wedding anniversaries and blithely trust those future celebrations to wait for us.

Enough of that, I told myself. Shake it off. Liz still has a chance.

My eyes sought a less sanguinary sight, the treetops across the street.

"Remember the time you and Marc and all of us Barneses went on that picnic to Valley Forge?" I asked my friend's unconscious form. "It was right after we met, and both of us went to a lot of extra trouble trying to impress each other—fried chicken, potato salad, which I had never made before, pickles and olives and carrot sticks. And you baked a big flat butter cake?

"But right away Garry got stung on the lip by a bee, so

he spent the afternoon whimpering and holding an ice cube on it. Chelsea chose that day to play at being a vegetarian. Marc and Rip, who were both there under protest, could scarcely find anything to say to each other, which was how we found out this would be a wives-only friendship. Remember? Anyhow, my potato salad was inedible, and your butter cake melted into a really gooey mess. It was probably the worst picnic I've ever been on.

"Well, listen up, girl," I told Liz emphatically. "I want another shot at it. Okay? I'll bake brownies, which I know how to do, and you make the potato salad. We'll loosen up the men with liquor or something, and we'll all play Wiffle ball. You hear me? We'll get it right this time. I promise. So . . ."

Margaret stepped into the yard from the driveway. She pretended she wasn't thinking I was crazy. Patsy cautiously followed.

"They're coming," Margaret said, although I could already hear a siren.

When I nodded, something tickled my jaw. I wiped at it with my shoulder and my blouse came away wet. To my surprise, I was shivering.

Wendy and Gail waited in the driveway, neither of them quite sure what to do with their hands. Camilla and Bonnie had remained inside, and belatedly I realized that back when all this started, all of five minutes ago, I had heard Bonnie gasping her way into some serious hysterics. Camilla, I supposed, had stayed behind to administer to her.

The police and an ambulance arrived simultaneously. Tuesday mornings are probably about as busy as Saturday night in our township, which is to say not busy at all. Yet we maintain a complete police department, fully capable of investigating anything from purse-snatching to homicide. I had reason to know.

The paramedics moved in and helped me out from under Liz. While they swiftly checked Liz over, the single cop who took the call, Sgt./Det. Kriebel, approached me to ask, "Can she speak?"

Speak? I could scarcely speak. "No," I answered.

"What happened?" he asked. We stood several feet back, away from the other women. Kriebel's hat was awry, but his snappy black uniform looked fresh from the laundry. He folded his arms across his chest while he listened to what I knew.

"Interrupted burglary?" I suggested. The rest of the women had formed a corridor to the ambulance's back door for the scurrying medics.

"So it would seem," Kriebel agreed. "Early to say for sure." He eyed me a bit more intently. "And you are?"

"Ginger Barnes," I replied. "Last house in the cul-de-sac. Will you be notifying her husband?" A backup police unit had parked in front of the Kelmans' and three officers began to fan out around the house. I noticed they carefully avoided the crooked swath of crushed grass between Liz's front door and Margaret's.

Kriebel gifted me with a wry smile. "You want to call him?"

I shook my head and, with what I considered admirable efficiency, told him, "He works for Myertech, but I think he's in Albuquerque. The phone number is probably on their refrigerator."

Liz kept track of Marc's whereabouts on a large homemade grid, yet she never ever phoned him with those wifely questions most of us have, the "Where did you put the washing machine warranty?/When can you see the eye doctor?" communications that sew our lives together. Liz was the ultimately competent and undemanding executive wife, capable of assembling dinner for six in twenty-five minutes or less. If she were conscious, I wasn't entirely certain she would tell Marc about this.

The cop thanked me sincerely enough and returned to his squad car.

The medics had shifted Liz onto a stretcher and rigged

up an IV of some sort. Now they were carrying her to the ambulance, stepping carefully over the edges of the cement walk, balancing carefully down a slight slope to the drive.

Just before they closed the ambulance doors, I glanced inside. Margaret was in there with Liz, lightly touching her arm, exuding grandmotherly comfort whether Liz was aware of it or not. The doors slammed. Gaudy lights flashed, and the vehicle slowly drove away.

After that, Kriebel questioned us remaining women individually. Had we seen any strangers casing the neighborhood? Anything out of the ordinary this morning? Anything odd anywhere ever? A pessimism seemed to pervade the familiar routine, as if the sergeant/detective was acutely aware that burglars were only caught about fifteen percent of the time.

With nothing more to say or do, I felt hollowed out and limp. Our names and addresses had been dutifully recorded. Those of us remaining were free to leave.

Bonnie did, immediately, as well as Wendy and Gail. Camilla lingered, wearing a patient philosophical expression on her professorly face. Patsy stood by me with more animation than Camilla, and the three of us watched as the police secured Liz's house and yard all the way down to Margaret's door, listened to their hopeless communications as extra men searched an ever-widening area until any possibility of finding anything useful became extinct.

Finally Camilla left, her pearl-buttoned cardigan held on her shoulders by a thin, liver-spotted hand. She said nothing, just shook her head and walked toward her home.

Patsy's breathing remained quick, her nearly black eyes bright with either caffeine or emotion. She sidled up, plucked at a fold of my skirt. "Brandy," she announced decisively.

"For the skirt?" I replied with confusion.

"For you. Cold-water soak for the skirt." Trust a mother with two rough-and-tumble boys to know what to do. We assessed each other appreciatively, and I realized I would enjoy knowing more about her.

I thanked her and lumbered inside Margaret's for my purse, pulling the door, locked, behind me. Then I went home and took Patsy's advice, followed by a sandwich. My mental functions needed downtime before rebooting. I slept soundly for an hour then woke with a sense of suspended animation, as if Liz's hospitalization had put my life on hold as well.

Consequently, the afternoon stretched before me as wide and flat as Iowa. I made a huge batch of Slope Soup, a concoction consisting of sausage meat, kidney beans, potatoes, onions, and tomato sauce, mindless work that produced food to be eaten without thought—with a spoon. I set it on our shady slate front step to cool before saving it in the refrigerator.

When I glanced up, I noticed Sgt./Det. Kriebel staring at the Kelmans' from the middle of the street. It seemed like a good moment to wander up there, see what he knew about things.

"Burglary?" I asked again, interrupting his contemplations.

He rubbed his smooth, young chin and settled his feet farther apart. "Robbery. Higher classification. Husband's going to see what's missing when he gets back."

"From Albuquerque?"

"From the hospital," Kriebel corrected me. "When we called the office, he was there. Flew back early this morning on urgent business and phoned his wife from the airport. I guess that's why she went out for groceries."

"Could he have done it?" I blurted.

The police officer stiffened and stared. "You just got a suspicious mind? Or do you know something?" He was now irritated and wary of me, but of course, I'd asked for it.

I tried to minimize the damage. "I guess I figured if

Marc had an alibi, I could concentrate on feeling sorry for him.''

''You do that. Either way you can't go wrong.''

As he strolled toward his squad car, he eyed me over his shoulder. Even as he slammed the door and turned on the engine, his warning gaze never broke.

Chapter 5

When he got home—early for a change—Rip blanched when I told him about the attack on Liz. In fact he hustled me into his office to question me about it out of earshot of the children. "Will she be all right?" he asked.

"I called the nurses' station a little while ago. They said her condition was 'cautiously optimistic.' "

"Poor Marc," Rip lamented as he unloaded his briefcase and sport coat onto his desk chair. "Where was he this time?"

"As a matter of fact, he was local. Just got back this morning."

The way Rip took that in stride reminded me of Kriebel's stiff response to my query about Marc's alibi. "You just got a suspicious mind? Or do you know something?" Rip had accused me of becoming excessively suspicious—maybe he was right.

A couple minutes later the four of us settled around the plank table for dinner, a somber family forced to feel profoundly close by the day's events.

Even the kids were visibly subdued. Garry actually behaved as if using a spoon required his complete attention.

"Anything happen at school?" I asked, just to be sure.

He shrugged one shoulder.

"You still bummed about track?" Chelsea pressed.

Garry stuck out his tongue. Baby books never acknowledge the real milestones—the day your youngest learns to get his own car door, the day he realizes sticking out his tongue no longer produces the desired effect. According to my calculations, Garry's "cute-clock" was ticking double-time. Soon he would need more sophisticated self-defense techniques—such as sarcasm.

"Yep, still bummed about track," his sister concluded.

When baseball soured for Garry, he switched to track. Unfortunately, he wasn't very good at that either. The argument that his body wasn't quite used to his new improved muscles cut no ice. All he really understood was that his best friend, Jordy, beat him out for the last spot on the team.

"This, too, shall pass?" I offered.

"Huh?"

I lifted my son's glass and set it next to his hand. "Drink your milk."

Garry cast me a thoroughly disdainful, relatively cute scowl.

I then addressed Chelsea. "Don't you like Slope Soup?"

"Yes. No. I'm not really hungry."

"I've got to make some calls," Rip told us, rising from the table.

"You kids have to do the dishes," I insisted. "I'm taking some dinner up to Mr. Kelman."

Yet when I scooped the soup for Marc into a plastic container, there wasn't as much left as I expected.

"Hmmm," I thought to myself. "Maybe Chelsea liked it better than I thought.

Walking through the dusk carrying my sympathy offering, I braced myself to deal with a man who was probably sick with worry. Consequently, Marc's anger came as a shock.

He threw the door aside. "Just look at this mess, Gin. It's no wonder they call them pigs."

"Who?" I asked, not yet adjusted to his mood.

"The police, of course."

To me, Marc Kelman's arms and legs had always seemed lengthier than necessary, making any movement an exaggeration. Tonight, his agitation made him look wild.

After I closed the door and took a deep, fortifying breath, I glanced around the living room as instructed. Every surface in sight had been dusted with something—white powder on dark items, black powder on light. Liz's collection of teacups displayed on the cherry wall unit were off their stands in no particular order. Drawers were slightly opened, incidental tables crooked, chintz cushions on the floor.

The police had done their job with zeal; and while part of me applauded their thoroughness, the uncharitable notion that they were underworked crossed my mind once again.

No fair, I chided myself. Perhaps this mess, for it really was a mess, meant they were frustrated by a second robbery with assault in the area within a week. Maybe they just plain hated the idea of burglars operating in their jurisdiction. Maybe they were just as human as the rest of us.

Marc pounded a yellow throw pillow with the flat of his hand and threw it onto the yellow printed sofa. "Unbelievable," he informed me as he began to pace.

Fortunately, I knew of another husband who became furious when his wife got sick—my Uncle Jack. When I mentioned what I considered to be an inappropriate response to my mother, she explained that Jack felt helpless, and that his frustration made him angry. I tried to keep that in mind now.

"How's Liz doing?" I asked.

Without looking at me Marc merely shrugged, and I had the impression he was fighting off tears.

My own breath caught, so I changed the subject for both our sakes. "I brought you some dinner. Did you eat yet?"

"Humph? Oh, eat? No. Not hungry." Marc had high cheekbones, disheveled brown hair and horn-rimmed glasses. Beneath his square chin a loosened burgundy tie hung from an unbuttoned white collar. A heather-toned V-neck sweater had probably dressed him up comfortably for his flight from Albuquerque. High altitude and April in Philadelphia probably felt about the same.

"I'll just put it in the refrigerator then. It's easy to heat whenever you're ready."

"Humph? Okay. Thanks." He shook his head in a what-am-I-going-to-do? manner.

"You want me to help clean?" I offered automatically, as I habitually do. My own house needed work, but this was psychological housekeeping as opposed to ordinary sanitation. Much more worthwhile and rewarding.

Marc looked at me as if he required more information before he could possibly answer.

"Somebody's got to do it," I said. Marc continued to stare.

"I don't think it should be Liz, do you?"

Eventually Marc shook his head.

"So do you want me to give it a shot?"

"Yes. Sure. That'd be great. Thanks."

"No problem."

The phone had begun to ring, and Marc was drawn to the receiver, a white slimline reposing on an end table. Blinking, he picked it up.

"Yes? This is Marc Kelman."

He listened only a moment before his lanky body folded onto the sofa. An unearthly groan emanated from his gut. Sweat beaded his brow. He sank back against the cushions.

The receiver hung in his limp hand. For a moment he just gasped out some very masculine, very frightening sobs, then abruptly he scrambled upright and rushed from the room.

I picked up the phone. "This is Gin Barnes," I said to the person on the other end. "I'm here with Mr. Kelman. Can I help you?"

"No, but maybe you can assist Mr. Kelman," a professional-sounding female replied hesitantly. "We've asked him to come in to the hospital. His wife . . ."

I drove him there myself, waited in the hallway while his wife's doctor spoke to him privately. Afterward, the doctor guided Marc out through the doorway and waited for me to take charge of his arm.

When I touched him, Marc looked down into my face without any apparent recognition.

"She's gone," he said to the kind stranger I had become.

Much later while I lay awake working through my own grief, struggling to understand, the reason why the police had been so thorough collecting evidence finally occurred to me. From experience they knew they would need everything they could get to convict a possible murderer.

Chapter 6

When I phoned Wednesday morning, Marc was out, so I grabbed the keys I had borrowed before I left last night, clipped on Barney's leash, and went over to assess the extent of the cleaning chores.

Now, with my dog dozing out under the Kelmans' red maple, I stood in their disheveled living room. Marc had done little to straighten the disarray, nothing to remove traces of the police. Perhaps it was merely that I was there alone and my imagination came into play, but something about the appearance of the place dissatisfied me. Something seemed off. But what?

After quickly scanning the kitchen, I progressed to the dining room, where I peeked into the drawers of a cherry hutch. I had the sensation that Liz was looking through my eyes, groping for explanations. She seemed to nudge me into following the killer's probable movements, to urge me to visualize the convergence of events that ended with her death.

Her family silverware remained intact inside a mahogany box. Maybe the robber had considered it too heavy or too easily identifiable. Maybe there simply had been no time to grab it after Liz came home and interrupted the overall search.

Yet the other inconsistencies I found were not so easy

to explain. Liz's wallet was empty of cash—I blatantly checked her purse for that—and a small, delicate French clock had disappeared from the dining room mantel. A diamond watch Liz must have set on the kitchen windowsill while she cooked remained, but an ornate antique letter opener was gone from the desk in the hall.

Was the inefficient burglar an amateur? Or was he so spooked by his confrontation with Liz that he panicked and ran, swiping a couple of random items on his way out?

None of this information seemed to be of much use, however; so I forced myself to be practical, to wet a dishtowel to drape over the horrible three-by-five-inch bloodstain near the front door. Revulsion only permitted me to drop it from a two-foot height and adjust the coverage with my toe.

"You did it again." I wagged my head and clucked to myself. To satisfy my curiosity I had volunteered—conveniently forgetting what I had actually volunteered to do.

The usual cleaning supplies were in the pantry, and in no time I was sponging fingerprint dust off every surface in the kitchen—boring work that freed my imagination. Soon I felt Liz guiding my hands in and out of the water, watching over my shoulder as I lifted the salt and pepper shakers to wipe under them.

After half an hour of that, I sat square in the middle of the kitchen floor and cried.

Eventually, I went over to the wall phone.

"Is Marc Kelman available?" I asked his company's local receptionist. "This is his neighbor calling."

"You bet," she answered. "Don't know why that man came in today." Her tone summoned an image of Marc sitting with his chin in his hands.

"It's Gin," I told him when he came on the line. "You doing okay?"

Silence.

"Yes, no, maybe?" I prompted.

"No," he said.

"Well, here's an idea for you," I said. "Your place

needs more work than I can possibly manage before the funeral. And to be honest, I'm having a little trouble . . . being here. How about we call Margaret's cleaning service, and you come home to keep an eye on them?''

Silence.

''Marc?''

''Whatever you say.''

''Okay. I'll arrange for the cleaners—you come home.'' I made him answer me a couple more times until I was certain he understood the plan, then I said good-bye and proceeded to make the appropriate phone calls. When I explained that the house needed to be ready for visitors after a funeral, Margaret's service obligingly agreed to juggle their schedule.

Preparing to leave, I automatically checked the back door, but it refused to hold. A close examination of the lock revealed that a toothpick had been jammed into the gap around the latch, effectively preventing it from popping into the locked position. Anyone who gave the door a shove could get inside. Even a stiff wind might open it.

With a skinny knife I pried out the little sliver of wood so the door was once again secure. No doubt the police had noticed the problem—they were thorough about everything else—but if they had mentioned it to Marc, he must have forgotten all about it.

Of course, last night he had had plenty on his mind.

I placed my borrowed key on the counter and departed through the front door.

As I untied Barney from the red maple, the mail truck passed by, its brakes squeaking to a stop at the end of each drive. Since I knew Letty often appeared soon afterward, I decided to approach her about her yard so I could scratch that onerous chore off my list.

Right on time, my next-door neighbor emerged from her house like a mole from its burrow, blinking at the light while scanning her surroundings for danger. She wore yet another shapeless housedress under the brown cardigan.

Her toes shuffled forward in order to accommodate her loose black shoes. Her palm batted the weeds that encroached upon the driveway ruts as she passed.

Barney easily accomplished what I set out to do. He tugged me toward the old woman as if I were missing the social event of the day—and would I please get the lead out?

Letty, the dog, and I arrived at her mailbox simultaneously. Our Irish setter eagerly reacquainted himself with the smells on Letty's skirt and shoes, plus every flavor on her hands.

"Barney," I scolded, hauling him a polite foot away by force of his choke collar, a temporary and not very effective gesture.

"Oh, let 'im be," Letty remarked. She seemed tired and careworn today, as if she had not slept well last night. The gnarled fingers she ran around the dog's muzzle moved more slowly than before, and she lowered her face for a friendly licking as if her joints were stiff.

I watched carefully for a signal of how to accomplish my mission. Honesty seemed to be my only choice.

"Letty," I began. She apparently liked dog kisses, because she endured Barney's licking much longer than I would have.

"Lord, he's a mess, in't he?"

"Yes. I'm really sorry."

"No matter." She was smiling wearily, her plain white face a swag of cheek wrinkles and thin lips. Her ears protruded from wispy strands of mostly gray hair confined by yet another blue rubber band. I could see now that the dress had been brown-and-white striped in previous years. Of the ten buttons down its center front, one was misaligned and one was missing.

"Letty," I began again. "Letty, I have something I have to ask you."

Her eyebrows rose, or I should say the flesh where eyebrows usually were arched with mild surprise.

"You got somethin' to axe me?"

"Yes, Letty. Some of the neighbors were wondering if you would mind maybe cleaning up your yard a little."

The non-eyebrows arched as she cast silver-black eyes across the mess that was her domain.

"What for?"

Oh, dear. "Well, your property doesn't exactly look like most of the others on the street . . ."

"So?"

". . . and a couple of the families are trying to sell."

"Yeah?"

"So they're hoping you will agree to pick up the trash and cut the weeds out front, at least from the wall out to the curb. Twenty feet. That isn't much." That wasn't all they asked, but it would be a start. At least the rest of the jungle would remain behind the front wall.

Letty's fists set on her hips and her eyes stared at asphalt. Her scowl could have been consternation, but I thought it best to finish my spiel before finding out.

"If the work would be too strenuous for you, my kids and I would be glad to help."

"Nope."

"I'm sorry. Do you mean no, you don't need help?"

"I mean nope, I ain't gonna do it."

My jaw went slack.

"Me and me friends likes the place just as she is," Letty elaborated. "Ain't that right, doggie?" She patted the top of Barney's head and the turncoat grinned back at her.

I sighed, imagining myself repeating Letty's answer to Wendy and Gail. "What friends?" they would retort. "The old bat doesn't have a friend in the world as far as we can see."

It pained me anew that of the people on Beech Tree Lane I was the most sympathetic toward our eccentric neighbor, and here I was stepping on her proprietary toes.

She reached into her mailbox as if our conversation were over.

Remembering how I had portrayed her to the complainers—as a penniless recluse—I spoke somewhat more softly than before. "If it's money you're worried about . . ."

"What? What did ye say?" Her eyes snapped like a Sunday school teacher demonstrating the wrath of God. She clutched a handful of junk mail to her breast. I spread my hands and backed off, physically and metaphorically. My face burned. My heart hammered.

"Letty, I'm truly sorry. I hated giving you their suggestions, but I had to let you know how they feel around here. I hope there aren't any hard feelings . . ."

She backed up her drive until her heel hit a rock, then she spun and scurried as if pursued by antagonists from every angle. I was sorely sorry to be numbered among them, but at the time I could think of no way to separate the messenger from the message.

I hurried home to nurse my guilt—and anger that I had allowed myself be pushed into such a position in the first place.

Later I realized I should have told Letty about Liz so she could be on the alert. If others suspected, as Wendy and Gail did, that Letty had money stashed somewhere in her house, the old woman might be in danger.

Yet the likelihood of a thief returning to Beech Tree Lane so soon after Liz's murder seemed remote—too remote for me to disturb Letty with another upsetting bit of news.

I played catch with Barney instead.

About 1:30 someone knocked on my door. Sgt./Det. Kriebel waited for me to respond, notebook in hand.

"Just following up, ma'am," he told me without any trace of his previous rancor. "Is there anything more you remember about yesterday morning? Maybe something you overlooked during the commotion?"

I stepped outside and folded my arms thoughtfully. ''You know about the toothpick in the lock, right? I found it when I was over there cleaning.''

''Yes. That was how the assailant gained access to the house.''

I made no effort to hide my confusion. ''I'm not sure I understand how that worked.''

Kriebel spread his feet and thrust his chin forward. ''Not that common a trick, but common enough,'' he lectured. ''The burglar probably came to the door, maybe the day before, gave some excuse to Mrs. Kelman—glass of water, something like that—then when she's not looking he breaks the toothpick off in the lock. Unless she's lucky enough to notice, he can get back in whenever he wants.''

I must have swallowed a rock. ''But that means . . .''

''Yes, ma'am. That means Mrs. Kelman spoke to her assailant prior to the attack.''

My cheeks sizzled. ''So do you think she was killed on purpose?''

Kriebel shrugged. ''Maybe. Maybe not. Technically, it's murder either way.''

I liked that idea so little that I immediately asked, ''Would a regular person, not a burglar, know how to do the toothpick thing?''

''I suppose so,'' Kriebel admitted.

''What if somebody just wanted to, to kill Mrs. Kelman, wouldn't the toothpick make a good cover-up?''

Kriebel scowled, his wariness of me back in full force. ''That's a bit far-fetched.'' He wagged his head to dismiss the idea.

''But you're not ruling it out?''

''We're pursuing the robbery idea first, Mrs. Barnes.''

''But don't those guys work an area and then move on?'' I had read enough newspaper accounts to learn that; and even if I hadn't, it was ordinary common sense.

''Yes, ma'am. But we have feelers out in all the places he's likely to go.'' Kriebel squinted impatiently.

"He," I said. "As in one guy."

"We saw no indication of an accomplice. Did you?"

Kriebel's red-faced indignation almost shamed me into silence.

Almost, but not quite. Whoever killed Liz was out there somewhere, and I wanted him caught. At the moment, the police were the only ones in a position to do that, and before I could sleep soundly ever again I needed assurance they had every angle covered.

"Could a woman have done it?" I pressed.

Kriebel shook his head again. "Unlikely. Possible, but unlikely." Reading between the lines, I assumed he meant that women more frequently obtain money by other illegal means, that breaking and entering was statistically a man's crime.

"And her husband's still in the clear?" I didn't like to think ill of the man, but most murders do tend to be domestic quarrels, and the Kelmans' marriage had endured some strain. Marc's traveling. Also, their difficulty in conceiving a child had increasingly become a source of anxiety and contention.

"Not that again," Kriebel snarled sarcastically.

"I'm just asking. You're not investigating Marc, right?"

"Not at this time. But if you think we should . . ." His sneer completed the sentence.

I threw up my hands. "I'm sorry," I apologized. "You're the professional."

But even as I said that, my uneasiness from that morning returned tenfold. Liz's death just plain didn't feel right. Her house just didn't feel right . . .

"Gin has been a bit of an alarmist ever since she solved that murder."

I kept quiet. If the robber/murderer theory failed to pan out, the police department would be forced to investigate Marc and everyone else who had the slightest motive to kill Liz.

While Kriebel lumbered back to his squad car with almost comic casualness, I reminded myself to let the man tend to his business.

Meanwhile, I would try very hard to mind mine.

Chapter 7

Occasionally I feel like a pit bull with my teeth in the mailman's leg. I would gladly release my grip if only someone could offer a compelling enough reason to go against instinct.

Liz's death was beginning to look and feel like yet another mailman's leg, and I knew from experience that I had better find myself a reason to let go. The police were probably right. I was quite probably wrong. And yet I envisioned a batch of sleepless nights lining up to get me if I didn't do something to banish them, preferably as soon as possible.

About five minutes after Kriebel left, I chose my course of action. It was safe, easy, and only slightly out of my way. But best of all, no one would know about my prospective wild-goose chase unless I told them myself.

Feeling equally foolish and self-satisfied, I grabbed my car keys and drove toward Bryn Mawr.

Sunday night's newscaster with the pink suit had referred to the 6000 block of Argonne Avenue, and it was a simple matter to locate the collection of driftwood cubes connected by glass where Mrs. Corinne Novak had *''walked into the business end of a blunt instrument.''* I parked in the driveway and rang the buzzer next to the dark red door.

While I waited I glanced around to see if the neighbor

in the white shirt had changed her mind about moving. Apparently not. Another FOR SALE sign graced a nearby lawn.

Yet even considering the recent robbery and assault, the block looked pretty much like paradise to me. Custom-designed homes of brick, stone, and tastefully stained wood were set onto ample lots among ancient oak and poplar trees. Backyards were secluded by ornamental shrubbery and discreetly designed four-foot fencing meant to protect the unwary from wandering into a swimming pool. The usual real estate ads would read ''ctrl air'' and ''4 fire-places, mstr bth w/sauna,'' and so on. The husbands would be on blood pressure medication and the women would suffer from migraines, but anyone in the world who had not lived the life would envy them. And why not? Stress symptoms were not exclusive to Bryn Mawr.

A casually dressed housekeeper answered the door; I knew she was a housekeeper because her clothes were familiar Kmart stock, and there was no bandage on the back of her head. Also, she said, ''May I help you?''

''Would it be possible for me to speak to Mrs. Novak? I'll only take a couple minutes of her time.'' Since only a bionic woman would have recovered in less than a week, I felt certain she would be at home.

The housekeeper cocked her head of steel-gray curls and narrowed her brown eyes. ''Does she know you?'' she asked. Looking devoid of any profession was an asset now and then—if I had been carrying a clipboard or briefcase, the door already would have slammed.

''No,'' I admitted, ''but I'd like to talk to her about the robbery. You see, it just happened again on my street.''

As I listened to my own words, my temerity abruptly deserted me. I gulped noisily and tears stung my eyes. I crossed my arms to hold it all in, but my emotions betrayed me.

''Sorry,'' I apologized quickly. The tears spilled over,

and I wiped them hastily with a sleeve. Then I shrugged because I could think of nothing to say.

Actually, my loss of composure accomplished what mere words probably would not have. The housekeeper realized I was not the typical pesky stranger, and Mrs. Novak became curious enough to grant me an audience.

''She's just home from the hospital,'' her employee whispered as she led me along the slate-floored hallway into a living room situated on the right. Her pointed glance warned me to be brief. Then a few steps into the high-ceilinged spacious expanse, she abandoned me. She might eavesdrop on my conversation with her boss, or she might not.

Regardless, her departure made me feel trusted and almost welcome. Recovering from an injury was tedious stuff, and perhaps Mrs. Novak's housekeeper was glad for a few moments alone.

Corinne Novak pressed the remote control to a wall unit and turned off *Days of Our Lives.* She wore a white peignoir and the expected bandage, and her honey-blonde hair fanned out from her face in a neglected frizz. Unbecoming bluish sacks that she probably hid beneath makeup hung below her eyes, but she wore no makeup now and looked every minute of sixty or more. Yet there was a vigor waiting to return, a physical strength that had probably saved her life. I suspected tennis or perhaps water aerobics on a regular basis.

She patted a blue-seated chair at right angles with the sofa on which she reclined, and I obediently sat down.

''Who are you, and whatever do you want to ask?'' she said with a forthright smile.

I had been distracted by the tall cubes of windows, the African artifacts hanging on the walls above Native American rugs. The vibrant red and gold and black decor was both eclectic and highly personal, as bold as the architecture of the house. When I took a breath to speak, I discovered there was still a lump in my throat.

"I'm . . . excuse me." I cleared my throat. "I'm Ginger Struve Barnes, and I live on Beech Tree Lane . . . where another woman was attacked earlier this week."

"Yes, I saw it in this morning's newspaper." Corinne Novak's expression conveyed her knowledge of Liz's death; I had no need to mention it aloud.

"She was a friend of mine," I said over the lump.

"Take your time," the woman draped on her sofa assured me. She sounded so professionally patient that I looked more closely at her eyes. This was no frivolous, old-fashioned helpmate; I suspected a complex and far-reaching history all her own. "Would you like some tea or a cold drink? I'm afraid we only have instant coffee." Whatever her background, she relied on her instincts about people, even now when she could just as easily have chosen to hide.

"Oh no," I reassured her. "I won't be staying. In fact I can scarcely believe I'm here, but . . ."

"But you are here, and you must have had a very good reason to come." She patted the knee of my slacks, which for once were something other than denim. Brown wool I realized, although I could not remember putting them on.

"Would you like to start at the beginning?"

I nodded, and considered which beginning pertained.

"This morning," I said, "I went to my friend's to . . . to clean up after the police. There was fingerprint powder everywhere and tomorrow is the funeral, and anyway I had this feeling that the Kelmans' home had been invaded, which may just have been what I knew combined with what I saw."

Corinne Novak nodded slowly, although her expression remained neutral.

"But the more I looked around the less it felt to me as if a burglar had been there. It felt as if someone had come into Liz's house for another reason, maybe even to harm Liz, and then they stole a few things to copy what happened to you." I shook my head. "Now that I'm here it sounds silly, especially since I don't have any facts to back it up.''

''But that's why you're here. To compare. Am I right?''

She was so right that I straightened up in my seat. ''Yes,'' I agreed enthusiastically. ''I'm afraid I had a rather . . . unsatisfying . . . conversation with the policeman in charge a little while ago. I questioned his reasoning, and he took offense. Before I make a fool of myself again, I thought I'd better get my information straight.''

''Quite right. Always arm yourself before combat. So what do you need to know?''

''Were many things taken? Was the thief thorough?''

The woman nodded decisively. ''Quite thorough. He didn't take anything too breakable or bulky, but he took most everything else—jewelry, furs, my husband's coin collection, cash, even a small antique lithograph that was quite valuable.''

''So would you say that the thief knew what he was stealing?''

''Most definitely.''

''The police seem to think that Liz's arrival prevented her intruder from taking very much from the Kelmans' house. Do you have any idea whether you came home at the beginning or the end of the robbery?''

Corinne Novak became thoughtful. ''I can't say for sure, of course, but I do know my arrival didn't phase him much. The lithograph I mentioned used to hang to the left of the front door, and I habitually noticed it whenever I came home. I'm almost positive it was there when I came in with my suitcases, and it was gone when I woke up.''

My excitement had grown as she spoke; and despite my former embarrassment at behaving so brashly, I was glad I had been given an opportunity to ask questions.

''Suitcases? You came home from a trip?''

''Yes, exactly. My husband was out of the country on business, so I went to visit our daughter in Denver. The thief was very happy for the suitcases.''

I took a large breath and let it out. "Just one more question. How did he get in?"

"The police thought he ran a thin knife vertically between the upper and lower windows. They're screwed shut now, but until this week we just had those half-circle locks in the middle. Apparently, they're easy as pie to open with a narrow knife."

"Did you find any toothpicks in your door locks?"

The woman's forehead creased with confusion. "No. Nothing like that. Why do you ask?"

"Because that's how Liz's robber got in."

"The crimes don't sound much alike, do they?" the woman remarked with a skeptical squint.

"Night and day," I agreed.

She insisted on walking me to the door, and just before I left I asked her what kind of work she did.

She smiled and gestured toward a bookshelf displaying about twenty oversized paperbacks with her name on the spines.

"Self-help books," she confided, almost as if we had something in common.

I wished her a speedy recovery.

"You, too," she said, and finally I got it.

Humph, I thought all the way home. How about that.

Chapter 8

Liz's Friday morning funeral was an unsettling affair with probably a hundred twenty people milling around in the uncomfortable, overcrowded chapel. The humid, overcast weather seemed to press everyone even tighter together, and the priest perspired openly.

Rip had attended the viewing with me the night before and felt he wouldn't be missed in the throng of relatives and Marc's co-workers. Plus his taking time off for any reason invited every teacher Bryn Derwyn employed to do the same. I couldn't remember a day Rip had missed since he had become a headmaster.

Personally, I was glad for the freedom to feel how I wanted to feel without my husband watching. As it turned out, he would have been mortified by my behavior.

Like most everyone else, initially I was subdued and reverent. Leaning inconspicuously against the wall near the entrance, I assumed a reflective pose that discouraged conversation while allowing me to observe everyone else.

Marc in particular caught my attention when he had a lengthy dialogue with a young woman who looked slightly familiar. Yet her medium-length brown hair was nothing special, her face pleasant but not especially noteworthy. I felt certain I had never met her . . . Liz. She looked like a young version of Liz. Whoever she was, she had plenty to say to Marc; and he was intent on every word.

Eventually the cluster of others waiting to express condolences cut the conversation short. Marc leaned over to touch the young woman's shoulder and kiss her cheek. He made one more parting remark. She nodded and turned away, followed by his eyes. Only then were the waiting sympathizers able to obtain his attention.

"Please be seated," intoned the priest only moments later. Recorded music with no identifiable tune shushed the crowd and reminded anyone whose attention had strayed why we were here. I shuffled along with the other stragglers and found a single seat halfway back on my side of the room.

To my left were two older women linked to Liz by some fate beyond my comprehension. To my right sat a seven-year-old girl who squirmed and noisily chewed gum. I shut my eyes and permitted my mind to escape both the lofty formalities and the flawed flesh of the congregants. Instead I concentrated on fond memories of my comparatively brief, but genuine, friendship with Liz.

"Corporate relocations," she had once explained, "teach you not to waste time." So by mutual consent we skated past the tentative acquaintance stage to become instant confidantes. We could say anything to each other, and usually did. At least until Monday.

Despite her effort to behave normally, Liz had seemed different, as if she were keeping something to herself despite being unused to deception. I wanted to believe she might have shared that something with me one day, but perhaps that was expecting too much of any friendship.

"Although God never blessed Elizabeth Kelman with children, she would have been an excellent mother," the priest informed us, and the woman next to me clucked critically to her friend. "She hated children. Told me so herself."

My jaw muscles rolled with the clenching of my teeth; the mailman had stepped into my yard.

The disrespectful speaker felt something and glanced toward me. Our eyes engaged.

"She did want children," I snapped. "She just didn't want people like you to know how much."

A rustling seemed to ripple through the room. Three rows ahead a scandalized face stared me down. Behind her to the right another woman's forehead creased with disapproval.

Had I spoken too loudly?

I seemed to be standing. Everyone's eyes were on me, even the priest's. I held my breath, regretting there was no way to reassemble my molecules someplace else via willpower.

The priest recovered instantly and proceeded with his homily. The gathering once again faced forward, leaving me standing like a lighthouse on a pile of rocks.

Mortifying as it might be, there was only one way to take my molecules out of there. My face flaming, I grabbed my purse and pushed past the seven-year-old and her mother until I reached the aisle free and clear. Seconds later I was outside in a fresh, gusty rain shower and running toward my car.

Disoriented, humiliated, and soaking wet, I preferred not to return home. The next hour or more belonged to Liz, and it felt wrong to get caught up in my own life before that time elapsed.

I began driving at random—left, right, straight. It didn't matter. The pointlessness of my decisions reminded me of those Girl Scout penny hikes in which the whole troop flipped a coin at every corner. I realized now that the leader probably hadn't known what else to do with us.

Well, I didn't have anything better to do either.

In a mile or so the massive King of Prussia mall lay before me, a labyrinth of parking lots surrounding a maze of department stores and shops.

Primarily to get out of the rain I parked and went inside, immediately becoming an anonymous woman on an anonymous errand. To my amazement, the mall felt more private than the chapel had. The decor was prettier, too—an elegant combination of pearl-gray and green marble warmed by wood. I chose a bench next to a palm and began to watch everyday life flow around me.

Among the sparse selection of shoppers were a few older men. Most were women. Some walked and talked casually with a friend, either pushing a stroller or not.

After a while, I closed my eyes and said good-bye to Liz.

Soon a calm came over me, and I realized it was time to return home.

Gusty spring breezes had broken up the clouds, leaving Beech Tree Lane freshly washed and fragrant in a steaming haze of sunshine.

Unfamiliar cars clustered around the end of the Kelmans' driveway. I considered stopping in to apologize to Marc, but decided not to intrude. My decision-making faculties were obviously out of kilter; I feared I might make matters worse. Rip was right—Gin *had* been a bit of an alarmist ever since she solved that murder. Time to realize it wasn't my job to right every wrong I encountered. Time to step back and wait for my equilibrium to return.

My own responsibilities were quite enough for me to handle—beginning with that garage door I must have left open.

Chapter 9

The trouble was—I never left the house through the garage, and neither did anyone else in the family. It was cluttered and dirty as an attic and not any more convenient to the cars than the front door.

I climbed out of my relatively new Suburu station wagon and hugged myself for warmth. The garage was two cars wide and stuffed with everything from tools and furniture to bags of old drapes and baby clothes. It faced the driveway sideways, which was why the house would have looked normal if I had glanced in my rearview mirror on the way out.

Since we had only one broad white garage door, an electric opener was a necessity. If the opener was broken, we had to disengage it before anyone could lift the door manually.

A tug on the overhead handle confirmed that nobody had disconnected the electric opener. The door didn't budge and wouldn't have budged without someone pushing the switch in the kitchen or using the remote I kept in my car.

So it must have been absentmindedness on my part, possibly even from yesterday.

Still, I glanced around to see if anything appeared to be missing. I even rattled the interior door to the kitchen to see if it was locked. Everything seemed undisturbed except my peace of mind.

Sam Browder stood at his mailbox reading a pink flyer. He crumbled the page and turned to go, so I shouted to him.

"Wait! Hold on a minute."

I hurried out my drive and the twenty yards farther to where he waited, his expression both patient and concerned.

"Sam, this may sound silly, but my garage door was left open and I don't think I did it. Did you happen to notice anybody around while I was out?"

Today he wore jeans and a turquoise golf shirt that flattered his olive complexion. The premature gray curls among the brown were the flaw that pointed up his physical perfection. He squinted thoughtfully toward my house.

"Sorry. I was working—trying to work—and I'm afraid I just didn't look outside." He hung his head. It swayed with the weight of a heavy disappointment, making me switch from my improbable problem to his real one.

I looked at him closely, and I was reminded quite suddenly why I had sought out Liz's sisterly advice.

For a lingering second Sam also studied me. Fortunately, I had dressed for the funeral in a tailored brown suit—clean, neat, and asexual. On the outside.

Inside, my warning lights pulsed frantically, but I had ventured this far, I figured I might as well follow through. "Do me a favor?" I requested.

Sam lifted an eyebrow.

"Come check the house with me? There's a door into the kitchen from the garage . . ."

"Sure, if you're nervous about it. Be glad to." He stashed his mail back in the box.

On the way past I picked up mine, a bunch of junk mail and another pink flyer.

We went through the hazardous walkway down the right side of the garage, and with Sam Browder breathing easily behind me I unlocked the door to my kitchen. He stepped inside and I followed.

Sam walked to the right along my narrow boxcar of a kitchen and peered through the rectangular opening into our living room. "Want me to . . ." He circled a finger in the air to finish the sentence.

"Yes, please." What else could I say? That inviting him into my house had been a colossal error in judgment? That surprising a burglar might have been safer? That I wished he'd leave me more of the kitchen air to breathe?

He wandered on out into the front hall, peeked idly into the coat closet, then glanced back at me and shyly smiled. He stuck his head into Rip's little office, then continued down the hall, walking first into Chelsea's room, next into Garry's, then turning into the TV room from which we had overheard him arguing with his wife.

With every foot that stretched between him and me my breathing eased. The man's presence stunned me. My own audacity stunned me. What was I doing? Was I really afraid someone had broken into my house, or was there something else on my subconscious agenda?

Sam returned to the hall and pointed upstairs. His eyebrows inquired whether he should proceed.

I shrugged. He proceeded.

I darted for the downstairs bathroom, I was that nervous.

When I emerged, Sam was waiting. He had leaned against the plank table on the living room side of the kitchen pass-through where I'd dropped the mail and my purse.

"Everything looks good," he told me. It was just an observation, not a compliment. Not even close.

The oxygen from my sigh stabilized my pulse.

"Thanks, Sam. Can I offer you a cup of coffee?" Since it was lunchtime, he'd probably interpret that as courteous but not encouraging. Offering him a sandwich would have been tantamount to a proposition.

"No, thanks. I better get back. I didn't get much work done yet."

I repressed another sigh, relief this time, and nodded instead. "Well, thanks for humoring me. With all the stuff that's been going on lately I guess I'm pretty jumpy."

"We all are. We should be."

I nodded again, gratefully.

"Bye," he said.

"Thanks again," I replied, but this time I meant "Thanks for leaving." I'm pretty sure we both breathed easier when he pulled the kitchen door shut behind him.

After his departure, I picked up the pink flyer that had been with our mail. It announced a meeting at Margaret's house next Monday night regarding the formation of a neighborhood "townwatch."

All things considered, I thought I should go.

Chapter 10

If your kids are too young to drive but happen to attend a private school, their social lives probably begin (but do not end) several miles away. A round-trip just for an evening of popcorn and Arnold Schwarzenegger might conceivably add fifty miles to your odometer. Getting your kids invited somewhere overnight was an emergency maneuver not unlike crying wolf.

However, if my response to Sam Browder was any indication, it was time to cash in some chits. Chelsea was already scheduled to be gone Saturday night to Sunday. One little phone call to suggest some reciprocity, and our son was all but packed for Jordy's.

I gave him the good news at dinner on Friday night.

''Aw, Mom . . .'' he complained. The rest of the thought obviously went, ''Why'd you have to do that?''

I poked at my salad. ''Jordy's one of your best buddies. You haven't seen each other lately, and I happened to be talking to his mother . . .'' Then I glanced again at my son.

In a few years he would no doubt use English to tell me to butt out, but for now body language came across loud and clear.

Too late, I remembered about that track thing, that it had been Jordy who made the team instead of Garry. So for the moment Jordy and Garrett Ripley Barnes appeared to be ex-best buddies. Obviously Jordy's mother had been equally as dense about it as I.

"Don't you think you should be bigger about this situation?" Rip suggested.

"If I was bigger, it wouldn't have happened." Garry snorted at a forkful of mashed potatoes.

"You know what I mean," Rip told him. "One of you has to be the first to forgive the other one."

"Not me," Garry said. "He called me a shrimp."

"I'm sorry, Gar," I told him. "But your father and I have plans for tomorrow night, and I've arranged this, so you'll just have to . . . to get through one night. If it goes really badly, you don't ever have to see him again." As Scarlet said, *Tomorrow is another day*, and with luck both boys would soon forget all about track.

After I took a bite of meat loaf, I noticed Rip staring at me quizzically. I squinted back hard so he wouldn't question me out loud until later.

"What was the funeral like?" Chelsea asked out of the blue. It took me a moment to answer.

"Very nice," I said. "Long." A safe assumption since all Catholic services seemed to run long.

"So what's this party we're going to tonight?" I asked Rip to elevate our collective mood.

"Tenth grade parents."

"Ah." The first year Rip was at Bryn Derwyn we held get-acquainted wine-and-cheese parties at our house for each grade, including kindergarten—thirteen parties within three weeks. By the fifth one I couldn't have recognized anyone I'd met if I'd plowed into him or her with a shopping cart. Mercifully, these evenings were now held in the homes of various good-hearted couples. Sometimes Rip and I were in the mood for them. Sometimes not, depending.

"You don't have to go," Rip told me, "if you don't want to."

My husband's concern helped me realize that as rough

as my day had been, accompanying Rip to a cocktail party wouldn't hurt me—and it might help us.

When we were upstairs dressing a few minutes later, Rip finally got to ask what we were doing Saturday night that was so hush hush.

I spun toward him and my skirt swished around my knees. "Spending time together," I announced.

"Oh?"

My greenish-eyed husband treated me to a crooked grin, and I gravitated toward him. We kissed rather nicely for a couple so out of practice. Go to hell, Sam Browder.

Rip waited downstairs for me to finish dressing, and I did my best to make an entrance. His response was to set aside the sports page and walk toward the door.

"Okay," he said. "Let's go to work."

At our destination Karen Lindsey, our hostess, greeted me with surprise. "Ginger, how nice. We weren't sure you'd make it." A white staircase wound toward the second floor. Fresh flowers overflowed a painted bowl set on a side table of the spacious hallway.

I glanced at Rip—he must have mentioned that I'd been to a funeral on the off chance that I would decide to stay home. An understandable precaution; but Karen's awareness of my day meant others might also know, so I would have to be especially careful to steer conversations away from my personal feelings. The whole purpose of the party was to acquaint the tenth grade parents with each other and give them yet another reason to like their child's school.

"Come. Let me introduce you around." Karen directed a graceful wrist toward the dining room. She wore a sheer, broadly striped black dress over an opaque slip. Heavy gold shell jewelry that would have been appropriate for either business or this evening's child-related social affair struck the perfect balance. Karen looked responsible and slightly motherly, but also soft and welcoming enough to encourage her first-time guests to enjoy themselves in her home.

Several couples stood drinking and eating around a mahogany table loaded with hors d'oeuvres. The food, I saw, was catered, although some of the parent parties had been potluck—hostess's choice. I noticed four different cheeses, three dips, and two pâtés, plus small rolls and a plate of turkey and ham for making miniature sandwiches. Rip said hello, then detoured into an adjacent study where a bar was overseen by Karen's husband, John.

The two nearest women introduced themselves, and I eased into a conversation about how the school year was going for their children. Rip brought me a low plastic cup half full of red wine as I listened to raves about how happy "Kevin" was at Bryn Derwyn compared to last year at his previous school.

"I love to hear stories like that," I remarked, for it was true. And I was the one who always heard them. Rip would be singled out for concerns—complaints really—which was why he viewed school events as work. However, the seriously disenchanted families rarely attended a party such as this one.

The evening proceeded, Rip speaking one-to-one with as many of the twenty in attendance as possible. I moved between groups, nibbled pâté and crackers, and waited for the inevitable.

It came when I was alone by the celery sticks. Rip had been cornered in the kitchen by a father with a bald head and black mustache. Most of the others had drifted into the living room across the hall.

"I'm sorry about your loss," Karen said softly so that others would not overhear.

"Thank you," I responded, hoping in vain that that would end that.

"Awful, what happened."

I wanted to refuse the bait but could not without appearing rude. "Yes," I said, then I waited.

"Do the police have any leads?"

"On the robber?"

"Yes."

"They think he's left the state."

Rip's expression as he listened to the man in the kitchen seemed inordinately grim. Perhaps a seriously disgruntled parent had opted to brave the social scene solely for the opportunity to bitch at him.

"Did they get much?"

Much what? Oh—much of the Kelmans' stuff. "No, not very much."

Karen shuddered. Her eyes flicked toward a collection of crystal displayed in a case in the corner of the room, and she seemed to envision losing her life over the precious pieces of glass.

I glanced at my watch. Rip had been standing with an empty cup—the universal passport to the bar—for easily twenty minutes while the mustached man lectured him.

"Excuse me, Karen," I said. "It's getting late—our son's home by himself."

She nodded her complete understanding and approval of my excuse. Private school parents may have other flaws, but they rarely ignore the needs of their children.

I sashayed into the kitchen and put my hand on Rip's sleeve.

"I think Garry's been alone long enough, dear. And Chelsea will be home soon." She actually had a ride to and from a movie, while Garry was probably safely into his personal notion of bliss—old gangster movies on cable.

"Oh, yes," Rip agreed promptly.

"Look into it," the man told my husband ominously.

"Yes, of course," Rip replied seriously.

We said good-bye to everyone as we inched our way through each room, and outside we each breathed in a relaxing chestful of crisp April air.

"Beautiful house," I said. "Nice people."

"Not bad," Rip equivocated. So the kitchen-man had been a bear.

"Comes with the territory," I hinted.

Rip made no reply.

Once home, I thought Rip would shed his weekday attire and tumble right into bed, but instead he loosened his tie and stepped into his little office. A second later the computer screen lighted the room like a miniature shuttle to Mars.

"I'm going to bed," I told my husband's back.

"Be right up," he replied without turning his head.

Talk about depressing.

Apparently, Rip planned to share whatever trouble the mustached man had discussed with him with his computer—but not with me.

Chapter 11

When I awoke Saturday morning, Rip was snoring softly and deeply into his pillow. I let him sleep; I wanted him well rested for our private night. Yes, I wanted his attention, and we deserved the time together. But most of all, Rip obviously needed to step away from the firing range, rub his eyes, relax, refocus. I didn't know anything specific, but I recognized the signs. With a little time, a little privacy, maybe I could get him to talk it out . . .

After breakfast I went out to the garage, in part to straighten up but mostly to check once more whether anything was missing. The clear weather was an ideal fifty-eight degrees, April's finest, and I was back in jeans and a sweatshirt. Garry and Barney kept me company with a bonding boy/dog ball game in the front yard. Too late I noticed that their game left skid marks on the struggling grass.

Tripping over our large bamboo rake reminded me that if I didn't soon clean the leaves off the flower beds, I would be decapitating daffodils. Tomorrow maybe. Right now I wanted to look inside a few more boxes.

About ten, when Rip and Chelsea emerged from the house, I dug my way out of the clutter to see what they had planned. Both wore serviceable old sweat suits, making Chelsea's brand-new white running shoes with black-and-purple reflective stripes impossible to miss. They appeared to be as well engineered as a sports car—and comparatively speaking, just as expensive.

"When did you get them?" I inquired with heavy meaning. Only last weekend I had forbidden her to spend the money.

Chelsea glanced at her feet and tucked back her face. You're not going to make me feel bad about this, she conveyed quite effectively. "Last night before the movie."

Now I remembered. She and her girlfriends had been given a ride to a nearby shopping center. Apparently, it contained an athletic shoe store as well as a theater.

Garry had drawn close, bouncing with curiosity. "Where to?" he asked with transparent envy.

"I'm going to run over at Valley Forge Park," Rip replied. "Chelsea wanted to come along."

So it appeared that our daughter was attempting to scorn calories and contour her baby fat with exercise. There was proud resolve in the dark brown eyes that met mine, plus a hint of defiant confidence. Get ready, Gin. Your daughter has become interested in boys.

"Can I bring my bike?" Garry begged. The park included a paved path five miles long.

Some day, fairly soon, I would pick a moment to question Chelsea about the money for the shoes. For the time being I wanted my daughter to hold onto that modicum of confidence, at least long enough to memorize its feel. As I well knew, the bill would come due soon enough.

Rip glanced at Chelsea, who shrugged off her brother's question. "Sure," Rip told our son, who had hurried around the car to peer into the garage.

"Hey," Garry complained. "Where's my bike?"

And so Rip and Chelsea went running in Valley Forge Park while Garry hid behind his bedroom door—probably to deal with his emotions in private.

I got to wring my hands and earnestly tell the police how

someone in the family might or might not have left our garage door open.

About five, I was doing something clever with hamburger (adding mushroom soup) and contemplating my long-awaited adult evening, when the phone rang.

"Gin, this is Kit. Jordy's coming down with a cold, and it probably isn't such a good idea to have Garry over. I'm really sorry, but . . ."

"No problem," I hastened to interject. "You can't do it, you can't do it."

A sigh was audible over the line. "Thanks for understanding."

"Sure." What else could I say? That Kit should thump Jordy upside the head for being as immature and unforgiving as Garry? "I hope he feels better Monday."

"I think he will."

"I think so, too." So there it was. Garry's best friendship mortally wounded and my attempt to reconnect with my husband on hold—again.

We all ate the hamburger concoction and instant mashed potatoes with the gusto they deserved.

When the phone rang again during the Gelatin/Pudding Surprise (the surprise being that I remembered to fix it in advance), I leaped from my chair in the hope that Kit had talked some sense into her son. Hope literally springs eternal.

"Hello?"

The line remained silent. Then it went dead.

"What?" Rip asked, when he noticed my consternation.

"Hang-up call."

"Probably a wrong number."

I grunted and kept my thoughts to myself. If it had been a wrong number, it was the fourth one we got this week.

Interrupted by only one other call, Garry, Rip, and I spent the evening holed up in the family room. Garry watched a medley of music videos and sitcoms, which from my perspective sounded like rapid mood swings at loud volume. I replaced the buttons on assorted items of clothing and tried not to pine over my lost interlude.

Rip sat with his feet up and a novel in his lap—*The Gold Coast* by DeMille, which was engaging enough for him to tune out the TV.

It is an unwritten law in our house that I answer the phone when Rip is home. This allows him a moment to brace himself before getting hit with any ice water.

On occasion I get doused.

"Did you talk to her yet?"

"Eunice?"

"Did you?"

"You mean Letty?"

"Damn right I mean Letty." Eunice began to cry large alcohol-intensified sobs.

"I tried. She wasn't very receptive."

"Try again, will you? I want to sell that property and get that bastard out of my life."

I had one of those fleeting insights you sometimes get that sounded so possible it was probably true. Eunice needed the proceeds from the house to pay for a divorce. Adding to the desperation in her voice was a sluggish economy, one that had been driving real estate prices down for years. Midpriced homes like the Vickers' languished behind the plastic pages of the multiple-listing books. New houses simply did not get built.

And then I remembered that Eunice sold midpriced houses, and Sam designed single homes.

"She isn't the easiest person to talk to," I remarked a bit more gently, "to say the least."

"Just do it, Gin. Please? I'm not there anymore or I'd do it myself."

I thought of my earlier sympathy for Sam and realized that until I had both sides of the story my compassion should be more evenly dispensed. Fat chance, I know, when divorce is involved, but I had to try.

"I'll do my best," I told her.

"You're a dear," Eunice gushed into the phone.

"Sucker" was the word I probably would have chosen.

When I returned to the family room, Rip stood up and stretched.

"I think I'll throw a few things into a suitcase and then turn in."

"What!" My pulse pounded. My palms began to sweat. I glanced at Garry to check his response to my fear. He laughed along with the television sound track. I permitted Rip to see my dismay.

"Don't you remember?" he asked without much concern.

"Remember what?"

"The conference."

"No."

"There's a financial conference in Baltimore tomorrow afternoon through Monday night. It's on your calendar."

"Didn't notice."

"So you want to help me pack?"

I kissed Garry goodnight and followed Rip upstairs.

I watched him pack, but I didn't help, a subtle and not especially satisfying form of protest.

Chapter 12

Distance is a state of mind.

As soon as Rip left for Baltimore late Sunday morning I felt displaced. My attention span rejected even simple tasks, so I buzzed from one to another.

After I picked up Chelsea from her overnight in Ardmore, I turned her loose on laundry and commandeered Garry to help me rake the flower beds. Almost immediately a gusty breeze kicked up, making the job inefficient and irritating. Yet we persisted; the daffodils had grown half an inch since yesterday.

Trying to keep Garry entertained, I began to speculate about the occupations of the people attending the open house at the Browders'. With mock assurance, I declared the first couple to be a race car driver and a financial analyst.

''Baseball coach and cheerleader,'' Garry said of the next two prospective neighbors.

''Fixes widgets,'' I guessed for a tall, serious man climbing out of a Volkswagen.

''The man or the woman?''

Since his wife was all eagerness and energy, I switched to her.

As expected, Garry asked me what a widget was.

''A widdle gadget with a gween wight.''

For some reason that ended the game. Garry launched

into a report of a TV show so detailed that it might as well have been verbatim. I only half listened while I continued to monitor the nearby stream of home hunters.

Their cars glided to a slow halt. Eyes on the house, the couples would make quiet remarks to one another as they hesitantly opened their doors. Like tourists they would proceed up the Browders' driveway where they were greeted with the professional warmth of Eunice's associate. I noticed more than one person scowl in the direction of Letty's unkempt jungle.

"How many people do you think have gone through so far?" I quizzed my son after his recital finally ended.

"Ten?" he guessed.

"Eight couples at least," I informed him. Garry was not impressed; however, I was. I doubted that Gail and Don Vickers' house had seen that much action in a year.

Eunice must have called in a lot of markers. Poor Sam.

By early evening Rip's absence was so tangible he might as well have been there. Wondering what he was doing right that minute in Baltimore, what he was having for dinner, I shouted to the kids that our pizza was ready.

"Mom, I need five bucks for Mrs. Norton's gift," Garry announced as he took his place at the plank table. Mrs. Norton, his school's popular music teacher, was having a baby.

"Get it for you right after dinner," I told Garry as I contemplated whether or not to use the opening he had given me. Chelsea had taken the table with a faraway, fairly receptive look, so I gave it a shot.

"Which reminds me," I said to her. "I'm curious. Did Dad give you the money for the sneakers?"

"Running shoes," our daughter corrected me.

"Well?"

"Hunk-uh. Baby-sitting money." She had already taken a bite of the pizza.

"That's a lot of baby-sitting." Who had hired her? And when? I simply could not remember.

"Yep."

Careful, Mom. "You didn't tell me why you wanted new . . . running shoes."

"You didn't ask."

Advantage, Chelsea.

That night I stayed awake an extra hour waiting for a peaceful closing to my day. Like Godot it did not arrive, so I wandered downstairs for a glass of wine, something to ease that odd feeling that accompanies Rip's absence from my bed.

My purse on the kitchen counter reminded me of the five dollars I had forgotten to give Garry for his music teacher's baby gift. If I didn't set the money aside now, neither of us would remember in the morning.

Trouble was, there was no money in my wallet. Change, but no bills. Disconcerting, to say the least. On Monday I'd taken one hundred dollars out of the bank. I'd bought gas, picked up some dry cleaning. There should have been about eighty dollars left.

My first thought was of the opened garage door, but my wallet had been with me when that happened. If that happened.

That left Rip's trip and Chelsea's new running shoes. Rip usually informed me when he borrowed cash out of my wallet, and he had not said anything. Also, since he was traveling on business, he had probably taken Bryn Derwyn petty cash.

That left Chelsea, a possibility that seriously rattled me. To my knowledge she had never been dishonest before. I couldn't explain how I knew that, and I suppose I might have been wrong. Yet my money was missing, and I did not remember her having that many lucrative baby-sitting jobs recently. Was this to be the start of a major problem? I simply could not say.

One way or the other, the matter required some thought.

Getting it right was paramount. In a day or two maybe I'd come up with the absolutely dead-center perfect way to handle it. If such a thing existed.

Sleep became even more elusive after that, so I was doubly annoyed when Barney started barking sometime after midnight.

"Mom!" Garry complained from his room. "Barney!" Chelsea scolded from hers.

"I'll go," I told the kids, flipping on a dim light so I wouldn't walk into a piece of furniture. Barney often cried wolf, so I wasn't overly concerned.

Stomping down the stairs, I tried to gauge which sort of bark it was. Not the one for deer. Definitely not the one for another dog trespassing into his space. It was the deep-throated, full-out threatening roar he used when something caught him by surprise and he needed to save face. A sharp noise would do. During daylight a bird landing on a branch would probably do. But it wasn't daylight; it was 1:00 AM.

The ruckus seemed to come from the family room, so I headed there. The house felt drafty. Objects I knew perfectly well looked wrong in the dark. My nightgown tangled around my knees and caused me to stagger into a wall. By the time I got to the dog I was fully awake, and totally annoyed.

His relentless voice had taken on lionlike timbre. I grabbed the beast's nylon choke collar and led him from the family room into Garry's adjacent room.

"Go to bed," I ordered the dog. "Go to sleep." I shut the door. If Barney couldn't see what upset him, he would quiet down; and as long as he kept quiet, Garry wouldn't mind an overweight bed-hog.

I padded back into the family room and parted the curtains. Streetlight from the end of our drive oozed a moony glow across our grass and an equal distance into the cul-de-sac. Shadows trembled. Crickets squeaked. Wind hissed curses into the treetops. Nothing moved that reasonable human vision would consider out of place. No abnormal noises recurred that I could hear.

Still, you buy dog food year in and year out for that one time it isn't a trash can blowing over or the neighbor's cat. Irish setters are rotten guard dogs, true, but sometimes . . . sometimes.

My skin felt as cool as the furniture I touched to feel my way around the house. In Rip's office I hugged myself while I peered out the window, trying to pick out any movement, any change in the tree-shrouded backyard. What unfortunate timing the dog had—Rip was so seldom away overnight.

The thought reminded me of something, something a friend always said.

Liz. Lord, how I missed her. She had always joked that Marc was never home when she needed him to shovel snow or climb a ladder . . . or to frighten away a burglar.

Although I stared even harder into the darkness, I saw nothing unusual. I progressed through the obstacle course of our living room to check the northern side of the house, then into the kitchen for a better look at the drive. No unwelcome lights. Nothing. I returned to bed.

In the morning when I rubbed my sleep-deprived eyes and opened the door for Barney's constitutional, he pushed past my leg and took off. My eyes widened. My mouth dropped open. The dog was gone.

"Chelsea," I shouted. "Barney's run away again. I'm going after him."

Wearing only a shirt over her underwear, our daughter stepped into the hall. "Need your car keys?" she asked. The old remedy. In his younger days horsepower had been the only way to catch up with Barney.

I scanned the empty yard. "He's so out of shape," I said. "I think I'll try on foot first." Fortunately, I was already dressed. "Okay, Mom. Shout if you need help."

I stepped outside, began calling the dog's name. His path through the dewy grass was clearly visible but ended under the trees between our property and Letty MacNair's.

Letty MacNair. The fragile, stubborn woman who could take care of herself, thank you very much. No. I thought as I ran. Not Letty. Nobody better have hurt Letty.

The weeds along the uneven drive slapped at my arms. I was forced to slow before I fell. Which door? Where *was* a door?

The front entrance was centered beneath a sagging portico, but Barney was not there, nor were there any wet paw prints on the porch.

I pressed through the encroaching weeds and back to the driveway, which continued along the length of the sturdy stone house. At the left rear corner stood another small, covered porch. Its door to the kitchen gaped open, and Barney's muddy tracks led inside. I could hear his worried whimpering.

Wiping sweat from my eyes, I inched along in slow motion, finally pushing the door wide enough to enter.

Letty MacNair lay facedown in filth, her wispy hair and ragged clothes caked with blood.

The muscles in my throat went rigid. Memories of Liz knotted my stomach, doubled my fear.

Barney urgently nudged the woman on the floor, stepped back and implored me with his eyes. Then he flopped onto the floor beside Letty, eyed me and whimpered.

I stooped down beside the animal, forced some words through the tension in my throat. "Good dog," I said. "Stay."

That close to Letty I could better see the wound, a swollen area on the left side of her head with a jagged cut two inches long. Fresh blood oozed into the dried crust. Again, that meant Letty still had a pulse, but I touched her neck to confirm it.

Yes. Still alive. I breathed deeply for the first time since I saw the gaping back door. Just like Liz. Too much like Liz. Alive—but for how long?

Frantically canceling out the dingy clutter, the hopelessly

old-fashioned appearance of everything, I scanned the room for a telephone.

Nothing. If I hadn't seen lights in the windows at night I would not have believed the house had electricity.

"Stay, Barney," I repeated. "Stay."

I had no choice. I fled for home, picking my way along the rutted drive, running full out across the few feet of street on toward my front door shouting, "Chelsea. Chelsea! Call an ambulance."

Chapter 13

It unsettled me, to say the least, how often the police had been called to Beech Tree Lane recently. What? Four times in the last week? For Liz, for the thefts of Bonnie's television and Garry's bike, and now for Letty's assault.

I thought about the unlikelihood of all this while I waited in Letty's driveway for the paramedics to examine her and gently lift her onto their gurney.

I stayed because I could not leave. Maybe it was only second-guessing, but I felt awful for not calling the police during the night when Barney had begun to bark.

"You riding along?" asked the driver as he prepared to shut the ambulance door. Perhaps he misgauged the concern on my face, perhaps even mistook me for a relative. He waited for my answer.

His question was a good one. Just how much responsibility was I willing to accept for my reclusive next-door neighbor?

I glanced back over my shoulder. Right now in Letty's indescribably squalid kitchen, a kitchen that could have been outfitted in nineteen hundred or the Middle Ages, police technicians struggled to separate evidence from the roach eggs and mouse droppings among the empty Doritos bags. Letty conducted her life in that kitchen and I never imagined, never asked, never cared . . .

* * *

I informed the driver that I would follow along in my car.

Due to the competitive trend in the medical care business, Hobbs Memorial Hospital had recently become more compact and efficient. Emergency registration consisted of a tidy mauve-and-blue cubicle centered behind the initial reception desk, which was open to attack from all directions. Plastic chairs lined the perimeter of the waiting room. The floor was blue-and-white harlequin tile, the treatment areas behind white curtains on the left, windowed metal double doors into the main building to the right.

Ambulance delivery bypassed the harried receptionist as did I, but in due time the red-haired, freckle-faced farm girl in the cubicle crooked a finger at me and reeled me in.

''Are you here with Letty MacNair?'' she asked after I was seated.

I admitted I was.

''Are you her daughter?''

I shook my head. ''Next-door neighbor. Actually, I scarcely know her.''

The freckled face puckered with puzzlement and chagrin, so I elaborated. ''I found her this morning, and I don't think there's any family, certainly nobody I'd know to call.''

''I see. Then why don't you tell me what you know, and we'll see what else we need to find out.''

''Sure.''

''Name?''

''Letty MacNair.''

''Is that short for Letitia?''

''I don't know.''

''Okay. Address?'' I recited the address. ''Is that a single dwelling?''

''A house? Yes.''

''Does Ms. MacNair own or rent?''

I thought about that. ''I think she owns.''

''But you're not sure.''

''Right.''

Freckles was beginning to distrust my information, but her fingers remained optimistically poised over the computer keys. "Health insurance?" she challenged.

"Actually," I said, "I'm ready for that one." Before I went to fetch my car, I had requested permission from the policeman in charge to check Letty's wallet for insurance ID. Her purse, a maroon plastic relic from when plastic was thick and nearly indestructible, had already been dusted for fingerprints. Her "wallet" happened to be a grimy petit point change purse that did not retain prints. The technician gave it to me as well as Letty's house keys so I could deliver them to Letty later.

I extracted the change purse now and snapped it open for Freckles to view the quarter and three dimes inside.

The registrar pinched her lips to chastise me for my sense of humor.

"No health insurance." She tapped on a few computer keys.

"Person responsible for her bills?" She raised an ironic eyebrow.

"Not me."

"No relatives."

I shrugged. "Nobody comes around. Maybe I could look around the house for letters, something like that."

The woman grunted.

"I don't mean to be impertinent," I said. "Really. I don't know Letty very well, but I like her. I'm the only person on the street who's ever talked to her."

Freckles managed to thaw a little. Maybe her curiosity was finally piqued. "Reclusive?" she suggested sympathetically.

"Very."

"Eccentric?"

"Think of bag lady," I said to cut her speculation short. Already one person too many mistook Letty MacNair for a wealthy eccentric.

The pert nose flared, perhaps as she imagined Beech Tree

Lane harboring weird, dirty women. After kneeling down in Letty's kitchen, I wasn't especially tidy myself.

The registrar and I looked at each other a minute before I broke the silence.

"So I'm wondering. If Letty's as broke as I think she is, will she still get good care? And who will pay?"

Freckles smiled with half her face. "You will. The next time you come in."

I winced.

Finally, the woman abandoned her computer pose and leaned toward me on her elbows. "She'll get excellent care even if she doesn't have any more than what you showed me. We'll try to find relatives, of course, who would know her circumstances. We'll also check into Medicare. If she has any assets, such as a house, we'd use that as collateral."

"She'd lose her house?"

The woman wagged her head. "Highly unlikely."

"Last resort?"

She nodded.

"Thank you." I realized I had sighed with relief.

After I reminded the harried nurse at the centralized desk that I was waiting for information about Letty MacNair, I parked myself on a plastic chair. Not much activity in an emergency room on a Monday morning. Just a housewife whose finger probably needed stitches and an old couple, the husband's painful leg propped on a chair. Both parties had drawn tight inside their problems. No one met my eye.

I distracted myself with an old issue of the *Main Line Times*. The police blotter listed a trash can fire and some smashed mailboxes. Also, a car was broken into, not Bonnie's; and, of course, there was no mention of the attack on Corinne Novak because the paper was dated last Wednesday. Next week's local news would probably cause a small sensation.

In about ten minutes a young man in a blue chambray shirt and white coat emerged blinking from Letty's cubicle.

He carried a Bic pen and a stainless steel clipboard. He mumbled to the nurse and she waved a hand toward me.

"Ms. . . . ?" he prompted, extending a slender hand.

"Mrs. Barnes," I obliged.

"Dr. Rosen," he said. "And you are? . . ."

"Letty's neighbor." I said it in syllables as if answering a second-grade quiz. I'm not fond of aloof doctors.

He blinked more vigorously while he studied my face for real. Since most of the people he spoke to were more emotionally involved than me, and therefore more interested in what he said than how he said it, it brought him up short to be mocked.

"No relatives?" he asked, glancing behind me hopefully.

"Nope. I'm it."

"We don't usually give out information to . . ." He had brown eyes and thick glasses and one of those short, scruffy beards they hand out in medical school. He looked exactly like my gynecologist and the orthopedic surgeon whose boy is in kindergarten at Bryn Derwyn. I think of it as the "generic doctor" look.

"Doctor," I said a bit impatiently. "I found Letty this morning. I've been waiting to find out how she is. There are no relatives that I know of. Nobody but me. How is she?"

Pathetic. I'd been listening to my voice raise, and it struck me that the situation was pathetic. Here was a human being who appeared to have nobody more interested in her welfare than me. And who was I? A near stranger too friendly not to say hello, whose dog apparently cared more about the woman than I did.

That is, until I heard myself.

The generic doctor sighed and met my eyes and allowed himself to share his own feelings for a minute.

He shook his head and glanced at the floor. "Sorry," he said. He pressed his forehead with his thumb and middle finger, and I knew it was a headache, knew he hadn't slept.

"Concussion," he told me. "Broken wrist. Vital signs

weak but already responding to plasma. She wasn't in real good shape when this happened. She's going to be here awhile."

"But she's going to be okay?"

"She's elderly. She's got problems. But, yes, I'd say she's going to be okay."

"Thanks."

During our parting handshake his eyes strayed toward the patient waiting in the next cubicle. I was glad his head was turned and even gladder to get my hand back quickly. I needed to reach into my purse for a tissue.

Chapter 14

After I finished blowing my nose, the curtain of Letty's cubicle parted, and an orderly and a nurse wheeled one of those tall gurneys out with Letty on it. Bandages swathed her head. A bag on a hook dripped clear fluid into her arm. Her skin looked fresh-washed and white, her eyes very vague.

"Please," I said. "Give me a second. I'd like her to know I'm here."

The nurse nodded to the orderly. "Just say hello," she advised. "She's a bit upset about the robbery. Keep's saying, 'Give it back. It's not yours,' something like that. So go easy." I assured the woman I would be very brief.

"Letty?" I said. "It's Gin from next door. I'll be back to see how you're doing."

Letty turned her head toward me without recognition.

Then I realized she might not be seeing well. For that matter she might not even know my name.

"Ginger Barnes with the big red dog. From next door."

Nothing. I shrugged defeat. Maybe I'd been doing it for myself anyway.

The nurse nodded again and began to push the gurney toward the door leading into the hospital corridor.

"Wait," said a feeble voice. Letty's. Her eyes had taken

on an intensity. The nurse raised her hand for the orderly to stop.

I moved in close so I wouldn't miss anything Letty had to say. "Who hurt you?" I asked.

She waved her hand impatiently. "Hide me mail," she said.

I looked at the nurse. She shook her head; she didn't understand any better than I.

Letty pawed at my sleeve, grabbed on, pulled me closer. "Hide me mail."

Did that mean what it sounded like? Better ask. "You want me to hide your mail?"

"Yes."

"Sure, but first . . . ?" I didn't get to finish the question. Letty pulled me closer and whispered.

"Garbage can."

"What . . . ?" I started again.

"Out back. Promise." Unusual request under the circumstances. It crossed my mind that Gail and Wendy had been pressuring Letty about suburban etiquette after all, otherwise why insist that I put out her trash and take in her mail?

"Sure. But first, did you see who hit you?"

"Promise," she said emphatically.

The nurse began to fidget. "She really shouldn't . . ."

"Promise!" Letty insisted, her hand still tight on my sleeve.

"I promise. No problem."

Letty released my arm and lolled into what looked like instant sleep. Apparently she had no intention of telling me more about what had happened, if indeed she knew anything more to tell.

I felt both disappointed and unsettled. If our reclusive neighbor didn't wish to tell the police what had happened, that was her business. But my family was my business, and for their safety I wanted to know—needed to know—what was going on around us.

I watched until the gurney was out of sight beyond the double doors.

There seemed to be a wet tissue in my hand. I tossed it into a wastebasket and drove home.

Chapter 15

When I phoned to ask, the police officer in charge of Letty's case assured me that they were finished with her house, and yes I could do whatever I wanted to get it ready for her return. "Good luck," he added emphatically.

"Same to you," I said, since we both were faced with formidable tasks.

I took a few minutes to regroup with coffee, toast, and aspirin, to reassure the dog, and to put away the peanut butter and jelly the kids had used to pack lunches. Then I changed into the jeans and sneakers I reserve for my filthiest chores, possibly sealing the driveway or something equally ruinous, in preparation for searching through Letty's house. I had told the hospital registrar I would look into the possibility of family, but my motive was partially ulterior. If Letty had even one relative, I could gracefully retreat.

A chair under the doorknob prevented the kitchen door from opening. This time I noticed that the doorjamb was splintered where it had been forced. Apparently the last cop to leave did the chair trick and exited out the front.

That particular lock was stiff from disuse, but with a little pressure the key I found in Letty's purse worked. Soon I stood inside a musty vestibule facing broad stairs and a hall leading through to rooms at the back. The scale was grand, from the pre-petroleum crunch/chamber-pot era. There would be an attic, a full basement, and a servants' section by itself upstairs. A dining room with a hint of mahogany lay to the left, and on the right behind double doors a living room dominated by a fireplace spanned the depth of the house.

Closing the front door was my first mistake. The dust and mold—for the carpet was a damp thickness of mush—nearly choked me. A glance at the ruined ceiling explained the water. The MacNair residence was in serious need of a new roof.

I gave the living room a quick run-through. There the ceiling appeared dry and unmarred, but everything else was covered with more cobwebs and dust than I've ever seen outside of a vampire movie. Two sofas with soft cushions flattened by age bracketed the fireplace. The brass candlesticks on the mantel had blackened from neglect. On three walls musty books stood perfectly aligned on their shelves. Although there were recent tracks on the Oriental carpet, probably made by the police, anyone could see that Letty had not used the room in years.

For my purposes I wanted Letty's living quarters, not this rotting museum of yesteryear; so I bypassed the dining room, which reeked with decay, and aimed for the back of the house.

The broad, rectangular kitchen possessed four doors—the one propped closed with the chair opening onto the small, square porch that faced the backyard, one into the dining room, another to a staircase probably leading to the servants' quarters, and the fourth to a storage pantry full of dishes, which in turn led to a sitting room. This appeared to be where Letty lived.

I heaved a big sigh to quash my feelings of horror and revulsion. The kitchen had been the worst, but this was scarcely better. Letty owned a radio for entertainment and a dirty blanket and pillow on a long sofa for sleeping. Three housedresses hung on a clothes tree, and a heavy wool coat drooped from a hook against the wall. Hose and underwear clumped together in the top drawer of a bureau. Everything was threadbare. Everything was dirty. Letty's own odor remained strong, mingling with the musky smell of old furniture and very old food.

The closet in the corner must have been converted into a powder room with the advent of indoor plumbing. A towel I preferred not to touch hung on a nail hammered into the back of the bathroom door. Inside were a rust-stained porcelain sink and a bucket on the floor next to the toilet.

I held my nose, extended a finger, and pressed the lever to flush the toilet. Nothing happened, which explained the bucket. I imagined the old woman hauling water from a deeper sink to perform the necessary function, but I did not imagine her doing it more than once a day. Pinching the towel between two fingers, I shut the door then kicked the towel close to its base to minimize the stink. Then I turned my attention to the modest-sized room Letty called home.

The braided brown rug had been spared water and mold but little else. If I wanted to be complimentary, I'd say the floor remained remarkably free of clutter. Perhaps Letty liked an unimpeded path to her favorite chair, a green slip-covered thing with grease stains.

"Get on with it," I admonished myself out loud. "This isn't a garden tour."

I proceeded to finish searching the few drawers of the bureau, the two occasional tables. There was no desk, no scattered mail, no personal papers of any kind.

"Hide me mail," Letty had implored in early twentieth century uneducated English. Perhaps all her papers were hidden—or stolen!

I wondered more than ever how Letty had come to live in this relic. Had the household simply died off one by one until she was the only person left? Did anyone in an official capacity even know she was here?

My housekeeping sensibilities had reached the gagging

point. Before I faced Letty's kitchen I thought a glimpse of my own suburban castle, for that was surely what it seemed by comparison, might put me back in touch with reality.

Farther back a crumbling stone wall surrounded the worst of Letty's jungle, but standing on the small back porch where Letty's attacker had entered, I could just see my front door through the strip of trees and bushes that edged the front halves of our properties. Breathing marvelously fresh air and gazing at our silly red pseudo-barn with its crabgrass lawn and mismatched patch on the roof made me feel almost maudlin.

As usual, my father came to mind. "Emotions," he often reminded me, "are only useful for determining action."

Yes, Dad, you coldhearted intellect. You're probably right again.

While I was outside I walked down to pick up Letty's mail, and by the time I returned to her living quarters I had a better grip on what I was doing—and why.

"Resident," said the supermarket flyer. "Resident," said the ad for mailing labels and also the course list for summer classes at a nearby college.

I lay the three items on a corner of the tin-covered worktable centered in the kitchen. Surely Letty didn't expect me to hide her junk mail. If a thief came in and took it away, she would be lucky. The same with most anything else left in the house. I couldn't imagine that the upstairs held any surprises.

I propped open the outside kitchen door, fluffed out one of the trash bags I'd brought, and set to work on the litter of Doritos bags and other assorted debris that covered much of the available space in Letty's kitchen. After I made a dent in the accumulation of trash, I would see about replacing that splintered doorjamb, my favorite kind of challenge. I thought we had a board about the right size in our garage. Hammer, saw, nails, chisel . . .

Before I knew it I heard the kids coming down the street

from the bus stop, arguing loudly about whether some boy named Tim liked Chelsea or not.

My spirits lifted. If the kids were home, Rip would soon follow. His conference had ended at noon. He had probably driven straight back to Bryn Derwyn Academy from Baltimore.

Time to transform the work-worn Cinderella into version number two.

Rip sipped a drink and watched as I finished cooking dinner. ''Conference any good?'' I asked, trying to humor him into a good mood. He came home so preoccupied that I decided to postpone mentioning Letty.

He shrugged.

''You get one idea from it? You always said if you got one idea from a conference, it was worth the trip.''

Silence.

''Why do I feel as if I'm poking at a turtle with a stick?''

''One or two,'' he said in answer to my original question.

''You miss me?''

Rip tossed me a mischievous grin and took hold of my hands. His rump leaned against the counter, and I anticipated him pulling me in close.

Instead he allowed me to watch his grin fade along with his attention.

''What's the matter?'' I was frightened now, not just worried.

''Tired, that's all.'' He looked into my eyes when he said it, the better to appear completely honest. I loosened his tie some more and snuggled in until my temple rested on his collarbone. He lowered his chin onto my head.

''What aren't you telling me?'' I wondered into the front of his shirt.

As if pulling himself out of it for my benefit, Rip became more animated. ''Just ordinary shit, Gin. Nothing unusual.''

''You sure?''

"Yep. Come back here. That felt good." I melted myself against him.

"Oooh," Garry leered from the doorway, his older sister close behind.

Shyly, Rip and I separated. He led the kids around to the dining table. I set our food on the shelf of the pass-through, then joined them at the table.

After a round of personal reports, I finally told Rip about Barney's fuss during the night and how the dog had led me to Letty this morning.

"I called the nursing station just a little while ago, and she's still sedated from getting a pin in her wrist. I'll probably go see her in the morning."

His own concerns had temporarily recessed, and Rip gazed sympathetically into my eyes.

Reassuring. My husband still lived here; circumstances had been keeping us apart, nothing more. Be patient, I told myself. Just another detour along the marital road.

We finished the meal, and Rip and I began to clean up.

"Can you take it easy tonight?" I asked.

"Going to. I'm beat."

"I'm going over to Margaret's for a little while. She's invited everybody on the block to talk about starting a townwatch."

Rip clapped me on the shoulder. "Say hi for me." He put the last dish in the dishwasher and wandered across the front hall to his office. The computer chirped.

"I hope this detour turns back soon," I muttered to myself, shaking my head.

After I dried my hands, I grabbed a jacket out of the closet to wear to Margaret's. Around here April evenings can really have an edge.

Margaret's smile became pinched when Richard Diamond refused her home-baked cookies with a curt wave of his hand. His square, commanding face suggested that he was distracted by more important matters—such as finding a new livelihood—but Margaret seemed disappointed just the same.

The Shannahan family was represented by Nelson, a pudgy, prematurely balding blond man with probing hazel eyes, who took two cookies from Margaret's plate with a boyish smile and allowed Margaret's motherly face to warm once again.

Probably Patsy Crouthamel also wanted a cookie because the effort it took to decline produced a scowl. She clamped her hands under her folded arms. "We better get on with it," she said. "Some of us can't stay too long."

"Yes," Margaret agreed, immediately stowing the cookie plate on a side table. Her husband Sol sat on the wing-backed chair, and she settled on the sofa between Patsy and his knee.

I noticed that our two hosts seemed connected and compatible in the way only years together will join two individuals. Thinking of Rip at home complaining into his computer caused me to envy the Raymonds intensely.

With gentle command, Sol addressed the people gathered in his living room. "In addition to Liz Kelman you may have heard there's been another attack on our street," he said. His unbuttoned business shirt revealed wattles of excess skin. His hands displayed the blotches of either old age or certain strong medications. "Someone entered Letty MacNair's house and knocked her unconscious. The police don't know for sure whether anything was taken, but the assumption is that the intruder expected to find money hidden somewhere."

"Does anybody know how she's doing?" asked Neil Grogan, the computer science professor. He was a bulky middle-aged man with thinning gray hair and thick silver-rimmed glasses.

Margaret gestured toward my spot against a wall.

I straightened on my dining room chair so I wouldn't mumble. "Her doctor told me she isn't in the best of health, but she's going to be okay."

Neil nodded solemnly, as I expected he would—he's a nice, decent guy—but my focus strayed toward the ever-critical, honey-blonde Gail Vickers, who originally complained about the condition of Letty's property. She remained appropriately silent, even grim.

Her husband, Don, was also present. Tall and even blonder than his wife, wearing investment banker glasses and a pinkie ring, he relaxed in his black pin-striped suit, sans neckwear, the way actors relax in character—the form looked perfect, but you knew it was faked. "Don't forget our trash can fire on Saturday night," he reminded Sol.

Trash can fire? Hadn't I just read something about that?

Patsy Crouthamel's sea blue jumper clashed with the Williamsburg blue sofa. She lifted a hand and asked whether anyone had been getting hang-up calls. To her right, prim and perfectly dressed, Margaret perked to attention, her eyes darting from Gail and Don Vickers to Nelson Shannahan to Richard Diamond, Professor Neil Grogan and me then back to Patsy. That was our group. Naturally, Marc Kelman had not come, and of course Letty was missing. Apparently Sam Browder told Sol that he subscribed to a security service and that that would have to do.

"I've gotten hang-up calls," Gail admitted. She quickly took her own visual survey. Every head nodded, even mine.

"Our mailbox was smashed," Neil Grogan offered.

"Ours, too," said Patsy. "Anybody else?"

Negative head shakes. "You live at the end of the street," Nelson observed. "Maybe some kid just drove along Monroe and kept going."

"What's the difference?" Don asked. He seemed to be the most anxious of the men present, perhaps because his house was still unsold.

"The point is that crime in this neighborhood has suddenly increased," Sol continued patiently. "The police aren't much help . . ." Neil began to grumble disagreement, but Sol merely raised the volume. ". . . With prevention, so I propose that we do something about it ourselves."

"What?"

"A volunteer townwatch committee."

"How's that work?"

"We take turns patrolling our street—two, three times a night."

"Every night?"

"I'd like it to be every night for a while, but we have to see how many participants we get."

"What'll it cost?" Neil asked.

"Nothing."

"How do you figure?"

"The paperwork for scheduling will be minimal, and I'll do that myself. When we patrol, we'll use car phones or portable phones, which I'm sure some of us already own. If the person patrolling doesn't own one, I'll lend him or her mine."

"What exactly does a patrol person do?" Richard asked.

"Checks for unfamiliar cars, open doors, suspicious lights. The police will teach us all that. If we agree this is something we all want to do, I've arranged for us to join the next training session in Tredyffrin, where they've had an active townwatch organization for years. In fact that's where I got most of my information."

"Suppose we see something? What are we supposed to do?" Nelson asked.

"Just phone the police—period," Sol replied emphatically.

Neil Grogan wagged his head. "I don't see how sporadic patrols will accomplish anything. If a crook is casing our street, won't he just operate around the patrols?"

"Maybe," Sol agreed. "But statistics prove that the word gets out quickly, and the criminals just plain bypass the area."

"That just doesn't make sense," Nelson disagreed. "Crooks aren't that stupid."

"But they are that careful," Sol insisted. "The Tredyffrin PR officer told me that it's the training that makes the most difference. Trained citizens are on the alert for strange vehicles in their area all the time, day and night. If something looks suspicious, they know the police are grateful to get a call—even if it turns out to be nothing. Believe me, I talked to our local cops and they *love* the idea. They can't be everywhere, and let's face it folks—we've got a problem.''

There were grudging grunts and nods, and Margaret seized the moment to pass out a sign-up sheet.

''I'll ask Marc and Sam if they're interested in helping us,'' Sol told us. ''The more participation we get, the easier it will be on everybody.''

''When do you hope to start?'' Patsy asked.

I had been searching my mind for the trash can fire connection, and suddenly I had it. This morning, while waiting for news about Letty, I had read about a trash can fire in the *Main Line Times*. The article also mentioned smashed mailboxes and a car break-in. What disturbed me most was that the crimes on our street reflected what had occurred elsewhere in the county during the previous week.

''The next training session is April 18, next Tuesday night at the Tredyffrin library,'' Sol told us. ''It only takes about an hour or an hour and a half. If any of you are interested in doing informal patrols this week, stay a minute; we'll have to clear it with the police. But I can't imagine they would object.''

I wondered if it would be too ''alarmist'' to say something about the newspaper coincidence. The meeting was clearly coming to a close; my opportunity would soon evaporate.

But what exactly should I say? ''Listen, folks, we seem to be getting a whole county's worth of crimes right on this block. Are we lucky, or what?''

I glanced around at my neighbors and once again chose silence. Perhaps it was the newspaper coincidence that made me cautious, but I believed that someone with a sinister agenda had singled out our block—a suspicion that engendered more than a few fears.

As Neil pointed out, crooks are not stupid. They particularly would not risk apprehension for a prank such as lighting some trash on fire or clubbing a few mailboxes with a baseball bat. Viewed separately, the theft of the television from the Diamonds' car, the bike from our garage, could be written off as random, relatively commonplace crimes—but not when they happened a day apart across the street from an assault and battery and only a few houses away from a murder.

I still had my suspicions about Liz's death, especially considering what I knew about her marital problems. But to me, the rest of the crimes pointed toward an amateur who wanted something very badly, and that something was probably on Beech Tree Lane.

Which further meant that the perpetrator just might be right in the Raymonds' living room assessing this new obstacle to his goal.

I glanced around a second time with a different perspective. Something dangerous was going on around here. I had no idea who or what or why, but either by accident or design one neighbor was dead and another was presently in Hobbs Memorial Hospital.

When my turn came, I signed up for the townwatch with a flourish and passed the sheet along.

Walking home in the dark, I warily watched for strange moving shadows and flashlights where they didn't belong.

Rip was in bed sound asleep when I found him. His suitcase of dirty laundry gaped at me symbolically from the bedroom floor.

Chapter 16

Tuesday, April 11, blustered in like an irritable goat. The staff at Hobbs Memorial seemed calm by contrast, professional caregivers braced for any sort of turmoil. Even if it happened to be a facade, I appreciated their effort.

After admission, I knew Letty would have been assigned a staff physician, not the original one from the emergency room; so I notified the nurses at the floor desk that I wanted to speak with that doctor when he or she had a minute.

''You want Dr. Ellen Bixnell,'' the nurse remarked after consulting a chart. ''I'll inform her that you're here.''

I thanked the woman, then I slipped into Letty's room to say hello.

Her roommate, equally as elderly as Letty, lay angled against her pillows watching a morning soap opera. Toothless mouth agape, her bony hand grasped the pillowcase so hard her enlarged knuckles were white. Letty couldn't listen in even if she wanted to because the woman was using earphones. It occurred to me to ask what television rental cost; it could be a small gift from me for the duration of Letty's stay.

I eased to her side and watched her milky gray eyes flutter open. The crisp white linens served to emphasize the unhealthy color of her skin. Her hair had been shaved away from her right temple to accommodate the bandaged stitches from her cut. Also, her face had been washed and her teeth cleaned; but it had been years since Letty had visited a dentist, if indeed she had ever visited a dentist. Maybe some arrangement could be made to repair the neglect before sending her back home. Another question to ask.

I stroked the fingers extending from the cast on her right wrist.

"Good morning," I said. "How are you feeling today?"

Letty turned toward me, blinking with confusion. "You're . . . ?"

"Gin Barnes from next door," I reminded her. "I found you yesterday. Or I should say our dog Barney found you. How are you feeling?"

Letty squeezed her eyes as if looking inward. "Been better," she admitted.

"Letty, do you have any relatives?"

She looked up again. "What?"

"Family."

"Just me friends." Her eyes grew moist.

That again. Maybe the blow on the head or some medication had caused her mind to go fuzzy. Or maybe vague was her normal condition. My previous conversations with her had certainly never gone the way I expected.

"Do you have any idea who hit you?" I asked, not particularly hopeful of an answer.

Letty moved her head fractionally side to side. No.

Since those two questions about summed up what we had to say to each other, I glanced around searching for small talk. In contrast to her toothless neighbor, Letty's side of the room was a desert of white, tan, and beige. No flowers or cards. No frilly bathrobe hanging on a hook.

"Would you like me to bring you some daffodils from your yard? They're the first ones on the block to bloom."

"Don't bother."

"I took care of the garbage from the kitchen as you suggested, but I wasn't sure I understood what you meant about hiding your mail. It was only junk yesterday, so I left it on the table . . .''

Letty's eyes widened. ''Hide it. Hide it all,'' she implored me.

''But . . .''

''In zuh garbage bucket out back.'' She lifted her head but had to drop it back. Still, she managed to grab my arm with her good left hand. The grip was firm, almost painful.

''Okay,'' I said. ''Whatever you want.''

''Promise.''

''Sure. I promise. You want me to put all your mail in the garbage bucket out back.''

Letty visibly relaxed.

I kept my confusion to myself. When I had finished stuffing three trash bags with the detritus in her kitchen, I looked outside in vain for a trash can or two to store them in until collection day. Instead I found a stinking mound of rotting foodstuff back in the corner of the walled kitchen garden—or what had once been a kitchen garden in a previous incarnation. Currently it seemed to be the site of the Cat and Rat Olympics.

A woman wearing a royal blue silk blouse, and a long lab coat over a gray wool skirt leaned against the doorjamb. She had a stethoscope around her neck, short, no-nonsense salt-and-pepper hair, and clean blunt fingernails.

''Dr. Bixnell?'' I asked.

''Yes. You wanted to speak with me?''

I excused myself from Letty and joined the doctor in the hallway. She unobtrusively closed the door.

I explained who I was, then I said, ''I'd like to help Letty get back on her feet, but I'm not sure where to begin. I can't find any evidence of family; and frankly, I can't see how she manages to stay in her house.''

''I can only tell you about her physical health, Mrs. Barnes, but the degree of malnutrition I've observed goes along with what you say. Nobody's been looking after Letty MacNair for quite some time except Letty MacNair, and she hasn't been doing a very good job.''

''Malnutrition?''

Dr. Bixnell nodded. ''I see you're skeptical, but I assure you the evidence is clear.''

''I don't mean to question you, doctor, but I'm trying to understand. If she's malnourished, why isn't she . . . thinner?''

'' 'Malnourished' means her diet is poor in nutrients. Often people who can't buy enough to eat choose filling food high in calories.'' I thought of the marshmallow feel of Letty's arm when I almost knocked her down in the street.

Also thinking of the empty containers I had cleaned up the day before, I remarked, ''Corn chips and doughnuts,'' mostly to myself.

''Exactly,'' Bixnell agreed. ''It's my opinion that her poor diet hastened the growth of her cataracts.''

I had been expecting to talk about the bump on Letty's head or maybe how long her wrist would be in a cast. ''Excuse me,'' I said, ''I'm trying to get up to speed. Cataracts?''

''Yes. Advanced ones. Letty MacNair is nearly blind.''

I slouched back against the wall.

''She needs surgery to see well again.''

My whole body sagged. After a moment, I met the doctor's gaze. ''Can that be done while she's here? I mean before she's released?''

Bixnell gave me a smile, my reward for finally catching up. ''Definitely. My choice would be early next week.''

''What doctor would she get?''

''Anybody with time . . .''

''. . . who wouldn't mind waiting for their money.''

Bixnell shrugged, but the smile held firm.

''Let me ask around,'' I said. ''I've got somebody in mind.'' A Bryn Derwyn parent who happened to be connected to Hobbs Memorial.

''Letty will have to agree . . .''

"You sign her up, and I'll find a willing surgeon." At least I hoped I would.

"Oh, and doctor, I need a little favor."

"What's that?" she asked.

"Letty's house is beyond filthy. I'm going to offer to clean it up, but she may resist. If she does, I'd like to tell her you won't let her go home until it's . . . sanitary?"

Bixnell's smile widened. "You may. And, furthermore, you won't be lying."

Our conversation was finished. Dr. Bixnell smiled once more over her shoulder and returned to the chart rack at the end of the nurses' station.

I leaned against the wall a while longer, until I finished absorbing what I'd learned. Now at least the condition of Letty's place made some sense. Maybe she had always been sloppy, but nobody was quite that slovenly by choice. More likely Letty's living conditions reflected years of failing eyesight and poverty.

I caught myself shaking my head with amazement. A proud woman, destitute and nearly blind, living a baseball's throw from my front door, and I took so little notice from month to month that I hadn't even guessed.

I glanced inside Letty's room once more; but her curtain was drawn, and all I could see was the toothless woman watching television.

How many years ago had I hoped to escape simply by renting Letty a TV?

I called ahead to be certain I would catch Eunice Browder in the real estate office.

"I only need five minutes," I told her over the phone. "It's about Letty MacNair."

"Ten forty-five," my recently departed neighbor told me, always the businesswoman. "I've got an eleven o'clock showing." I opted for the traditional, "Thank you," instead of what I wanted to say.

Eunice stood restlessly at her desk flicking brochures

with her fingernail as if they were contaminated with something. Today's suit was the yellow of a Mercedes Benz or scrambled eggs. The subtle hue turned her complexion to porcelain and her hair to fire. Even the gold on her ears and fingers glowed smugly, but perhaps I was developing an attitude toward Eunice Browder that wasn't especially neighborly. I'm not fond of emotional drinkers telling me what to do. Or maybe I just wanted an excuse to dislike Sam's wife.

She folded her arms and brightened as I approached the desk.

"Did you speak with her?" she asked.

"Are you going to offer me a chair, or aren't we sitting today?"

"Oh, sure. Sure. Sorry." She gestured toward an aluminum and tweed thing for me and drew in a larger tweed thing that looked as if it would accommodate just about any pose. Forced attentiveness was the present choice.

"So is she going to cooperate?" I noticed the spacious room was discreetly dotted with desks. Ficus trees and other assorted foliage gave an impression of privacy.

When I finished glancing around, I addressed Eunice's question my own way. "Yes, I think so. Dr. Bixnell has a nice professional manner. And Letty doesn't give the nurses any trouble."

Creases marred the real estate maven's cameo pose. "Gin. I asked you whether Letty is going to clean up her yard. What's all this . . . business . . . about doctors and nurses?"

"Then you haven't heard?"

"Heard what?"

"Letty's in the hospital. I found her Monday morning in her kitchen. 'Assault and battery' I believe it's called."

Eunice grasped the arms of her chair and stared at me. "Another attack? That's awful."

"Yes," I agreed.

She swiveled a few inches off my gaze the better to think

aloud. "I just got an offer on my house!" Her face seemed to watch the offer disappear.

"That's nice," I said. "Letty's suffering from malnutrition, and she's almost blind."

"Oowhat?" Eunice confronted me again, rather angrily.

I feigned innocence. "That's what you wanted to know, wasn't it? The reasons why Letty's place is a wreck?"

The businesswoman had sunk into her cushions, too busy being dumbfounded and annoyed with me to sit up straight.

"She's destitute, Eunice, living on junk food and going blind in a hurry due to malnutrition."

Eunice's mouth, which had sagged open, snapped shut. "I don't believe it."

"Which part don't you believe?"

"The destitute part."

My turn to stare. "Are you saying you know she has money?"

"Well, no. Not exactly," Eunice admitted. "But I was curious, you know? I'm in real estate, so I looked up her house in the county register." Probably right after she put her own house up for sale. "I figured maybe she wasn't the owner, and maybe the owner would listen to reason. Maybe he's totally unaware of how neglected his property is."

"So . . . ?"

Eunice shook her head. "Dead end."

"What do you mean, 'dead end'?"

Eunice shrugged. "Letty owns the house."

It was one of the questions I'd come to ask, and still I was surprised by the answer. "Good," I said after a moment. "Great!" If Letty had assets, maybe it wouldn't be too difficult to convince a good surgeon to operate on her eyes.

I stood up and walked around my chair, grasping the back to steady myself as I asked one more question. "Eunice," I began carefully. "In your professional opinion . . ." I waited for her whole attention. ". . . exactly what would Letty's house be worth?"

The professional sat back and pondered, aided by a nicely manicured finger thoughtfully rubbing her lower lip. "I'd have to see inside, of course, but if it's as filthy inside as it is out . . ."

"Ballpark," I prompted.

"Three-fifty, give or take."

"Three hundred-fifty thousand dollars?" I asked, just to be sure.

"Give or take. They don't build houses like that anymore."

"Thank you," I said, with sincerity this time. I also reached out and shook her hand.

She looked dejected, so I took a stab at cheering her up. "If it's any consolation, Sam seems miserable without you."

She uttered a few invectives.

I tossed an ironic, "Have a nice day," over my shoulder as I left.

Chapter 17

Much of my early afternoon was spent by the phone tracking down the Bryn Derwyn parent who was an ophthalmologist and waiting for him to return my call.

From the three or four school parties he had attended at our home I remembered Dr. Gregory Kinderhausen as a short, dark-complexioned man with vigorous, curly black-and-white hair that appeared to need trimming daily. I also remembered that his daughter's third grade teacher at her previous school had been unfamiliar with the term ''auditory learner'' and, therefore, had difficulty assimilating little Kimmy's inconsistencies—a difficulty she often expressed at various volumes to Dr. and Mrs. Kinderhausen as well as to little Kimmy. Presently the child was flourishing in Bryn Derwyn's fourth grade, at least that was the cocktail conversation put forth by Mrs. Lydia Kinderhausen one night after a couple of inexpensive white wines.

Kimmy Kinderhausen was the only reason I expected her father to call me back, a courtesy I was careful not to abuse. That's why I kept my case matter-of-fact and succinct. I needed the guy to know that he could beg off if he wanted to.

He left me listening to him think for a minute before he said, ''Miss MacNair's in Hobbs, right? I'm there tomorrow morning. I'll give her a look and get back to you.''

I tried to say, "That's absolutely wonderful—thanks!" but my voice broke. "Uh, doctor," I managed to croak, "You realize there's no health insurance."

"We do a certain amount of pro bono work . . ."

"She owns a house. At least I think she owns a house." I suddenly realized there could be any number of stumbling blocks to prevent converting that asset to the payment of anything to anybody—back taxes for example. Plus Eunice's information, however likely to be true, was secondhand.

"We'll put my bookkeeper on that one," he said. "Let's you and me just worry about getting your neighbor's eyesight back."

By then I couldn't even croak, but the ophthalmologist didn't stop to notice. "Call you tomorrow," he told me. Then he hung up.

After my voice returned, I paged Dominick the plumber on his beeper.

"Do you ever do charity work?" I asked when he called back.

"Charity?" he said, as if the word were new to him.

I tried again. "How about a tax write-off?"

"What are you getting at?"

"You know the house next door?"

"Just moved in?"

"Other side."

"That architect guy?"

"The one in between. Belongs to Letty MacNair. Older woman, a little eccentric."

"Oh," he said heavily.

"It's a long story, but I'm trying to clean up her place some before she comes home from the hospital next week. Anyway, the toilet's broken and I'm not too sure about a couple of sinks. Will you look at them for me?"

A silence grew. "Hold on," he said. "I'm just checking my schedule here." I relaxed a little.

"You gonna meet me there?"

"Yes."

"About 7:45 tomorrow morning?"

"Sure."

"Get you all fixed up with an estimate."

"Great," I said, roughly the way he had said, "Oh."

"Finally find out what it's like in there," he finished.

And won't you be surprised.

Those details under control, I put on some more work clothes, gathered up some serious cleaning supplies and put Barney on a long leash for company. While I toiled at Letty's, he could wait out under a tree—where it would be cleaner.

Barney was thrilled to return to Letty's. He trotted up her driveway sniffing and admiring her weeds, watering a few, delving into overgrown clumps where chipmunks or mice had burrowed. I pulled him back from his explorations with a sharp, "No." He had gotten sick once from eating garbage he found just that way.

After I unloaded my supplies onto the back porch, I stood surveying the wilderness that the remains of the original Doland estate had become.

Most of what remained was the half-acre former kitchen garden that constituted Letty's backyard. Ringed by a slightly crumbling, five-foot-high stone wall, it was a tangle of paths through weeds, vines, and uninvited trees. Bugs and birds and varmints of every description seemed to thrive. The way Barney's eyes half closed and his nose wiggled, he probably had inventoried every species.

"You need a walk, or what?" I asked, but he paid no attention to my prompting.

Quite suddenly he lurched into a gallop, tugging my wrist sharply when he reached the end of his leash and pulling me pell-mell along Letty's path through the weeds. A rat leaped into a hole in the wall near the rotting garbage heap, the final resting place for food even Letty considered inedible.

I planted my feet and reeled Barney into control. He danced on his paws and muttered that I never let him have any fun.

"You don't pay the vet bills," I thought out loud. "Let's keep going."

The well-worn path to Letty's dump continued over a low pile of rocks where the wall had once offered a neat doorway to the rest of the Doland land. Instead of a woodsy vista, a nicely mown lawn edged with split rail fencing fell to the right, and a broad yard with a green-tarped in-ground pool spread to the left.

Although it was probably just a path Letty used to leave her property, I realized this might also be the route taken by her assailant, so I decided to see where it led.

The dog and I followed what seemed to be a trail along the fencing until it ended abruptly at Maple Lane, a road I used almost daily to get out of our secluded development. What I had never noticed driving by was the continuation of a footpath that lay directly across the street.

"Sit. Heel," I told Barney as I both looked and listened for other housewives hell-bent on driving somewhere or other in a hurry.

After only three cars whizzed by, we made it safely across Maple Lane and proceeded down the footpath, which now followed a row of prickly barberry bushes to our left. In the field to the right, green sprouts popped up among last year's bent, dry blades of grass.

Sixty yards later the field ended in barbed wire, and the path dropped down a slope to the left onto a macadam parking lot edged with three green dumpsters. We were at the back of our nearest "strip mall," a row of four stores a mile by car from our house.

The back of a square white refrigerated truck faced the butcher shop at the nearest corner. Wearing a knit watch cap, blue short-sleeved shirt, and bloodstained white apron, a bulky man with a side of beef on his shoulder emerged from the truck and walked toward the building's opened rear door.

"Excuse me," I called. "May I talk to you a minute." He paused to glance toward me and my dog. "After you put that down?" I added.

He nodded to the truck driver, who began to close up and leave. "Sure, but hold that dog tight. He can't come in here."

"Discrimination," I told Barney while the man was out of sight. "You want to press charges?" Barney wagged his tail eagerly. His tongue dripped as he waited for the butcher's return.

In a moment the man reappeared, wiping his hands on a paper towel. He kicked the back door shut with a sturdy shoe.

"Don't have long," he said.

With the door safely shut it was possible for Barney and me to walk closer. "Oh, I know," I told him. "I just need to ask you something that will sound strange, but I promise to explain."

"Yeah?" His wide face above broad shoulders and a bull neck looked down on me skeptically.

"Do you know a woman named Letty MacNair?"

"Nope." He turned to go.

I touched his arm. "Elderly woman. Looks like a bag lady."

He turned back, thinking. "Housedress, brown sweater?"

"That's the one."

"What about her? She ain't in trouble, is she?" His formidable face had both softened and become protective.

"Actually, she got mugged in her home. She's in the hospital."

The butcher scowled.

"She's getting good care, care she probably needed."

My listener nodded. He knew Letty MacNair well

enough to like her. So far, that made two of us.

"You want some coffee?" he asked. "I need some coffee."

"Sure." Then I remembered Barney. "I'll just tie him to a tree." A row of scraggly mulberries grew uphill from the dumpsters. Barney would have shade and smells galore—pooch heaven.

Pete, for that was the butcher's name, served me excellent black coffee at a porcelain table beneath a window view of the trees to the side of his shop. Through a nearby doorway I could see that the shop was empty.

"Bell will ring if anybody comes in," he remarked.

The meat locker with its huge walk-in door hummed a few feet away. A single lightbulb dispelled the afternoon shadows.

A fleeting thought of dead and frozen flesh caused me to weigh my chances against the enormous man across the table. Yet his open, St. Bernard expression reminded me that, facing the risk of incarceration or extinction, the larger the dog the more gentle the breed. For the same reasons, extra-large men usually develop some body language to reassure, rather than intimidate, us women.

"So what's your question?" my new acquaintance asked.

"I guess I'd like you to tell me whatever you know about Letty."

"Like what, for instance?"

"Are you friends?"

He snorted, then sipped his coffee. "Nah. I just help the old broad out now and then."

When he saw that I didn't understand, he explained. "Meat I ain't gonna sell before the date, stale bread. Stuff like that."

"Does she ever buy food?"

"Oh, yeah. Beginning of the month she always has cash. I saw the envelope once, and it looked like a couple hundred. But a couple hundred don't go far these days."

"No." I was thinking of Letty's malnutrition and how her whole life probably revolved around getting food. A lump that was difficult to ignore developed in my throat.

"Funny thing," Pete continued. "Last month she didn't show up for a couple days. Then I saw her back where you came down, just having my coffee like this, but before I got outside she was gone. I run after her with the first thing I could grab, some bread I think, and when I caught up she was embarrassed as hell. Thanked me nice, but couldn't look me in the eye. Wasn't like her at all, see. Usually she's all spit and vinegar. Sort of turns cadging me out of stuff into a sport."

I smiled and nodded, thinking of the cinnamon buns Letty had wheedled out of me.

"But not last month," Pete lamented, wagging his head.

"You think it was because she didn't get her money?"

He considered that. "You mean like she was embarrassed that last month she couldn't pay at all? Maybe. Yeah, maybe."

The lump was taking on major proportions. I stroked my neck and blinked at the door to the meat locker. Anything to keep from looking into the baleful eyes in that big friendly face. I could see why Letty came here. It wasn't just the closest food store. Pete was a genuinely nice man.

While I finished my coffee, he solemnly punctuated everything I knew about Letty with appropriate comments of indignation and concern.

"Hold on a minute," he said when I finished. He lifted a finger to emphasize that I should wait. Then he disappeared into his shop, returning a moment later with something wrapped in butcher paper and placed inside a shopping bag with handles.

"To welcome Letty home," he explained. "After her operation. You'll be taking care of her, right?"

Inwardly I groaned. Would I? Was this the meaning of "friendly persuasion"? Amazing how compelling it felt.

Letty's butcher/friend and I parted with an empathetic

handshake, like the only two proponents of an unpopular cause. I hurried home to freeze what turned out to be enough steak for five, plus a bone for Barney.

All the while I was doing that, I kept thinking about the two hundred dollars Letty was forced to live without this month, and what I thought was that sometimes mailboxes tempted the younger teenaged boys. Too young to drive, hormones making them feel a little wild. What if a couple of kids wanted to start a harmless little fire? They dig into some mail, come across an envelope full of money. Celebration time! Another night they decide to smash a couple other mailboxes, light a trash can on fire . . .

Uncharitably, I thought of Patsy and Max Crouthamel's two sons. Right age. Right inclination?

Nope. No way. Banish that one right out of your head, Gin. How would you feel two years from now if somebody voiced suspicions about Garry based on nothing more than his age?

Chastened, I returned to Letty's. Before Dominick got up close and personal with the plumbing tomorrow morning I had some serious penance to perform.

Chapter 18

While Barney dozed out in the shade and I labored with Lysol, my mind escaped into speculation about everything that had been going on.

The loss of my friend continued to taint my days, much like a chronic injury you learn to acknowledge only periodically. Liz was gone. Although bringing her killer to justice would provide only minimal satisfaction, I yearned for the consolation of seeing him punished. It was a source of frustration to realize there was nothing I could contribute toward that outcome.

Even hinting to Sgt./Det. Kriebel about the differences between the Novak break-in and Liz's had been futile. Kriebel had easily dismissed the discrepancies, holding to his belief that the same robber who attacked Corinne Novak was responsible for Liz's death. If that interpretation proved to be false, he would move onto another theory. Since I had no concrete alternative to offer at the moment, all I really could do was wait for his investigation to proceed.

Fortunately, at least some good was coming from Letty's attack—she was getting medical attention that was long overdue. Yet much about that break-in remained unexplained. Although I didn't know whether anything had been stolen—except possibly the two hundred dollars Letty should have received earlier last month—there would have been, must have been, something her attacker wanted. Without knowing what that was or whether the robber got it, it was entirely possible that Letty might still be in danger.

Practically speaking, that made uncovering more about her situation even more urgent to me than finding Liz's killer.

And maybe, just maybe, learning more about what happened to Letty would tell me something about what happened to Liz.

For over an hour I labored mightily in Letty's kitchen and bathroom. Next—with buoyant spirits and great disgust—I removed the slipcover from the overstuffed chair, the drapes from the windows, and the blanket from the sofa, bundled them up and set them on some grass just off the back porch. Then, for good measure, I went back for Letty's clothes—all of them. By then I itched from dirt and twitched from fatigue, so I sat on the edge of the small, sheltered porch to rest a minute.

A few feet away at ground level an iron disk set in cement caught my eye. It had a handle and a latch and appeared to be a lid. I went over for a closer look.

Inside was a garbage pail, the kind the refuse collectors once walked back and emptied for you in the old, old days. At the moment this one happened to be stuffed with mail.

A voice behind me said, "Hi."

I jumped as if I'd been shot. Narrowly missing my fingers, the iron lid flopped down with a resounding clang.

"Sam!" I gasped. "I didn't hear you coming."

His arms were linked behind his khakis in a casual, aw-shucks fashion. However, his dark blue, deep-set eyes seemed thoughtful.

Also, they were aimed toward the lid covering Letty's stash of mail. Although I had no idea what could be important about a bucketful of junk mail, Letty was superprotective about it, and I respected her feelings whether I understood them or not.

Facing Sam, I deliberately wrinkled my nose with distaste. "Garbage pail," I announced, hoping the architect would lose interest in Letty's odd hiding place.

"What brings you over?" I asked as lightly as possible. "You certainly weren't jogging by."

Sam resisted a smile. "No," he said. "I haven't been jogging."

"Have you spoken to Eunice recently?" he asked.

So that was what this was about.

"Yes, I have," I admitted. The sympathy in my voice told him I was aware of his situation, that he didn't need to explain. "Just this morning."

The man nodded as if I had confirmed something obvious, such as the day of the week—peculiar because I scarcely ever spoke to his wife when they were together and had little interest in strengthening the friendship now.

"You're doing this for her, aren't you?"

"Doing what?" I asked.

"This." He swept his arm, indicating the pile of laundry and the scrub bucket setting on the porch.

My eyes widened. "Cleaning Letty's house for Eunice?" The idea seemed so preposterous that I could scarcely find words. "Hardly," I said. "The doctors won't let Letty come home to a pigpen—I suppose you saw the ambulance." He nodded grimly.

"Why should this have anything to do with you and Eunice?" I pressed.

At last the man looked abashed, and I was able to remember how self-involved every other divorcing person I've ever known became. Once again, I regarded him with sympathy.

"Walk down to the curb with me," I suggested. "I've got to bring in Letty's mail." Deliberately leading Sam away from Letty's stash felt equally silly and satisfying.

"So are you managing okay?" I asked, wondering whether my question would strike Sam as neighborly—or overly familiar.

To my surprise, the scorned husband began to talk. Not freely, though. More as if he had convinced himself it would be therapeutic.

''Eunice refuses to listen,'' he complained. ''She's set on getting a divorce despite anything I say. Ridiculous. And totally unfair. Did you see those people trooping through the house? I wouldn't be surprised if she sold it right out from under me.''

''She does have an offer,'' I told him.

The invective Sam used was so vile that I hoped never to be angry enough to use it in my lifetime. I waited for its effect to burn off before I added, ''She thinks it'll fall through because of what happened to Letty.''

Sam's grimace eased, another divorce symptom—nobody else's pain may surpass or even approach yours.

Meanwhile, I had already spoken too honestly. I was tired and didn't especially care what I said, which is why I rather peevishly remarked, ''What is the matter with you two anyway? You could have posed as the Yuppies of the Year poster couple.''

Sam's arms folded barrier style. He wagged his head woefully.

Now I was embarrassed. Sam had come over to talk because he suspected I had sided with Eunice, and perhaps because he was lonely and hurting. My response had been blunt and insensitive. Why? Had I wanted to punish him for being attractive and unattainable? Was my prickly mood a deliberate foil to keep myself out of trouble?

I sat down and patted the strip of curb to my left. Sam settled himself beside me like a kid facing a piano lesson. Communicating seemed uncomfortable to him, and for some reason he had chosen to practice with me. I wanted to think it was my inviting smile, but more likely it was the fact that we had heard some of the Browders' arguments from our family room. It also occurred to me that working in isolation at home probably had prevented him from cultivating many male friends.

"You ever want kids?" I asked, trying for a soft topic or perhaps unconsciously thinking of Liz.

"Nah," Sam replied. He kicked at some sand in the gutter left over from winter. I played with a stick.

Too late I realized I had done it again. My devilish subconscious might as well have written "sex" in the sand with the stick. Even my oblique reference was enough for our instincts to shoulder a gap between us.

That and the confidential nature of our talk. We fell silent for several moments.

I shrugged. "Maybe you'll both meet people who suit you better," I said, clearly backing off with my voice. Platitudes, our social scissors, cutting one free when one really needs to go. Thank goodness for platitudes.

Sam grunted, stood and stretched his magnificent frame, then began to wander along home. The last I looked he seemed to be examining the street for cracks in the macadam.

After I returned to Letty's back porch, I flipped the heavy lid off the former garbage pail and lifted out the bucketful of mail. In the kitchen I cleared off the central worktable and began to examine what my eccentric neighbor considered valuable enough to hide.

I put today's three third-class offerings facedown on the table and began to go through the bucket in order, top to bottom.

Among the first things I came across was the pink town-watch flyer the Raymonds had distributed, which told me only that Letty had been faithful to her surreptitious routine right up until her attack Sunday night.

Supermarket ads predominated. The rest were mostly opportunities to purchase things of little or no usefulness, especially to Letty. There were two unopened letters from a bank, just as likely to tempt her to overspend as any other piece of junk mail.

About a third of the way through the mound of trash I came across the only truly personal correspondence in the whole can, a white piece of copier paper with a typed message, probably printed off a computer:

> "Dear Ms. MacNair," it read. "Since living a lifestyle compatible with the rest of Beech Tree Lane is clearly of no interest to you, we—your neighbors—recommend that you move.
>
> P.S. We would be happy to tell you where you can go."

There was a tall wooden stool nearby. I sat on it.

Then I reread the message, moving my lips with disbelief.

A pair of grimy side windows above the double sink looked out at an overgrown pyracantha bush and the driveway weeds. I stared at them and swore with amazement. The message in my hand was a very state-of-the-art, very sarcastic, very Main Line threat.

I couldn't believe it. Someone on our block had actually pulled a chair up to a PC, tapped out a few clever, vitriolic lines, printed them up, and delivered them to a starving, nearly blind old woman who just happened to detract from the veneer of comfort projected by the rest of the street. It even implied that Rip and I concurred!

I think I was actually more astonished by the insensitivity manifested by the note than I had been by the violence directed toward Corinne Novak or Liz. As potential witnesses, at least their presences had imperiled another person's freedom. Letty's lifestyle was tragic, but it was difficult to imagine it seriously hindering anyone else's objectives.

Despite the comic "go to hell" implication, the message was no joke—Letty had just been attacked in her home. Learning who wrote the note could become essential to her future safety.

Someone embarrassed by Letty's mere existence? Someone who couldn't get what they wanted because of Letty? Either, neither, or both?

Judging by the cancellations on some of the junk mail, the note had been delivered during this past week. Logically, it must have been written after Margaret's tea, which was when the condition of Letty's property had emerged as such a hot topic. Perhaps one of the women went home, stewed about what was said, maybe mentioned her feelings to her husband, then one or both of them decided to play with Letty's mind.

Under normal circumstances I'd have thought that Liz's death would have preempted any such discussion about Letty. So why hadn't that happened? And why so many minor crimes in such a short period of time?

Again, I was confused by what seemed to be a convoluted, localized, but very deliberate agenda. Again, I felt that no one and nothing would be safe until the reasons for it all became revealed and the person, or persons, responsible were stopped.

And once again, I imagined others scoffing at my fears.

I smoothed out the unsigned message and put it in place in the pile of mail. The grocery flyer at the bottom of the bucket referred to the week of March 5, which meant that Letty must have received it approximately the time she had expected to receive her monthly cash.

I thought about what I learned from Pete the butcher, and my heart ached for Letty. Either last month's money simply had not come, or someone had stolen it out of her mailbox. Either way, I finally understood her paranoia about hiding whatever came in the mail. The money had meant a poor subsistence. It's absence meant hell. I pictured her going through the mail over and over, desperately hoping that this time the envelope would be there.

Almost as an afterthought I decided to look more closely at the unopened envelopes from the bank, the only mailed items specifically addressed to her.

"Ms. Letty MacNair," the first stated clearly at the head

of her correct address. The heft of the envelope suggested more than a two-page come-on for a credit card. In fact, the stiffness at one end *felt* like a credit card.

So what if it was a federal offense. I ripped open the envelope.

Inside a computer-generated letter congratulated Letty on being a fine customer. "Enclosed is your complimentary Money Access Card. Please watch for your preassigned Personal Identification Number in a separate mailing."

I skimmed the rest. "Promotional campaign . . . trying to acquaint customers who have never requested a MAC card with our quick and convenient automated machines . . ."

"Whatdaya know," I said to myself. Until now the only way I thought Letty could ever access bank money with plastic was by attaching a lump of it to a detonator.

Inside the second envelope was the promised preassigned PIN, plus an explanation of how to change it if she wished.

A MAC and PIN. Commonplace strategy. Get the customers accustomed to the machines for simple transactions so the bank could employ fewer tellers. Less expense for them put forth as convenience for their customers.

And no doubt it would prove very "quick and convenient" for Letty—as soon as I told her she actually had a bank account.

Chapter 19

Chelsea picked at her dinner, a ham/string bean combo done with 7-Up, her favorite when she was eight. Time perhaps to update my menus, figure a way to afford lobster, maybe learn how to use tofu—but maybe not. More likely it was time to intensify Chelsea's cooking lessons.

Meanwhile, nothing impeded Garry's fork. Chin down, elbows spread, while he ate he fidgeted as if the need to bolt equaled his sister's need for an eighteen-inch waistline.

"What's up?" I asked him outright.

"Hockey playoff," he muttered through a mouthful.

"Big bet?" I asked, and to my surprise he blushed. Rip noticed too, and his eyes widened ever so slightly. Our son was indeed growing up.

"How much?" I inquired.

"A dollar," he mumbled. Maybe there was time left yet.

I patted his hand. "Good luck," I told him.

"And you?" I asked Rip. "What's your excuse?" There was symptomatic rigidity to his spine.

"What?" He blinked.

"Where is your head? You look as if you're facing a firing squad. Is my cooking that bad?"

"Not quite," he conceded. "I was thinking about the dance at school Friday night. You going, Chelsea?"

"Maybe."

''Invite a couple of your buddies,'' I suggested, watching Rip as I spoke to Chelsea; dances at school were rarely a source of tension before. During, yes. Before, no.

''Round out the field,'' I added, offering biscuits around, which nobody took.

''Maybe,'' Chelsea hinted, her eyes sparkling a little brighter. Bryn Derwyn's middle school ratio was two to one favoring boys. Our daughter had researched the statistics personally, pretending to wait for her dad by watching soccer, basketball, lacrosse. Never field hockey, volleyball, or softball. I kept my observation quiet, however, as any good mother should.

Instead I brought the family up to date on Letty's situation, describing Pete the butcher in detail, skipping the threatening note and the nitty-gritty of my cleaning efforts, mentioning the offer on the Browders' house and Sam's vehement displeasure.

After the meal, Rip adjourned to his office with coffee. The kids helped me clean up, then hastily disappeared.

Attracted by the soft wrinkles on the back of my husband's blue oxford shirt, tempted to rub his shoulders and kiss the nape of his neck, I carried the coffeepot into Rip's study, ostensibly to refill his mug.

As soon as I entered the room, Rip twisted a knob and darkened the computer screen.

I felt slapped.

''Why did you do that?'' I asked. ''Rip, what's going on?''

''Nothing,'' my husband asserted. He turned to face me, spreading his hands.

Chastened by my expression, he started over. ''Nothing. I'm just writing something I'm not ready to show anybody.'' His line of vision strayed beyond me past his bookshelves to the twilight outside his window.

After an absent moment, his eyes challenged me. ''I'd just like a little privacy, that's all. Is that too much to ask?''

''No,'' I said. ''No, of course not.''

I retreated. After I set down the coffeepot, I realized I had neglected to refill Rip's mug.

Privacy? I thought. *Privacy!* In all our marriage Rip had never once requested privacy.

I wanted to scream. I wanted to cry. I wanted to call my mother or call Rip names.

Instead I crossed my arms and contemplated the red light on the coffeemaker. Eventually my hurt feelings would ease and I could focus on something else. Eventually, I would get some sort of explanation out of Rip. In the meantime I might as well move on.

To what? When things were not right with one of the kids—or Rip—it took willpower to focus on anything else. But surely there was something I could be doing.

Letty. I suddenly remembered I had business to discuss with her. The oven clock said 7:14. Hospital visiting hours ran a while longer.

I called across the hallway to tell Rip where I was going.

Letty glowered at a spot on the wall. The blue wraparound hospital gown she wore looked as faded and soft as one of her housedresses. Tonight her wiry gray-and-white hair seemed gnarled and dingy in contrast to the crisp, white pillows. I asked her what was the matter.

She grimaced and gestured toward her cheek with her good hand. "Toof pulled," she said, which explained the sourball-sized lump on her lower left jaw. Getting her to pay attention would be impossible until someone addressed her discomfort, so I walked back to the central nurses' station and found someone to bring Letty an ice pack and two aspirin.

"You're running up quite a bill," I teased after they were delivered. I referred to a fragment of a long ago conversation—somebody's complaint that aspirins dispensed in a hospital cost two dollars apiece. But the awkward way Letty swallowed the pills, wincing and gulping water through a straw, reminded me that that sort of humor was wasted on my next-door neighbor. She probably didn't know what aspirin cost ordinarily, let alone what it might cost here.

She cast me eyes filled with concern. "Gud wull provide," she said, but not as if she believed it.

God will provide. "The one who used to send you two hundred dollars a month?" I asked.

Letty glanced sharply at me, then quickly away.

"Exactly who gives you that money, Letty? Do you know?" Although there was a hard, wood-and-metal chair nearby, I stood restlessly by the bedside.

The white ice pack had reddened Letty's left cheek. Now her whole face flushed. Shrunk into her pillows, her eyes conveyed a bewilderment, as if this fear had been with her for months, possibly years.

"You don't know, do you," I realized.

Letty's head jerked, giving me my answer. She was unaware of her donor's name or why the money was sent; and because of her ignorance, everything about the mysterious "gift from God" was surrounded by worry and superstition.

"It comes at the beginning of every month, doesn't it? You really don't know who sends it?" Grappling with my own disbelief, I couldn't resist the urge to ask again.

Letty blinked, a supplicating gesture. Please, her expression said. Don't talk about it. As if talking about it might ruin everything.

I took a deep breath and smoothed the blanket next to her hip, stalling, reaching for words. Finally I pulled the chair over and sat, leaning far forward, elbows on my knees.

"I understand why you're worried," I said. "You're afraid the money will stop coming," I held her gaze. "Especially because that's already happened once, hasn't it."

Letty's lips moved, but no words came, just tears. Angry, frightened, frustrated tears.

I lifted her good hand into mine, the one without the

wrist bandage, stroked it as if it were my mother's.

"I think we should find out about this, Letty," I told her. "Why the money comes and why it didn't come last month. You have a right to know what's going on. You need to know what to expect in the future." Her life practically depended on it.

She stared at a spot on the wall. The ice pack had slipped from the crook of her jaw onto the covers. I picked it up, scraped at its frosty condensation with my thumbnail.

"Letty, do you know what a MAC card is?"

She turned her gaze toward me, carefully shook her head.

I put the ice pack back against her jaw. She watched me warily, still afraid I would bring her bad luck.

From the envelope in my purse I handed her the dark blue card with the raised numbers, the eye-catching rainbow, the electronic strip that knew more about her financial status than she did.

Letty held it with small curved fingers. After glancing at both sides, she rubbed the numbers with her thumb then handed it back.

"This little card can get money out of the bank," I said. "*Your* money out of *your* bank. There has to be an account or they wouldn't have sent you one."

Letty's brows squeezed close to her eyes, with doubt or fear or disbelief I couldn't tell.

"There is an account, Letty. There has to be. So how about it? You want me to check it out?"

Letty considered the little blue rectangle, then looked at me. She did a slow smile, which I returned in kind.

"Yes," she said, pronouncing the affirmative word perfectly despite her recent tooth extraction.

"Okay," I said. "Here's what we do. I get my lawyer to draw up a power of attorney. You sign it, and I go to that bank and demand some answers."

"Whut?" Letty muttered.

I realized she had no idea what a power of attorney was.

"Oh, sorry. Would you be willing to sign a paper that

says I'm allowed to look into your financial . . . that says I can ask the bank about your money?''

The older woman looked at me with puppy trust that almost made me ache from the weight of implied responsibility.

''Yez,'' she said, nodding painfully.

I snatched a tissue from the flat blue box on her nearby dinner tray. Handed it to her. Took one myself.

''What have I done?'' I wondered all the way home. ''What on earth have I gotten myself into?''

At 7:45 the next morning Dominick the plumber met me outside Letty's back door. Wearing his signature maroon Phillies cap with a short-sleeved gray work uniform, he toured the place with awe, examining the kitchen sink and both the downstairs and upstairs bathrooms with grunts of pricey proportions.

''Jesus,'' he said when he stopped to take in the room where Letty spent most of her time. Without curtains, sharp morning sun cut through the window grime, tickled the dust motes, and revealed the indentations where Letty sat. It disgraced the threadbare rug and highlighted the brown pattern in the peeling, tea-colored wallpaper. I made a mental note: Bring window cleaner.

Dominick informed me that the bathtub needed all the mechanical parts replaced, and that was pretty much the story with the toilets, too. Naturally, the kitchen drain was clogged and corroded, and the faucet needed washers desperately. The estimate came to a conservative three hundred seventy-five dollars. Perhaps Dominick grasped the notion of ''charity'' after all.

I thanked him and promised to call as soon as I figured out how to pay him. There was Letty's pride to consider. According to Pete, she had been mortified not to have any food money at all last month. So getting that power of attorney was top priority.

Some genius once suggested that teaching a starving man

to grow wheat was much better than offering him a bagel—something like that—so I didn't even consider asking Rip if we could donate Dominick's fee. Of course, short term, the hungry guy would probably be grateful for the bagel, too.

Back home, as soon as the business hour of 9:00 AM rolled around, I phoned Norman Demig, the lawyer who did our wills after Chelsea was born. His father happened to be exceptionally fond of my mother, although she offered him little encouragement. Yet because of our parents' friendship, Norman indirectly knew Rip and me pretty well.

I sketched in the situation, emphasizing Letty's dire needs and the possibility that she might still be in danger.

Demig grunted often enough to prove he was listening. After a moment's thought, he assured me that the legal procedure was simple, but he had to verify that Letty understood and agreed to what we were doing.

"Will you have to be there when she signs?" I asked.

He thought about that. "All things considered, maybe that would be best."

"I'd like to get started," I reminded him. "She might be coming home soon."

Sighing, he went off the line to check his schedule. "I've got forty-five minutes for lunch. I suppose Ms. MacNair's problems deserve thirty of them. Meet me there at twelve-fifteen."

I told him her room number and thanked him profusely.

For a busy man, Norman Demig was amazingly prompt. He bustled into Letty's hospital room with a minute to spare. I expected him to be breathless, but he slowed down with a sigh, placed his briefcase on the hard wood-and-metal chair, tugged at his lapels and addressed Letty. "Well now, we've got a mystery to solve. Or I should say, Mrs. Barnes does. You're in good hands. Did you know that?"

My mouth dropped open. Unaware that Norman Demig knew anything about my investigative luck in the past, and considering that I wanted to keep much of that private, his statement came as a shock. Yet learning any more about what he referred to was not to be.

"That bump hurt?" he abruptly asked Letty. He was no more than my height, five-foot-six with receding black curls, a solid belly that suggested a regimen of doughnuts and exercise, exercise and doughnuts. He exuded enough spare steam to paddle a riverboat.

Until now Letty had been squinting at him with distrust, but the question dissolved her stare into a flutter of blinks. She glanced at me to see whether to answer.

"This is my friend, Norman Demig," I said. "The man I told you was coming. He has that paper I need you to sign so I can find out about the money." We had been through all that only minutes before, but Norman Demig had come on so strong that it seemed prudent to go back to the beginning. Fortunately, Norman responded instantly, breathing deeply to relax himself, exhibiting a willingness to adapt to the moment. In a minute you'd have thought he didn't care whether he ever got lunch.

"Pleased to meet you," he purred at Letty. "Now tell me, dear, does that bump bother you much? Looks to be a bad one." He pouted a lip and stuck out his chin.

"Aye."

"And my friend here says you had a tooth pulled yesterday. That better today, is it?"

"Aye."

"Fine. Fine. Now Ms. MacNair, I need to know for sure if you understand what you're doing here."

"Signing a paper," Letty told him, more distrust slipping back into her eyes. Clearly, his intelligence was now in question.

"Yes, but do you understand what that paper does?"

Letty glanced toward me. "Lets Gin here look into me money." Why is he asking me this? she seemed to wonder.

Norman smiled. "Yes, ma'am. That's exactly right. And act on your behalf as well."

What do I care? Letty's shrug replied.

"And is that all right with you?"

"Aye."

"Okay then." Norman's energy picked up as he went to his briefcase. There might be time for lunch yet. "Grab us a couple of nurses, will you, Gin?"

I hurried to the nurses' station and explained what was needed.

When I returned, Letty held a legal-length document encased in thick blue paper in her good hand. The duplicate hung down and covered Norman's belt buckle. His chin was once again tucked in, his lips pursed. "Take your time," he encouraged Letty.

Two nurses stepped into the room and waited by the door. Norman acknowledged them with a nod, then returned his attention to their patient.

"Speak up if you have questions. When you're ready, sign on this line." He indicated the spot with the tip of a gold Cross pen.

Letty stared at the one-page document for perhaps half a minute, then she accepted the pen with her unbandaged left hand. Next, she smoothed the paper on her lap and wrote a large X on the indicated line.

Norman glanced at me with concern.

"Excuse me, Ms. MacNair," he said. "Do you usually write with your right hand? Is that why you signed with an X?"

"Not at tall," Letty said with dignity. "That's me usual mark. That's me signature."

"Very good," said Norman. "Now if we can just get you to sign this second copy for our files, we can let you get some rest."

"Fine," said Letty as she repeated the procedure. A moment later the nurses had finished witnessing the documents and hurried back to work. Norman did something official looking with a seal, then we both stepped into the hallway, letting the door shut behind us. We shared our astonishment in silence.

"Beginning to make sense, is it?" he asked with widened eyes.

Yes. No. Maybe.

"Some," I answered, thinking as he was that it's never difficult to cheat a person who can't read. "Candy from a baby?"

Demig handed me my copy of the document that would allow me to ask questions on Letty's behalf. Then he spun toward the elevator in pursuit of his lunch.

"Give 'em a bellyache, Gin," he called over his shoulder. His metaphor surely suggested by how fast he would have to eat.

"Hell, give 'em appendicitis." I figured that was the hospital influence.

Chapter 20

The sloped parking lot of the nearest First Commonwealth reflected the Wednesday late-lunch-hour lull. I picked a shady slot and hurried into the brick-and-glass shoe box that contained Letty MacNair's mysterious stash of cash.

The only available desk worker had a beige helmet of hair and a militaristic veneer. She altered her forbidding expression into a semblance of friendliness as I approached.

"May I help you?" she asked over her half-glasses.

"Yes. I hope so." Where to start? I handed her the form letter with the Money Access Card in it. She peeked inside briefly.

"It's one of our MAC cards," she stated. "Is there some problem?"

"No. No problem. It's just that my neighbor received it. She's in the hospital, and I'm taking in her mail." Wrong direction. "Anyway, when I checked her into the hospital, they asked me about her finances . . . Can you please tell me about this account?"

"Is it your account?" The woman's face pinched.

"No, my neighbor's."

"Are you an immediate relative?" She held the envelope about shoulder height, right above a wastebasket.

"No. Just a neighbor."

Her head waved. ‘‘I’m afraid I can’t release any information . . .’’

I reached out and snatched the envelope from her fingers. Then I stuck it in my purse and whipped out Norman Demig’s notarized blue legal form. ‘‘I have her power of attorney,’’ I announced, shocking the woman into momentary silence.

‘‘May I see it?’’ she recovered.

‘‘Certainly.’’ I passed the document across her desk while she tried to devise her next stumbling block. Either something was lacking in her training, or she had a reason to be uncooperative. She handed back the document. ‘‘May I see some identification?’’ she asked.

‘‘Listen . . .’’ I began, but a man, probably the branch manager, poked his head out of the office just behind the woman’s desk.

‘‘Anything I can do, Miss Detweiler?’’ About my age, mid thirties, and still in possession of his boyish good looks, he leaned forward on one foot while holding the doorjamb with both hands.

‘‘You can help me,’’ I offered a bit testily. His clear view of my expression had probably been the reason he hopped to Miss Detweiler’s rescue. Now he made another executive decision and waved me straight into his glass-and-wood cubicle. His smiling complacency told me he was prepared to stand by that decision, come what may.

‘‘Calvin Windermere,’’ he said, extending his hand. ‘‘What can I do for you, Ms. . . . ?’’

‘‘Barnes. Ginger Barnes.’’ I shut the glass door behind me. Miss Detweiler made a show of reading a piece of paper, but I caught the narrowing of her eyes when I glanced back at her.

After our greeting, Windermere stuffed his hands in the pockets of his gray herringbone suit and casually strolled to the back of his desk. He had medium-brown hair, medium-brown eyes, and an ordinary nose.

‘‘I need some information about an account,’’ I told him,

sliding the folded power of attorney across his blotter. He unfolded it, gave it a quick look-over, and dropped it on his desk. Then with his right eyebrow raised and his hands clasped together he sat down and invited me to use one of his lavender chairs. I had no choice but to use the chair; however, my ironing board offered more padding.

"What is it you need to know?" Windermere asked.

"Whatever you know," I replied.

The banker reread the names on the document, then pressed a button on the intercom. "Catherine?" Then to me he said, "I'm not personally familiar with the details, but Miss Detweiler can fill you in."

As the woman joined us, I evaluated her clothing. Wisely, she had tried to soften her edges with some puffy sleeves, but the geometric print blouse was tucked tightly into a straight mauve skirt. The effect was that of a square peg in a round hole.

"Ms. Barnes requires some information about the MacNair account. Will you please tell her what she needs to know?"

"Certainly." Catherine Detweiler arranged herself on the edge of another lavender chair, giving me time to wonder again why she had been so uncooperative before.

She raised an eyebrow, prompting me to ask for what I wanted.

"Okay. For starters, is it a checking or savings account?"

"Checking," she answered slowly, as if I already had asked too much.

"Thank you. Are deposits made regularly?" The keepers of Letty's cash communicated nonverbally for a moment.

Then Miss Detweiler gestured that she needed to consult her boss's computer, so he gave her his seat. While she tapped and waited, tapped and waited, her boss read over her shoulder. I saw nothing but their cloaked expressions.

"Are deposits made regularly?" I asked again.

The two First Commonwealth employees met minds

once more and finally Windermere caught up with Miss Detweiler.

He straightened and said, ''Sporadically. Listen, Ms. Barnes. I know you have the power of attorney for Ms. MacNair, but technically this account belongs to her trustee. Until I have time to get some legal advice on this, I think it would be best if you asked your questions of him.''

I took a long breath. ''Fine,'' I said, hanging on to my composure with two tight fists. ''Who is her trustee?''

Again the glances. ''Tell the woman, Catherine.''

''Edwin Markus O'Callahan.''

''And how do I find him?''

''We only have a post office box number,'' Miss Detweiler answered with no accompanying expression for me to read.

I waited, but the two stone walls stood firm.

''If it won't sprain your wrist, you want to write that down, Miss Detweiler?''

Wearing a tilted smile, she scribbled on a Post-it.

I looked at the note. ''No street address?''

''We can't give you what we don't have,'' the woman replied.

You're not even giving me what you do have, I thought.

''Can you at least tell me whether Ms. MacNair can use the MAC card you sent her?''

Miss Detweiler squirmed slightly and lowered her eyes. I think she was embarrassed on behalf of First Commonwealth Bank.

''She shouldn't. She received it by mistake.'' Her eyes lifted apologetically toward her boss. ''I explained that to Mr. O'Callahan when he called. A new employee did the promotion. Unfortunately, she thought she was supposed to send cards to anyone who didn't already have one, including all the names on the trustee accounts. That's why Mr. O'Callahan and Ms. MacNair each received one.'' Madam finally looked back at me and my purse. ''You really should return it.''

Not bloody likely.

"When did Mr. O'Callahan call to ask about the card?"

Miss Detweiler blinked. "I don't remember exactly. A couple weeks ago I guess. Right after he received his. I remember because I thought he called to complain about Ms. MacNair receiving access to the account, but all he really wanted to know was why he got one when he hadn't requested it."

"I'll bet he was just delighted to find out Letty got one too."

Miss Detweiler gulped in a ladylike way. "No," she admitted. "He was not pleased." She glowered at me, then glanced again in Mr. Windermere's direction. They really should try talking to each other. Maybe after this they would.

"Is that all?" the woman asked her boss.

"Ms. Barnes?" Windermere forwarded the question.

My temper demanded to inform these two that they might be party to a crime and were most certainly empty-headed jerks. However, calling these nitwits names constituted a personal indulgence, and I was cutting back on those.

I just snatched the power of attorney off Windermere's desk and snorted.

Outside, under a short awning attached to the side of the building was a MAC machine with nobody using it. I marched right up to it, took the card Letty had received by accident out of its envelope and stuck it in the proper slot—black stripe down and to the right. Then I punched in the preassigned PIN number and requested two hundred dollars from Letty's trustee account.

Cash fell into the bin behind the stiff plastic door. I took the money and put it in my purse while a white receipt emerged from another slot.

The receipt informed me that Letty MacNair's account balance was now $21,374.29.

Too late, it occurred to me that I might have made a serious tactical error.

Chapter 21

As soon the receipt popped out of its slot, I realized that the two hundred dollars I took out of the trustee account would show up on Edwin Markus O'Callahan's next bank statement—telling him that Letty, or someone else, was onto the account and would soon be onto him.

Bad or good? I wondered. Maybe such a shake-up would cause the secretive man to rush over and tell Letty everything.

I decided not to hold my breath. Letty had been living in the old Doland house alone for years. This O'Callahan character had probably been handling her money just as long. His habit of deceit was well in place.

Thinking of Letty's living conditions, her failing eyesight, and her overall poor health, my temper began to roil. Right then I might have gleefully shot Edwin Markus O'Callahan on sight if he hadn't been hidden behind that post office box.

A slender woman in bib overalls gestured to ask if I was finished with the MAC machine. I moved away while she went through the routine, and it occurred to me that now I would be able to make another withdrawal, a trick I learned one day by accident when I needed more than the machine's maximum allowance.

Soon another two hundred dollars of Letty's money

slipped into the cubbyhole, and another buff card showing the lowered balance emerged.

A second glance at the total made me realize that that figure might be all Letty MacNair had in the world—and it might not even be hers. The sporadic deposits the banker Windermere grudgingly mentioned could represent donations from O'Callahan or someone else who wished to remain anonymous.

With slightly less pleasure than I had anticipated, I walked to the public telephone around the corner and left my message with Dominick's wife. "Please ask him to fix my neighbor's plumbing as soon as possible—I have the money." I just hoped Letty wouldn't be needing it for food.

There was only one way to find out.

The traffic driving east on Lancaster Avenue in the early afternoon reminded me that the Main Line—in addition to being Philadelphia's wallet pocket—was also a flourishing business area. Vans carrying such things as upholstery fabric and meat jockeyed for starting positions at the traffic lights. A young woman with flying black hair in-line skated from the far sidewalk to the center of the street, speeding past me close enough to touch my door handle. All around were men and women speaking into car phones, ferrying preschool kids to the pediatrician, taking their stereos in for repair.

At the main intersection of Bryn Mawr I made a left, then turned right into an active parking lot. The slot I found nearest the post office was a bargain at twelve minutes for a nickel, but I drove my blue Suburu wagon a few yards farther to where the poles were red and the meters offered twelve hours for twelve quarters. Best to plan ahead. I fed it a couple of coins from the bottom of my purse, and turned to face the post office behind me.

A freshly painted brick edifice, it was trimmed with square marble columns embedded in the front wall and two globe lights supported by ornate brass stands to either side of the doorway. An Express Mail box sat at the edge of the brief garden to the left near the flagpole, and three regular blue mailboxes resided front and center along the curb. While I watched, a man parked in front of them.

I walked between his car and another, trotted up the several steps, and pushed through one of the two aluminum doors. Straight ahead was an elbow-high, fake walnut table with a pen and phone book attached and a row of special postal forms along the back. Beyond the table some postal boxes covered the back wall as well as the wall to the left. Glass-windowed rectangles of old fashioned brass, they further extended around a couple more corners right up to the postmaster's office.

I checked the phone book first. As expected, none of the five O'Callahans listed had a first name beginning with E.

Next I approached a middle-aged woman behind the stamp desk in the room to the far right. Graying curls brushed the collar of her light blue uniform blouse. Beneath her black-rimmed glasses extended a nose that was painful to behold. She dabbed at it with a tissue while I asked my question.

"Can you possibly tell me where I may reach Mr. Edwin Markus O'Callahan? He has a box here."

She turned away to sneeze into her tissue. When her face popped back up, her eyes were wet. "You mean you want his phone number?"

"Not his phone number—his address."

"Oh," she said. "We can't do that."

"Are you sure?"

"Quite sure. That's why some people keep a box."

"So nobody will know where they live." No salesmen or angry clients or thieves.

"Right."

"But I'm trying to locate his place of business. Surely you can tell me that."

"No. I'm sure I can't. Not if he has a box here." We looked at each other. Stalemate.

"Okay," I said. "Thanks."

"You want any stamps?"

"Not today." Not from the hands that held that tissue.

I knocked my wide wedding ring against the desk just for punctuation, and then threaded my way through the handful of incoming patrons until I was outside again.

Half a block along to my left—toward the actual "main line" train tracks—were a bank and a few shops. Overhead half a moon ornamented a clear blue sky. Across the street a large oak thought about showing some leaves. Salad-bowl-shaped cement planters containing freshly planted pansies dotted the border of the parking lot. Traffic on Lancaster hummed like "white noise."

The dozen or so strangers going about their business reminded me how urgently I needed to locate Edwin Markus O'Callahan. I began to examine my surroundings a bit more purposefully.

One of the nearby stores was called the Carousel Shop. HALLMARK CARDS GIFTS OFFICE SUPPLIES, said the overhead sign. Inside I rushed down one side of a long aisle of cards and back up the other watching for the biggest, brightest envelope available.

Lavender, mint green, aqua, hot pink, and yellow were in this year. In fact they were so popular that I rejected them all. I needed distinctive, if not unique.

A particularly large, pale pink envelope that accompanied, "For a dear goddaughter's baptism," almost swayed me, but at the last minute I spied an even larger, neon green envelope. Its card featured animals in gaudy clothes begging the recipient to, "Get well soon—the jungle doesn't swing without you."

Back inside the post office I addressed the oversized neon eyesore at the fake walnut desk, stood in line and handed the card and exactly enough money for first-class mail to the woman with the cold. She said nothing about my change of mind, just eyed me skeptically while she printed a postage tape and stuck it on. My smile probably irritated her almost as much as her nose.

I then located Edwin Markus O'Callahan's box, around the farthest corner of course, and stood watching through the glass for green neon. There would be no point in lingering if my card didn't get delivered soon. However, I need not have worried. Within five minutes it appeared.

I couldn't see whether the distrustful clerk put it there herself or not. She had disappeared from behind the desk for a couple of minutes; and as I left the building, I noticed she had not yet returned. If I was really lucky, she had phoned O'Callahan to warn him about me; if not, she had simply gone on break.

My next half hour was one of serious self-doubt. I spent it on a bench beneath a square green sign describing the parking choices in the municipal lot. Although the day was sunny, it got a bit cool there. I wanted to walk over to the car for a sweater but didn't dare. Edwin O'Callahan or his emissary might be coming to pick up his get-well card, and I might miss him—or her.

Or no one might come for hours. Possibly I might even have to come back tomorrow. That's where the doubt came in. Nobody was paying me to stake out the Bryn Mawr post office. In fact I had children to greet and eventually feed. True, they wouldn't be home until the late activity bus let them off around five. At this stage Chelsea merely nibbled lettuce, and Garry would eat the woodwork if I put it on his plate. Lately Rip had been obliviously gobbling his dinners and hurrying off to commune with his computer.

Thus I talked myself into staying parked on the bench, hoping as I began to shiver that the clerk with the cold had been suspicious enough of me to have alerted Edwin O'Callahan. Then, at least, something would happen soon.

Nothing did. As boredom set in, my reflections switched to Bryn Mawr itself. What was so special about the well-known town? The sound of the name? The college? The fact that it was the heart of the prestigious Main Line?

From my bench it appeared to be nothing special. Most other town centers in the other well-known wealthy enclaves I'd visited struck me as more demonstrably upscale. They had matching buildings nestled in township-funded gardens. The signs were tasteful almost to the point of invisibility. Cars vying for the elusive parking spots in those other places were mostly Mercedes, BMW's, and Volvos. This lot ranged from Jaguars to Buicks and Oldsmobiles to a Ford Taurus and a Dodge. Of course, a sign on the Taurus said it belonged to the assistant fire chief, and the only blue Suburu belonged to me.

So you could say Bryn Mawr held its money like a poker hand. The inhabitants might be flush, but their faces were as comfortable as the old clothes they wore to one of the six banks within a block and a half of the post office. And if their homes were filled with treasures, the treasures once belonged to Mummy and had simply become home. Ostentation was for the youngsters, the nouveau riche, who were permitted to crow briefly before settling down. They would get the message: If you've got it, there's really no need to flaunt it.

Off on that tangent, I almost missed a woman with a blonde pageboy carrying a white "Property of U.S. Postal Service" bin full of business mail. Her white flats clicking on the cement sidewalk, silky pale-blue shirtdress shimmering like polished silver, she hurried up the post office stairs. Glancing behind her with a worried expression, she ducked inside as if to avoid a cloudburst.

Based on her agitated behavior I thought it might be a good idea for me to hide. But where? The nearest tree was a skinny ginkgo. The largest object around was a postal truck parked twenty yards away. I sprinted for it and just rounded its rear bumper before the aluminum doors of the post office swung open and Sneezy emerged with the newcomer in tow. In Blondie's fist was a green neon envelope.

The postal clerk said something, waited for the woman's

nod, and retreated. Blondie looked left and right, then slowly descended to the sidewalk. She headed toward the traffic light at the intersection of Lancaster and Bryn Mawr Avenue, pressed the "walk" button on the post and eventually crossed to my side of the street at the corner of the municipal lot.

I could see all this without moving from my spot behind the mail truck. However, when she began strolling along the iron fence toward the next traffic light at Lancaster and Morris, I started walking past the backs of the parked cars in that direction.

Again, my quarry waited for the light to change, then crossed to her right to enter the extension of Morris, which was named something else—a bad habit of the area that makes giving and following directions something of a local headache.

I crossed Morris toward the Sunoco station before crossing Lancaster to the Texaco station, figuring that if Blondie saw me on the opposite side of the street, she would think I was going about my own business rather than Letty's.

She kept those white flats *click-clicking* at a good clip, though, and I had to trot to keep up when she wasn't glancing around. Since I was wearing jeans with my go-out-in-public white shirt and a well-worn pair of cross-trainers, my hurrying didn't make noise enough to turn her head in my direction.

The first block was a transitional mix of homes and businesses, and businesses in former homes. First I had the Philadelphia Suburban Water Company on my side with a huge Barnes and Noble bookstore visible beyond the parking lot. Then came a brick house with white porch pillars and green shutters, next a mostly stone house used for law offices.

Blondie scurried past the large, rectangular Prudential Preferred Properties office and lot, then a tan house containing an optometrist and two more law offices. In the distance the siren on an ambulance whistled up and down as it rushed a patient to the nearby Bryn Mawr Hospital. Birds hopped around the naked branches, squirrels chased each other, and I all but chased Blondie.

We passed an architect's place and suddenly she scooted diagonally across the street to my side, cutting the distance between us considerably. I tried to look casual as she glanced my way watching for cars, but we were the only ones anywhere on foot, and she finally concluded I was the enemy. She accelerated.

Arms pumping, neon envelope flashing from her fist, she power walked around a corner and took off at a sprint. I no longer wished for my sweater; I wanted shorts, a T-shirt, and a tall glass of water.

I turned the corner after my prey, lost her in a flash of sun off a windshield, hesitated, caught a glimpse of the neon card rounding a building. The woman was running outright now, trying to lose me with speed, straining the bottom buttons of that silk shirtdress just short of a major slip exposure. O'Callahan probably wasn't paying her enough for this.

I, on the other hand, had a cause and a pair of cross-trainers.

Blondie cut through a yard, bounced off a chain-link fence, duck-footed up a grassy incline, puffed between two close houses, rounded a maple tree, swung right and up some stairs on a pipe railing, yanked open a door, pounded up a flight of stairs, pulled open a glass door marked "Kyle E. O'Callahan, Attorney at Law," and thrust the neon envelope at a man who resembled Abraham Lincoln. I knew this because I was right behind her.

"Thank you, Ms. Hollyfield," said the man to the huffing woman, whose light blue dress was now stained dark blue in several unbecoming places. She glared at me like Beelzebub before leaving the reception area for parts unknown.

"And you are?" the man addressed me as if my presence was of little interest one way or the other. He held the card against the chest of his black, three-piece suit like a fan.

"Ginger Struve Barnes," I said when I was able. "Do you have a water fountain around here?"

"In the hall."

"I'll be right back."

"Yes, I'm sure you will."

There was a slim chance that he would lock the glass door behind me, but I was so out of breath and so thirsty that despite the odds I took the chance.

When I had gathered myself together and returned through the still-unlocked door, I asked the same gentleman whether Edwin Markus O'Callahan was there.

"No. What makes you think he would be?"

I indicated the bright green envelope in the man's hand. He glanced at the address and dropped it on the receptionist's desk.

"You've gone to all this trouble, you might as well come in." He opened a cherry-colored door leading to an office with light carpeting and more cherry office furniture, real this time. Beige drapes made a nice contrast to the wall of law books. An ancient typewriter on a spindly stand seemed to be a decoration in front of the window.

"This is Dad's office," he remarked. "I have a client waiting for me. Why don't you *briefly* tell me what this is about so I can decide whether or not to call the police."

"Have you noticed that people with something to hide always suspect others of being as duplicitous as they are? Have you noticed that in your profession, Mr. O'Callahan?" I don't often flaunt my vocabulary, but I thought a Bryn Mawr attorney might forgive me.

He did. Or rather he didn't. He began to bluster. So I said, "Letty MacNair."

Kyle O'Callahan stopped blustering and stared. "Who?"

"Letty MacNair. Your father has been sending her two hundred dollars a month for quite a long time, but this month she didn't receive it. What can you tell me about their arrangement?"

"My father is in Bryn Mawr Hospital recovering from a stroke."

"I'm sorry to hear that. Is that why Letty didn't receive her money this month?"

"Who are you exactly?" he asked.

"Ginger Struve Barnes. I have Letty's power of attorney."

O'Callahan extended long, thin fingers, palm up. Sunken cheeks, at least six-foot-four, probably sixty years old, receding hairline, black bushy eyebrows, black unruly hair going gray—Lincoln except for the nose. Somehow the nose was different. Puffier, maybe.

I extracted the folded legal document from my purse. He read it quickly and snapped it back onto my hand.

"How do you know this Letitia MacNair's trust is administered by my father?"

"His bank." As you well know. If your father has been ill for more than two weeks, you were the one who called to ask why he received a MAC card, so you were the one who found out Letty had one, too.

"When did your father have his stroke, if I may ask?"

The man sighed at the thought, and I began to see him as human. I also began to see myself as a tricky problem for him, an unknown, a potential threat. Or possibly just a very odd, very determined woman.

"The first one was six weeks ago. The most recent, last Friday."

"He'll recover?" I asked, worried that there would be an interminable delay in learning about Letty's trust if Edwin Markus O'Callahan died. There might be some facts no one would ever unearth.

The Lincolnesque son shrugged. He even tented his hands like the assassinated president, probably a studied affectation at one time, but an unconscious habit now.

''Letty is also in the hospital,'' I said. ''Hobbs Memorial. She was attacked inside her home.''

''Oh?''

''Yes. And the admissions woman there asked me about Letty's finances. That's one reason I'm here. Another reason is that two hundred dollars a month simply isn't enough to live on. Letty has a right to know whether more is available.''

''No,'' O'Callahan told me with assurance in his voice. ''I'm sure your . . . friend . . . is receiving every penny it's possible for my father to give her.''

''Then you know about the case?''

''No,'' the attorney said, wagging his head with regret. ''No, but I know my father. And he always does, did, everything possible for his clients.''

''Did?''

''My father retired fifteen years ago.''

I gulped. ''Then who . . . ?'' Who was watching over Letty's money?

In answer to my unasked question, O'Callahan said, ''Dad kept up with a few simple cases. Perhaps your friend's was one of them.''

''You'll look into it?'' I pressed.

''Certainly. I'll call Ms. MacNair in a few days.''

''How about calling me tomorrow?''

''In a few days. Now I really must attend to my client, Mrs. Barnes.''

I stood, well-trained girl that I was.

''You want my phone number?'' I reminded him.

''Of course.'' I wrote it on a pink While-you-were-out page in large numerals.

When I was finished, I said, ''Letty depends entirely on that money.''

''If at all possible, I'll see that payments are resumed. In the meantime, please apologize to Ms. MacNair on my father's behalf.''

I agreed to do so, but I was lying. I didn't shake Kyle E. O'Callahan's extended hand either. I muttered something about not wanting to give him a cold.

From the law office to Bryn Mawr Hospital was only a short walk, and naturally I didn't want to waste all the time I had left on my parking meter.

The lobby, with its grays and greens and glowing wood, seemed to possess all the polish of a fine hotel. I found Letty's trustee easily with directions given to me by a volunteer seated behind the first desk. Since it was still during afternoon visiting hours, my progress through the halls went unnoticed.

My five minutes spent staring at Letty's possible nemesis, or possible savior, also went unnoticed—even by the poor, shriveled man.

Edwin Markus O'Callahan didn't look much like Lincoln, more like a shrunken, bald corpse that drooled. He lay covered up to his chin with a sheet, and I couldn't even swear that he breathed.

''Will he be all right?'' I asked a passing nurse.

She glanced into O'Callahan's room and shrugged. ''Time will tell.''

My weary walk back to the municipal lot took me past Bryn Mawr Sports Medicine, past two tennis courts, past a garden dedicated to ''Philip Giagnacova for his tireless effort to the betterment and beautification of Bryn Mawr 1994.'' I suppose that meant if I spent a year planting pansies in cement salad bowls they would give me a garden, too.

I shuffled my feet, counted banks, puzzled about the black Cherokee Sport with the Sports Medicine logo and the dog barrier. I was pretty tired by then, but I had to wonder. Did those sports medicine people fetch their patients out of the woods, pluck them off the ski slopes?

Clearly, my balking brain needed a nap. I simply could not make it face the odds against Letty ever living a comfortable life.

Chapter 22

When Patsy Crouthamel saw me pulling into Beech Tree Lane, she frantically waved me over. Her hand held a bunch of sticks she had picked off her lawn, maybe in preparation for the first mowing.

"Have time for coffee?" she asked. She wore a yellow tunic over flesh-minimizing black knit pants. Big black earrings with lots of dangles drew attention to her beautifully made-up face. I should look so good on a weekday afternoon—but I rarely did.

From my car window I told her, "Why not?"

While she deposited the sticks into a trash can on her driveway, I pulled in and parked.

"Lovely having the kids a little older," I remarked, alluding to the confining elementary school years.

By mentioning our children, I also hoped to steer our conversation toward her boys. While I didn't care to accuse them of vandalism without knowing one thing about them, perhaps with Patsy's help I could cross them off my suspect list.

Her house seemed to be L-shaped, with the downstairs a continuous open space supported by an occasional post. As Patsy had mentioned at Margaret's, her kitchen and eating area indeed faced Beech Tree Lane and the bus stop right at the corner. An inviting living space with plenty of overstuffed furniture spread across the front of the house facing Monroe, and that's where we settled with mugs of fragrant coffee fortified with real cream and honest-to-goodness sugar. Patsy also placed a plate of chocolate chip cookies by my knee. After my encounter with Kyle O'Callahan, the comfort food was impossible to resist.

''I'd use that substitute sweetener if I wasn't eating cookies,'' she said, ''but you notice how if you eat anything with real sugar in it along with diet soda, the soda tastes really awful?''

''Yes,'' I agreed laughing. ''As if your mouth isn't fooled anymore.''

''That's exactly it.'' She smiled and helped herself to a cookie. ''So how was the funeral?'' she asked.

I blushed spontaneously. ''Liz's?''

''You went, didn't you?''

''Yes.''

''So how was it? Big? Small? Did she have lots of relatives?''

''Pretty big. Not very many relatives.'' I thought of Marc speaking at length with the attractive young woman. This was not a subject I wished to pursue.

''I left early,'' I said.

Patsy's right eyebrow shot up. ''Oh?''

''Can we talk about something else?''

''Death bothers you, huh? You think the police are getting anywhere?''

I thought about all the things that continued to occur on our street and said, ''No.''

''Me neither.'' She sighed and lolled back on her big blue chair. The sustenance had perked me up considerably. Perhaps another cookie would perk me up even more.

''We get hang-up calls all the time,'' Patsy lamented. ''I swear I jump every time the phone rings.

''And I can't find another mailbox like the one we had. The store where I got the smashed one went out of business like two years ago, and the ones I've seen other places are either too plain or look like Wendy Shannahan's house.''

My snort of laughter surprised us both. I did a quick dab job with the napkin Patsy had provided.

''She really goes for that cutesy stuff in a big way,'' Patsy chortled. ''So how about it? What do you think is going on?''

The woman's cut-to-the-chase style offered me two choices. I could be as open and honest as she was, or I could play my cards close to the vest. My instincts advised me to go for it. If Patsy scoffed, I could take it.

''I think somebody on our block has a very scary notion of how to get what he or she wants.''

''She?''

''He, probably.''

''Right. I don't think women go around clobbering other women, do you?''

''Nope.''

''So what do you think this somebody is after?''

''They could want Letty to leave.''

''Why phone me day and night? Why smash my mailbox?''

''Why steal my son's bike?''

We sat there appraising each other, thinking along the same lines, and gauging how honest to be.

''Some of the stuff might have been teenaged pranks,'' I said carefully.

Patsy threw back her head. Her brown bangs slipped down and her black dangles jiggled at her ears. ''You mean my boys? . . . Or your kids?''

My kids? ''Your boys are older.''

''True.''

''And stronger. Take somebody pretty strong to smash a mailbox.''

''Somebody driving the car, too. But listen here, sister. Just because Tony and Mike are the only teenagers on the block doesn't mean they're into property destruction and stealing.''

"How come?"

Patsy took that remarkably well. She simply leaned forward with a glint in her eye. "Because I know where my boys are when they're not here."

I leaned forward, too. Cookie crumbs fell off my chest onto my lap.

"Good. Wonderful," I said. "Where are they?"

Patsy had been ready with her answer before I asked. "They're at the Church of the Blessed Savior," she said. "Youth fellowship, tutoring math students, spreading the word, cooking for the homeless. You know where your kids are when they're not home?"

I thought of Chelsea managing to buy running shoes behind my back and the money missing from my wallet. Every day there was a gap between when Garry's intramurals ended and when the late bus brought him home. Chelsea, too. I always pictured them goofing around with their friends or doing homework—but were they?

"Not every minute," I admitted. Then I thought it all the way through. Hang-up calls had to be made from somewhere—somewhere other than our house. Someone *had* driven the guy with the baseball bat past the mailboxes that were smashed. And if Chelsea had taken Garry's bike, a preposterous idea to begin with, where would she have put it—and why bother?

Patsy and I eyed each other, both of us searching for safer ground.

Thinking aloud, I said, "The TV set stolen out of the Diamonds' car wasn't in the same category as the break-ins at Liz's and Letty's."

"Could have been done by the burglar, though."

"Yes," I agreed. "If it fit into his plan."

"What plan?"

"I don't know."

"But the bike and the calls and the mailboxes could have been kids," Patsy observed. Our kids excepted, we mutually agreed with our eyes.

"Mike and Tony's friends?" I suggested.

"Not their friends."

"Their enemies?"

Patsy shrugged, and I realized that two teenaged boys as religious as the two Crouthamels might draw a bit of harassment from their classmates, particularly ignorant rivals who might also try to set the "goody-goodies" up for some trouble. The pattern was as old as time.

"Or it could be one guy with an agenda we just don't understand."

"Back to that," I remarked.

"You really think somebody wants Letty out of here that bad?"

"She received a sort of a threat."

"Oh dear. That's awful. Did it upset her?"

"She couldn't read it."

"Well," Patsy said as she stood up, and I realized how late it was getting. My hostess probably wanted to start cooking dinner.

She shook her head and the earrings rattled. "Johnny Raymond wants his parents to move," she reminded me.

I started for the front door. "You think he might be doing it all?"

Patsy shrugged again. "He's weird enough."

I ran through the qualifications. By living alone, he could make hang-up calls anytime he liked, pretend to burglarize a house whenever he liked. He probably knew the inhabitants of our block well enough to know how to get to any one of us.

"Lock your doors," Patsy reminded me.

"You, too," I replied, and she did just that. I heard the bolt click.

The answering machine on my kitchen counter blinked at me.

"Ms. MacNair is scheduled for surgery at 8:00 AM Monday morning," said a secretarial voice. "Please call Dr.

Kinderhausen's office for postoperative instructions.'' Then she left the number. Ten after five, too late to phone now. I needed to adjust to the idea of Letty staying in our house anyway. Tomorrow morning was time enough to deal with that.

Garry emerged from his room down the hall. As usual, I watched each step, examined each facial muscle for clues, listened for nuances in his, ''Hi, Mom, what's for dinner?''

''They grow away from you beginning the minute they're born,'' my wise grandmother told me. ''So you better learn how to let them go.'' Somehow that did not preclude steering them around barriers or teaching them how to cope. Garry was tired tonight, or needed his dinner as much as I had needed Patsy's cookies. I reached into my own cookie jar—not my grandmother's treasured yellow one, for that was gone—but the blue glass one I had bought to replace it. When I put a fistful of Oreos into Garry's hand, his eyes widened with surprise.

''Live it up, kid,'' I said.

''Thanks, Mom.''

''Where's Chelsea?''

He wiggled two fingers like running legs, meaning that Chelsea was out exercising. Immediately I thought of the rush-hour traffic, but the fact that Chelsea left no note tipped me off. She was doing this for herself and wanted no mention of it, no encouragement, no acknowledgment whatsoever. Difficult as it would be, I promised myself to keep quiet.

Garry pivoted on his own jazzy, rather large, sneakers and lumbered back the way he had come. Barney raced along behind him. Cookies crumble—even Barney knows that—and sometimes the pieces fall onto the floor.

Since Tuesday when I found out about Letty's malnutrition, food had been reminding me of her. Now reading the back of a bag of noodles brought her presence right into my kitchen. What was it like not to be able to read? My eyes gobbled the written word. At breakfast I read cereal boxes. In doctors' offices I scanned articles on movie stars getting divorced or the newest technique for controlling a thyroid problem. Waiting in line at the bank, I saw the current CD rates whether I wanted to or not. Driving, I absorbed street signs, billboards, ads on the back of a bus.

What would it be like to be blind to all that information? My life could be in danger without me ever knowing it—from my household appliances, from my vitriolic neighbors. But also I might never learn about a sale on something I needed or the opening of what might well become my favorite movie of all time. What if I couldn't even cook noodles because I hadn't a clue how to begin?

Chelsea bounded in the front door, hair in ringlets, sweat gleaming on her cheeks and staining her sweatshirt. She seemed happy. I told her, "Hi." She kissed my cheek gratefully and asked if she had time for a shower.

"Sure," I said, and no more. She bounced down the hall with energy to spare. She had survived the traffic, she had avoided a maternal inquisition. Her life was good. Let her be.

I brought up the subject of illiteracy at the Barnes family dinner table. Rip quoted an old brochure by a beer company sponsoring a literacy campaign. "One out of five women can't read," he said. "And seventy-five percent of women with less than a high school education who head their own household are living in poverty."

"When did you read this brochure?" I asked, scarcely believing his statistics.

"Maybe 1990," he admitted. "But you think they all learned to read since then? These people can't fill out job applications, understand a bus schedule, read safety instructions—it's really a horrible problem." He shook his head and put down his fork. Both our kids were wide-eyed and silent. For maybe the thousandth time I was glad Rip was an educator.

Just before bedtime Rip volunteered to take the trash down to the curb. "Tomorrow's Thursday," I said with a palm to my forehead. ''I've got all that trash of Letty's to put out.''

''Better do it in the morning, babe,'' Rip advised. If they were not placed in tightly closed cans, raccoons ransacked every trash bag around. During the day cats, dogs, and crows completed the devastation.

''Hurry back,'' I urged as Rip headed out to do his chore.

He raised his eyebrows to ask if I meant what he thought I meant. I did. Maybe my fond thoughts at dinner had softened me toward him enough to show. Seeing his face then, he certainly seemed softened toward *me*.

We had a lovely night's sleep—eventually. The best in weeks.

I shouldn't have worried about the raccoons or crows. In the morning when I went to carry Letty's trash down to the curb, the bags had already been ripped open. Every Doritos bag and doughnut box—as well as every bit of filthy trash I had painstakingly collected around Letty's house—was once again strewn around her kitchen.

I bit my trembling lip. I folded my arms to keep from breaking something, and then I swore—lengthy strings of the best of my Uncle Jack's worst. Words that set my mother's finger wagging. Words that sent me to my room.

When I was low on breath, when I was sure I wasn't going to cry, I said, ''You'll be sorry.''

You'll be sorry. A simple, ominous sentence that was more of a curse than any of the rest. I said it again to seal it—louder—to make sure I was understood.

''Goddamn you, you're going to be sorry.'' I meant for it all. If anyone had actually heard me, they'd have known that.

Chapter 23

Walking—stomping—home for more trash bags, I came to a decision. No police this time. They would probably rush right over, take a look at Letty's kitchen disaster and think, "What's the difference?"

Or else they would laugh at me like Dominick's wife had over that bollixed plumbing attempt.

No thanks.

Due to my adrenaline buzz, reloading the trash bags went much faster than the first time. Of course, my mind was off in the wilds plotting revenge, so I worked more or less on autopilot.

Leave it to something mundane like a few—well, seven—large-capacity trash bags to put things into focus. Murder, assault and battery—my imagination refused to absorb those concepts. I dealt, but I did not understand. Trashing a poor old woman's just-cleaned kitchen was the sort of everyday nastiness I could grasp immediately. On a smaller scale it happened to me all the time.

In an hour I had hauled the heavy bags down to the curb, carrying them knee-high so they wouldn't rip on the jagged driveway. "Don't you dare," I told a crow passing by overhead.

Finally beginning to lose the worst of my anger, I went home to shower off the filth.

As it usually does, the water turned cold on me almost immediately, stunning me into a revelation. I stood staring at the white tile long enough to shiver.

"No prank," I thought aloud as I gradually warmed under the adjusted stream of water. "Somebody searched through those bags."

But for what? Another two hundred dollars? Probably not the MAC card. Nobody knew about it except Kyle O'Callahan, and he must have realized it was too late to get it back. Maybe whoever threatened Letty wanted to destroy the computer printout before he or she got accused of injuring her. One of the Vickers? Wendy or Nelson Shannahan?

I reached out for my towel. Letty might not have been the primary target when the crimes began, but she certainly seemed to be the center of attention now.

Maybe we would talk about that when I visited her that afternoon.

"Ack ah ah ah ah," she cried, both her bandaged and good wrists raised to fend off the doctor who had breezed in to check on her.

I had arrived only minutes before, promptly at two. My seat on the edge of her bed afforded me a great view of the total surprise on the doctor's face. His mouth dropped toward his dangling mask. One hand self-consciously covered his green scrub cap. He backed out the door staring at Letty's terrified stance mumbling, "I'll come back later." The nurse hurried out after him with only a scolding glance of scorn for Letty's theatrics.

Since the toothless roommate had gone home and the other bed was temporarily empty, Letty and I were left with blessed silence and privacy.

"Hey, hey," I said, smoothing down her hair, lowering her hands. "He just wanted to see if you're okay. They do that every day. What's wrong?"

"Green," she said. "The man in green. 'Twas 'im."

''What man in green?'' Letty's breathing was rapid, her eyes wide. I hunkered down close to hold her gaze. That close I could see the milky thickness of her cataracts, something I might have seen before if I had known to look.

''Something happened, didn't it? Tell me. I'll believe you.''

Letty's relief loosened her shoulders, straightened her back. ''He came for it. He shook me and said I were stupid and where had I put it—'twere 'is.''

''What did he want? Do you know?''

The woman wagged her head woefully, as if she truly felt stupid for not knowing.

''It doesn't matter, Letty. What else did he do? Did he hurt you?''

''He looked in me closet wid 'is flashlight. In me purse.''

I opened the narrow locker provided for patients. Her purse lay on the floor of the otherwise empty storage space. Obviously, the clothing she wore when she was attacked had been discarded. Letty would need new things to wear home. Something else for me to remember to do.

Except for the keys I borrowed, the purse was just as pathetically empty as when I had first checked inside for a health insurance card. Maybe when I learned more about the trustee account her purse would contain more than a change purse, a handkerchief, and a comb. Meanwhile, until I was certain I wouldn't be raising false hopes, I intended to keep Edwin O'Callahan to myself.

''Was he after a bankbook? Jewelry? Cash?'' Letty's blank expression was answer enough.

''When he was here, did you push the button to call the nurse?''

My neighbor's eyes widened again with fear, helping me to see her thoughts. ''You thought it was a real doctor because of his clothes?''

''It 'twas. I saw 'im.''

''He couldn't have been real, Letty. Doctors take a vow

. . . Anyway, no one here would have a reason to hurt you or steal from you.''

My arguments were weak, and even Letty could sense that. Doctors were human, and patients were easy targets for petty theft. For that reason nobody ever kept anything valuable with them in the hospital . . . unless they thought it was safer here than in their home.

I was aware that Letty had been unconscious when she was rushed to Hobbs, but maybe the ''green man'' thought otherwise. Awake, she could have brought something along for safekeeping, or a friend could have picked it up for her later.

''What did he look like, this man?'' I asked. ''Tall? Short? Young? Old?''

Letty's struggle to remember made me squirm. '' 'Twas too dark,'' she said finally.

''Don't worry about it,'' I told her, but I could see that she would be worrying about that and many other things in the future. If her peace of mind were to return, it would only be with a complete explanation of what had been happening. I yearned to provide that, but at the moment I felt just as bewildered as Letty.

''Be right back,'' I said.

At the nurses' station I explained that a man wearing a doctor's scrubs had frightened Letty sometime during the night. Although the two nurses listened attentively, their faces told me what they believed: Letty MacNair was one more daft old woman imagining that a doctor meant to harm her.

My temper responded accordingly. ''I'm telling you, someone wearing scrubs was in there last night trying to get something from Ms. MacNair. She's in here because she was hit on the head—remember?''

One of the nurses nodded, so there was at least a slim possibility of cooperation.

I threw up a hand to indicate a small concession. ''I'm not saying it was one of your staff,'' I told the women. ''In fact I'm saying it *wasn't*, but you better warn your doctors not to wear scrubs around Letty, because if they do they'll scare her all over again. Promise?'' I implored the two impassive faces.

''She's got surgery scheduled for Monday,'' said the least sympathetic one, a black woman with high cheekbones and a sarcastic sneer. ''You want the doctor to wear a three-piece suit?''

''I know it's a problem,'' I admitted. ''Just try not to scare her anymore, okay?''

They both nodded automatically. As I walked back toward Letty's door, I could sense them looking at each other and rolling their eyes.

Letty lay against her tilted pillows, a loosely joined doll compressed into a heap. Since she would have been unable to see it, I had never bothered to rent her a TV. However, today I had brought along two small presents.

''Are you comfortable?'' I asked.

''Aye.''

''Would you like me to brush your hair?''

The offer surprised her, but she nodded; and some tears she had been holding back escaped her eyes. She looked toward my face.

I smoothed her hair with my hand, carefully avoiding the bulky bandage at the side of her head. From my purse I extracted the soft brush I'd brought with me and began to stroke her hair. She turned just enough to make it easier for me, but silently she continued to cry.

''Does this feel good?'' I asked.

''Aye.'' She drew in a shuddering breath.

I stopped several minutes later, when her hair shone and her tears had eased off.

''Me ma used to do that,'' Letty told me.

I wiped her damp cheeks with a tissue. ''Tell me about your mother.''

''She was Mrs. Doland's cook, you know. Ma was a very fine cook.'' She inched up ever so slightly on her pillows.

"Mrs. Doland must have been very fond of your mother."

"Aye. And of me, too. A fine lady." Who Letty clearly missed even after quite an expanse of time.

"Oh," I said, remembering my other gift, a sample of my favorite cologne. "Do you like the smell of this?" I opened the little bottle and waved it near her nose.

Letty screwed up her face.

"Ugh," she said. "Not a bit." So much for that idea.

I returned to my agenda. "There's something else I have to ask."

Letty's non-eyebrows hunkered down over her eyes. "What?" she asked.

"Would you mind if I tidied up your house a bit? To get it ready for you?" Technically I had already started; it was about time I remembered my manners.

The pout deepened. "Dr. Bixnell said she won't let you go home unless . . ."

"She told me."

"Well, is it all right with you if I . . . ?"

"If you must, but . . ."

"But what?"

"What for, girl? What's in it for yer own self?"

By now I should have expected that question, but I never did. My mother always spent her free time doing whatever she thought needed doing; and much as I hated to admit it, so did I.

Tell Letty it was a personality trait? That it's impossible for me to hear about somebody's headache without offering an aspirin? How could someone living Letty's secluded life identify with that?

Tell her I liked crusty old women who tricked me out of sticky buns? Also true, but Letty wouldn't believe that either until she knew me better.

"I just found out my grandmother was friends with Mrs. Doland, and I know Grammy would want me to do anything I could for one of her friend's friends. Besides, we're neighbors."

Apparently my fib amused Letty. A smile I can only describe as "impish" parted her lips.

"Hey!" I said. "They did something else to your teeth."

The smile broadened. "E's a brute, but he give me relief, so I figured I'd let 'im at it again."

"Wow," I said, teasing her. "The royal treatment. Next you'll tell me you get egg in your beer."

"I wish."

Thus began our first real chat, and soon I found myself telling her about how much Barney seemed to love her, about Garry's athletic disappointments and Chelsea's self-improvement plan—all possibly to impress a pubescent boy named Tim.

"Are you worried about the eye operation?" I asked when we both fell quiet.

"Some," she admitted.

"Dr. Kinderhausen seems like a wonderful guy. Did you like him?"

"Aye."

"When you see him Monday, he'll be wearing those green scrubs you saw. Don't let that frighten you."

Letty remained silent, but I felt I had scored with my warning. Who knew how much of what I said made sense to her? Sometimes she seemed remarkably astute, other times my words might have been spoken in a foreign language. It was exactly like talking to my mother.

Searching for another conversational topic, my thoughts returned to the one thing we had in common—our neighborhood. Except this time I tried to view it from Letty's perspective.

"If you had the money, would you move somewhere nicer?" I asked.

"Never," she answered easily. "Mike and Tony is always fixin' me up with their mum's cookin', and that Raymond man never misses a bit of firewood. Those new folks over to you? Now they're a funny pair, but interestin'. Leave? Never. I wouldn't leave me friends.''

Them again. But wait a minute. ''Patsy's boys bring you food?''

''Nah. They put it atop the trash can long about dark. Their mum goes on about varmi'ts, but the boys know it's me. Caught 'em watching out their winder.''

''And what's so funny about the Diamonds next to me?'' If anything, they seemed to be the dullest pair on the block.

''He brings it in. She takes it out.'' Letty chortled. ''Funny pair.''

''You see them doing this?''

''Can't see whut's going in and out,'' she pointed to her eyes. ''Just see somtin'.''

She yawned, prompting me to accomplish my final goal without further delay.

''Letty,'' I began. ''After . . . after your operation on Monday, I'd like you to stay at my house for a few days.''

She rustled in her sheets as if gathering herself to protest, so I hurried to add, ''Doctor's orders.''

Her lower lip pushed out. ''I'm fine on me own.''

''I appreciate that,'' I told her. ''And we'll get you back home as soon as Dr. Kinderhausen says it's okay. But I'd really like you to be with us anyway.''

''Why?''

Because, poor vision or no, she seemed to know quite a bit more than she should about our neighborhood. Slipping from yard to yard in the dark, pilfering firewood, collecting a meal, watching through lighted windows, listening to everyone's trials and tribulations—on just about any block in the United States that was enough to earn a person at least one thump on the head.

''For your safety,'' I said solemnly.

Letty glanced at her wrist bandage, and her lower lip began to tremble. That's why I refrained from reminding her about Liz's death, or even last night's visitor.

''Until you see better and get your energy back, I'd feel

better if you were around other people. Okay?''

Letty sighed her acceptance, and for a moment she looked just like one of the pathetic specimens my mother befriended as regularly as she took in the Sunday paper.

And now I was doing it.

Damn.

Chapter 24

After I left the hospital, I decided to kill an hour at Appliance World, one of those over-advertised discount stores offering anything that ever plugged into a wall.

Centered among less assuming structures, this particular store was Gotham City cement in style, a tower of modernity that resembled a sand castle made with one of those pink plastic molds. A white Dodge sedan slowly oxidized at the far edge of the parking lot, confirming that Johnny Raymond was indeed on duty. I deposited my Suburu in a vacant slot and trotted through the cooling afternoon air toward the door.

Inside bumpy gray rubber paths led to octagonal patches of black carpet loaded with logically grouped products. Large yellow tags on the predominately black and white merchandise assaulted you with the "specially reduced" prices. I walked counterclockwise until I reached the washing machines.

"Hi, Johnny," I greeted Sol and Margaret's aging only son. As expected, his pants were black, his shirt white. Only his narrow, Buddy Holly tie hinted at individuality. "Congratulations on your engagement," I added.

"Hello," he replied. "Thanks." He continued to loiter at the edge of a Maytag in case I was teasing and really meant to look at televisions or a VCR.

"When's the big date? October 8?"

"Yes." His hair was parted and slicked flat, and his glasses frames came from Eyes 'R' Us, if there is such a place. I hoped his fiancée still possessed the first quarter she ever earned. Then they could pool their resources, maybe spring for a cup of coffee.

"That's just lovely."

"Thank you."

"Listen, Johnny. I thought I'd look at washers while I'm here. Which ones do you recommend?"

"John, please, Mrs. Barnes. Only my mother calls me Johnny. And we have several very good models."

"Gin, please. Only salesmen call me Mrs. Barnes."

His smile was scarcely tolerant. "Okay, Gin. What do you think you need?"

Something that washes clothes? I noticed a proud little notation in gold script on the back of one boxy machine. "Two speed," it said.

"Two speeds," I told the loving son who wanted his folks to move out of their house so he could move in.

John moved along a row of quite similar white metal contraptions, and said, "This is the bottom of that range; but for not much more, you can get yourself a number of other features."

I glanced at the cheapest two-speed washer, couldn't tell it apart from the ones right or left. I lifted the lid. Inside was a gray tub full of holes and a stem spiraled with fins.

John motioned me to the front end of the row. "This is your best bet, Gin. You got your optional second rinse, your delicate cycle, extra-large capacity."

It looked exactly like the other one except the tub was bigger and it was white. The price on the yellow banner had once financed the Barnes family for an entire week at the New Jersey shore. Years ago, but still . . .

"Does it sort the clothes, too?" I asked.

"Ahem," said *John*.

"This is my first stop," I quickly interjected. "I'll have to look a little further."

My grip on this conversation had never been tight. Soon I would be shuffled back to the bumpy gray path, so I lifted another lid and verbally sprinted for first base.

"I understand you think your mom and dad ought to retire," I remarked.

John Raymond narrowed his eyes and pulled at his nose. "I don't see what business that is of yours."

I closed the lid. Out. I hadn't even come close to crossing the bag. "What about these Maytags?" I asked, dancing around the corner toward the pricier brand.

"What about them?"

I became thoughtful. "Why do you feel so strongly about your folks retiring?" I mused. "Your dad doesn't have to mow the lawn, and your mother doesn't have to do heavy cleaning?"

No answer.

"These good washers?" I asked, returning to a question he might actually answer.

"Yep."

"I'll bet you say that about all the brands."

My neighbor's unpleasant son strolled all the way back down the row to the bottom of the bottom of the line and patted a lid. "This one will probably do for you, Mrs. Barnes," he said. "It just washes clothes."

"Got one at home, do you?"

I ushered myself back to the bumpy gray path, my backside scorched by the heat of Johnny Raymond's glare.

When I drove past the end of the Diamonds' driveway, I noticed Camilla Grogan's stoop-shouldered form emerging from Bonnie's front door.

How nice, I thought. They must have become friendly since Margaret's tea. Just like Liz and me.

Then naturally I remembered the rest.

Chapter 25

On Saturday, April 15, nature promised more than a politician with his hat in his hands. Lawns were greener than all the tax returns headed for the IRS at midnight, surely more laden with dew than any mail carriers would ever be with refunds. In between the Browders' and Kelmans' yards a magnolia tree proclaimed its intention to bloom in a day or two. Letty's brilliant daffodil heads glowed as if they thought litter and fertilizer were one and the same.

Even my yard offered a few optimistic sprouts—mayflowers shaped like torpedoes aiming at the sky, speckled dog-toothed violet leaves scattered under a tree, and mint-green day lily spears four inches tall under the lamppost.

In the morning Rip and Chelsea set off for another long run in Valley Forge Park. I conscripted the still-sulking Garry to help with Letty's kitchen and living room windows. If he was busy, maybe he would forget that elsewhere his best friends were practicing for the track team.

In the afternoon Rip helped lay a carpet remnant I found in our garage in Letty's upstairs bathroom where the tile had curled into sharp edges. We also did quite a bit more scrubbing while Chelsea and Garry picked up trash from among the weeds out front. We didn't dare mow or trim for fear of what Letty's imaginary "friends" would think.

By seven we Barneses had finished an early dinner and Rip and Chelsea were off getting dressed for Bryn Derwyn's dance. Garry had nothing to do, and I had nothing to do with him. I was tempted to rent something maudlin like *Bambi* so the miserable pre-teen could have an excuse to cry.

"Mom, where's my new sweater?" Chelsea called into the family room where Garry and I watched a quiz show. Seven-thirty approached; we were getting down to the all-or-nothing quiz question.

"Mom!" Chelsea prompted. "Dad says he has to be at the dance by eight."

Of course. The headmaster and permanent chaperon would want to be punctual, even if that meant Chelsea and her buddies would be unfashionably early. I hopped out of my seat to search for the sweater.

In short order I nodded my approval of Rip's Parental Prep attire, admired Chelsea's teenaged chic, and kissed them farewell. When I returned, Garry stared blankly at a TV commercial. I shut off the set.

"What'd you do that for?" he asked. "I wanted to see how they got that car up the mountain."

"You'll get other chances. Trust me." I extracted a deck of cards from the coffee table drawer.

"Aces and deuces are wild," I announced.

"What are you talking about, Mom?" Garry's practiced scorn was off a notch; he almost sounded interested.

"Poker," I answered. "Protocol of the business world."

"Huh?"

I outlined the rules, jotting a handy cheat sheet on the back of an envelope for reference. Garry donned a tennis visor after he won his first hand. Soon we were betting toothpicks and having a wonderful time.

At an appropriate moment I mentioned that his poker face needed work.

"What do you mean?" he obediently asked.

I concealed my elation. "Sometimes it's necessary to keep your feelings to yourself."

"Huh?"

"Part of the game is to get me to bet against you, right? Otherwise you won't win much money."

"I guess."

"I'm telling you. It is. So say you have a full house and I have three tens. I'm going to look at your face. If you're worried, smug, confused, or whatever, I'm going to use that information to help me bet. So what do you think you should do?"

Garry shrugged.

"You'll try not to show anything. That's a poker face, and believe me—it's part of the game."

Garry drifted into thought. "You and Dad do that all the time, don't you."

My son, the genius. "Yes, we do."

"Why?"

I sighed, folded my hand. "To protect ourselves, I guess. There are things you can't get if you appear to want them too much. A girlfriend. A sale to a big customer.

"Sometimes our feelings are nobody else's business. Other times our emotions may be inappropriate. We don't want others to think less of us, so we pretend we're feeling happy when we're really sad or sad when we're secretly happy."

Garry tapped his cards against his leg. Tears slipped down his face.

"The track team?" I asked.

He nodded. "Okay," I said. "Pay attention, because this is important.

"You are a very special person. You're bright. You have a wonderful sense of humor. You're good at math and spelling and you can remember lines from movies better than anyone I've ever met. But for some reason your body isn't suited for running track right now. Maybe you'd be better at tennis. Maybe golf. Maybe none of the above.

You're eleven years old. You've got to try new things to find out what's easy for you and what's hard, what you like and what you don't. As you get older, you have to keep trying, keep learning new things."

"But how come Dave and Jordy . . . ?"

"They're different people, Garry. They're learning about themselves by trial and error, too. Don't worry about them. Concentrate on learning about Garrett Ripley Barnes. And don't be too hard on him when he fails. Just steer him in some other direction.

"Now about your feelings . . ."

"I know. I should be happy for Dave and Jordy."

"Not exactly."

Garry gaped at me with astonishment.

I pushed the coffee table away so I could stretch out my legs and cross my ankles on it. Then I looked my son in the eye. "You're half right. If you can manage it, the mature way to feel would be to be happy for your friends.

"But suppose you're just plain jealous. You need to acknowledge that before you can decide how to behave."

Garry stared at me.

"If you're jealous, but you know you should be happy, then you know what you have to do."

"Act happy?"

"Right. Maybe by acting pleased for your friends, you'll begin to feel better about yourself and will actually get over your jealousy. And really, there isn't any reason to be jealous because you're just as good at something else as they are at track."

"Sure. What?"

"We don't know yet. Maybe poker. I call."

"Read 'em and weep," my son announced with a grin.

Pair of threes. I folded my three kings and feigned a heart attack.

Garry snorted with scorn. It was time to go out for ice cream.

On the way to the ice cream shoppe I detoured to look

in on the Bryn Derwyn dance—my idea, but Garry did not object. I think he wanted to see into his future as much as I wanted him to.

The school lobby was half lit, bestowing a welcoming evening glow. Alexis Kim, the eminently popular girls phys-ed teacher, sat at a table selling tickets. She winked us past without missing any of the flirtatious banter two youths leaning on the table worked so hard to deliver.

The auditorium, emptied of chairs, was scarcely lit at all. Primary-colored bulbs bounced beams off the ceiling, the walls, and the dancers in time to the frenetic music.

Bryn Derwyn had long ago discovered that disc jockeys capable of playing requests from a huge repertoire were the way to go for a school of its size. Live bands were too expensive and too inflexible. Even the junior/senior prom had gone the recorded music route.

Garry slipped through the door and opted to hold up the left-hand wall. He was mostly invisible except for the whites of his widened eyes.

If they were not dancing, students from Bryn Derwyn and their ''imported'' friends stood in mixed clusters and shouted their conversation directly into each other's ears. By instinct I found Rip near the three other teacher/chaperons and eased up beside him. Rip and I smiled at each other but did not attempt any conversation.

Chelsea and her girlfriends were at the opposite edge of the crowd, gesturing frantically at each other in an effort to communicate. Our daughter looked adorable. She fit in. She would never know I was there.

To my experienced eye, the dance appeared to be a success. No extreme segregation of the sexes that so often characterized a flop. More than a third dancing. I even noticed a senior girl grab the hands of a sophomore with glasses, pull him into the spotlights and jiggle his arms until he actually tried to dance, clearly his first attempt. He shared his infectious grin with everyone in sight.

I glanced at Rip to see if he had noticed the boy's rapture, but my husband's expression brought me up short. Arms folded, tight-lipped, his eyes glared toward the edge of the dancers where three young men cavorted almost ritualistically around one young woman. I squinted to identify her despite the darkened room; and when recognition at last came, my breath caught. It was the new science teacher, Lisa Burack, the daughter of Rip's mentor. When we had had Greg for dinner two weeks ago, I remembered Rip saying that Lisa was doing fine.

Of course what else would he have said?

At the moment Lisa concentrated on the internal, dancing as if she were inside the sensual music, oblivious to the three boys vying desperately for her attention. The way she moved, eye contact with any male would have been tantamount to a sexual invitation. Rip bristled with fury, while my mind raced.

Why was Rip so furious? Was Lisa's breech of discretion one isolated mistake? Or was her behavior habitual? Was Rip furious because the young teacher's conduct reflected on the school? Or was his response personal, on a level scarcely different from the gyrating young men?

For the remainder of the song I scrutinized Rip and Lisa with as much objectivity as I could manage. I concluded that I needed more information, which I planned to obtain at the earliest possible opportunity—no matter what.

Soon after the song ended Garry tapped my arm to go, and Rip walked us out to the Suburu. During our mutual silence I practiced my poker face with a vengeance.

As I drove into town, my thoughts were torn like scraps of paper tossed into my mental hat. Rip loved me, that I believed. Rip's ego was heavily invested in Bryn Derwyn Academy. How Bryn Derwyn fared would be how Robert Ripley Barnes and his dependents fared. The man and his work were inseparable.

How about the man and his family? Deep down I believed we were also inseparable, which was why I was able to take our son for ice cream with reasonable composure.

However, my confidence did not last.

Sunday morning I burned the toast and overfried the eggs. Rip was infatuated with Lisa Burack, I just knew it.

"Yuck," Chelsea complained. My response was to toss a potholder at her through the pass-through and leave the kitchen. "More eggs in the 'frige," I pointed out superfluously.

Rip wandered downstairs wearing jeans and a frayed oxford shirt with the sleeves rolled up. Outside it was raining, so inside was cool and damp. "Breakfast?" he asked tentatively.

"You're on your own," I advised him.

He shrugged that off like a champ, and headed straight for the bagels in the freezer.

If he were tired of me, would he be so easygoing? Wouldn't he grumble just a little? Was I wrong—again?

A little later he found me upstairs dumping clean laundry onto our bed. "Going to school, babe," he reminded me, his Sunday morning habit. Nobody interrupted him because only his family knew he was there.

"You think I can borrow Bryn Derwyn's Shop-vac this afternoon to do Letty's kitchen floor?"

"Just this afternoon? Sure. I'll bring it when I come home for lunch."

Why were you so furious at Lisa Burack last night? I wanted to ask. But I refrained. When it happened, I had been standing right there. He could have said something then, but he had not. In the interest of self-preservation it was time to face the truth. That meant speaking to Joanne Henry, Rip's secretary. She knew everything, and she was discreet. I would stop in, look her in the eye . . .

"Bye," Rip smiled pleasantly after he kissed me.

"Bye," I echoed as neutrally as possible. My family probably could survive one more morning of burned toast and bagels.

Unfortunately for my peace of mind, I realized Letty's eye operation and her release from the hospital were scheduled for Monday. My confidential conversation with Joanne Henry would just have to wait.

Chapter 26

About a block from every hospital is a street where people willing to walk a short distance may park free for an hour or two. Hodges Memorial had Mercer Street, and parking there made me feel frugal and efficient. As a restorative to equilibrium, it wasn't much against the helpless/fragile fears instilled first by Liz's death, Rip's odd behavior, and Letty's presently ongoing surgery. But it was enough for me to put on a bright face for the receptionist at the surgi-center.

She explained that outpatient surgery was running a little late and directed me to the nearby waiting room. "As far as I know, everything's going well. They just followed Dr. Brown and he tends to work slow."

"I guess Mondays are the same everywhere."

She smiled tolerantly, as if her real opinion were that hospitals were unlike anywhere else. "Right," I conceded.

The receptionist blinked.

One glance at the inhabitants of the waiting room turned me back to her.

"I'll just take a walk around the block."

Crossing in front of the parking garage, I strolled left again onto Mercer Street. This time I noticed the neat duplexes, their mirrored faces like twins desperate for their own identities. Blue with black shutters, white with red.

Tended yards and neglected ones, plantings as different as the inhabitants. In a corner beside a doorstep stretched a tightly curled fern eight inches tall. A row of ragged forsythia, new leaves overlapping the old blossoms, divided two yards. Further along a lacy white crabapple tree sheltered a white iron loveseat. Dandelions bloomed next door, but so did a row of red tulips lined up with military precision. Clenched maple leaves would open to the first rain. Soon Letty would see it all. Not today, but possibly tomorrow when the patch protecting the surgery on her worst eye would be removed.

I knew the procedure in imprecise terms. The doctor lifted the cornea, liquefied the cataract and expressed it, implanted a new artificial lens, stitched the cornea back in place and voilà—vision. Healing would be an individual matter. Glasses might or might not be needed for further correction.

Letty's second eye, her left, was not quite "ripe," explaining how she managed to take care of herself; but if the first surgery went well, the second could be done after six weeks or so.

My watch said 10:15. Time to wander back.

"Not yet," said the receptionist.

I took my place among the frowning, fretting few and chose the local paper for distraction. Perversely, I turned to the police blotter and once again read about the nefarious doings in our township. A driving under the influence at Lancaster and School House Lane, a broken windshield on Lincoln Court, another stolen bicycle, theft of a ladder left outside overnight. Liz's death was old news by now, but Letty's attack had its own paragraph—just facts with no inflections either way. Nothing about her deprived lifestyle, her medical problems, nothing about her unusual opinions or her quirky sense of humor. She might have been another mailbox or car windshield for all the emotion in those few sentences. I threw down the paper and glanced around for some other way to occupy my time.

Investigating the checkout procedure seemed worthwhile.

All by myself I followed the signs to Inpatient Billing, a cheery room of six paper-free desks manned with five competent-looking women and one wan male. Each operated a computer. I approached the nearest desk.

"Excuse me," I said, standard interruption procedure, although I didn't appear to be interrupting anything. "I'm here to pick up Letty MacNair, and I'd like to make arrangements for checking her out."

The woman tapped a few keys. "Letty MacNair," she repeated. "Here she is." She looked into my eyes just to be polite.

"All set," she said.

"You mean I don't have to do anything?"

"Right. Ms. MacNair's bill is paid in full."

"Oh," I said because that was all I could say. "Thank you," I added, the standard exit line.

After retracing my way back to the waiting room, I took my seat among the remaining frowning, fretting few and waited out Letty's release staring at the watercolor on the opposite wall.

"She didn't want to wear these clothes," the nurse wheeling Letty toward me explained. "Said they weren't hers. I told her it was them or nothing."

"They're a gift from my mother," I bent down to explain to Letty. "Don't worry about it.

"How'd she do?" I addressed the nurse. But Dr. Kinderhausen emerged through the double doors just then and smiled at me. "Went beautifully," he said. "Bring her to my office at nine tomorrow morning and we'll remove the patch." He clearly looked forward to the event.

"Well," I said. "Thank you, doctor." Not Pulitzer material, but genuine.

He handed me a prescription for an antibiotic eye drop to be administered every three or four hours. The nurse handed me a package containing a plastic protective shield Letty should temporarily wear while sleeping.

"Don't rub your eye," the doctor instructed Letty, "and don't get soap in it. Aspirin as needed."

Letty nodded vaguely, as if still somewhat dazed by anesthesia. Beaming, the doctor disappeared back through the double doors.

A moment stretched in which the nurse waited. Overwhelmed myself, I couldn't quite grasp what was expected of me.

"I'll just get the car," I said finally, and the nurse breathed. She began to ease Letty's good arm through the jewel-blue cardigan Mother had contributed from her stack of unused apparel. The matching dress was comfortably loose with a white collar, cuffs and a sash that, now that I noticed, was nowhere in sight. I made a questioning face and tying motions with my hands. The nurse reached into her pocket and gave me the sash while shaking her head. "Bone of contention," said her expression, so I refrained from asking more.

Oh dear, I thought. This was my new houseguest.

Memories of *The Man Who Came to Dinner* accompanied me to the car.

When Letty was strapped into her bucket seat inside my Suburu wagon, I asked if she remembered where we were going.

"Aye," she said. "Your house."

"Right." Partly realizing exactly how awkward her living with us was going to be, and partly remembering my promise to get her back home as soon as possible, it occurred to me that she would probably be needing groceries within the week. The MAC card? Why not?

"You be okay if I make one quick stop?" I asked. We were cruising along Lancaster again. The ubiquitous MAC rainbow symbol seemed to appear every other block.

"Aye."

A square brick Corestates Bank next to an Acme offered an easy parking lot, so it got Letty's business.

Card in, black stripe down and to the right. PIN number OK. Withdraw two hundred dollars from her checking account. Cash in the little recess. Receipt from the little slot. Balance $323.27.

My breath was noisy going in, slow blowing out. There used to be twenty thousand dollars in there. What had become of it?

I thought of Kyle O'Callahan, who knew nothing about Letty's affairs. Nothing except that she possessed a MAC card she had not been entitled to. Had he removed the money from her trustee account specifically so she couldn't get her hands on any more of it?

My conversation with Kyle had been brief, with very little information exchanged. As a possible explanation of why Letty had not received her monthly allowance, he had related that his father had suffered two strokes. I insisted that two hundred dollars a month wasn't nearly enough, and I had mentioned that Letty was also in the hospital, having been mugged in her home.

The hospital bill. Kyle O'Callahan had taken care of Letty's expenses. Damn. Maybe he wore a white hat after all. Maybe he was just as ignorant of her affairs as he claimed. Just because I didn't like him didn't mean he wasn't honest. Just because he was the only person available for me to blame for Letty's problems didn't mean he was responsible for any of them.

Sourly, I pocketed the two hundred dollars and walked back to my car.

Letty had fallen asleep with her head against the window. I sighed. Here she was in her upper sixties—give or take a few—fresh out of surgery, still recovering from a knock on the head and a fall, and I was preparing to send her home before she had even been in my house a minute.

I woke her just long enough to tilt back her seat and get her settled for the rest of the drive.

Then all the way back to Beech Tree Lane I tried to

reason through my impressions of Letty's trustee's son. No conclusions, just a truckload of doubts.

Although making binding decisions regarding Letty's assets had never been my intention, legally I knew the power of attorney authorized me to do so. I could, for example, order an audit on the trust Edwin Markus O'Callahan had been so secretive about for so long. That ought to tell me whether Kyle O'Callahan, Esq. wore a white hat or not.

As soon as I had a spare minute, I would leave a message for Norman Demig to call me. After all, wasn't dealing with other attorneys ninety-five percent of what they were trained to do?

Letty had no appetite for lunch. She kicked off her loose black shoes and tumbled into Garry's bed still wearing mother's jewel-blue dress with those ever-present white socks. She made quite a contrast to the geometric-patterned red, yellow, and blue comforter and the red sheets. A bit of American Gothic meets Mondrian.

Suddenly Barney wriggled past my knees through the doorway. Before I could grab him or shout, "No," he was on the bed next to Letty, circling for his notorious eighty-pound flop.

"Barney!" I finally managed. "Off."

Plunk, right into the spot between Letty's chest and knees.

"Ack. Let 'em be," Letty said, circling his rump with her arm. The contented smile looked good on her face.

What's the harm? I thought. Barney was our premier snuggler, and Garry's was his only permitted bed. Plus Letty's eye was thoroughly protected with bandages and that plastic sleeping contraption.

"You sure?" I checked.

"Aye." Already she was mostly asleep.

"I'm just going outside for half an hour," I said in case she awakened early. Bonnie Diamond had passed us in her

Volvo on her way out. "You know where the bathroom is."

"Aye."

I smiled and shut the door, confident at last that I'd done the right thing by inviting her. What we would do with a cantankerous, opinionated eccentric in our house, I had no idea; but come what may, it had been the right thing to do. Personally, I had already benefitted. Hadn't I had forgotten about Rip and Lisa Burack for a whole hour this time?

After leaving Letty and Barney to their naps, I changed into jeans, sneakers, and a sweatshirt, sighing with the relief of their comfort and grateful for their indestructibility. If I was going to skulk around my neighbors' bushes, peeking into their windows, I didn't want to be worried about ripping my pants on a branch or getting green stains on my sleeve.

Crossing my yard toward the back of Bonnie's, I noticed one of Barney's tennis balls on the ground and picked it up in case I needed an emergency excuse to be trespassing.

Close to the house the Diamonds' bushes were still wet from yesterday's rain. My sneakers also left incriminating patterns in the soft loam under their yews. Despite the tennis ball excuse, if Bonnie returned suddenly, I would still have some pretty dicey explaining to do.

With that in mind, I wasted no time. The garage that faced my house had one rear window that revealed room for two cars, a few yard tools, and two trash cans. Except for a tidy pile of moving crates, it looked remarkably neat—almost like new.

I hurried to the next accessible window, that of a laundry room. A plastic basket of clothes sat on the floor. A box of detergent sat on the drier. Big deal.

The kitchen possessed a sliding glass door opening onto a deck. I climbed the two steps and saw my shadow creep along the glass. When I got close, I cupped my hands around my eyes, and got my best view of the Diamonds' lifestyle I was going to get.

Inside were an oval table and four chairs. I noticed far less clutter than in my house. Even the living room—what I could see of it—seemed sparse and neat. There were some children's books in the magazine rack at the side of a recliner. Shadowed across the room as it was, I couldn't tell whether the television was old or new.

Nothing I saw suggested the pattern of items coming or going that had so amused Letty. All I knew for sure was that after Bonnie placed a defective new TV in her car, it had been stolen before she could return it. Of course, Bonnie could have been dispensing with the latest batch of unwelcome merchandise right then, and her house would look exactly this normal.

The green electronic numbers of Bonnie's oven proclaimed that it was nearly 2:00 PM. We had passed on the street close to noon. It was time to scoot around front where I might have a legitimate reason to be.

I emerged from the Diamonds' driveway just as Sam approached. He came from the left, the direction of my own drive.

"Oh, here you are," he said jovially.

My heart pounding, I related my story about getting Barney's ball back. Sam started glancing around for my dog, so I hastily asked, "Were you looking for me?"

"Well, yes," he admitted. He was all casual elegance in brown today, including a subtle, knitted tie. I supposed he had met with a client earlier, or some other businessperson. I couldn't help remembering him in running shorts, but this time the image repelled me. Lisa Burack's gyrations were too fresh, too irritating. At the moment sex was a four-letter word.

"I've been wondering if I might take you up on that offer of coffee?"

What offer? When? His dark eyes softly pleaded in a cautiously suggestive way that might have been completely innocent—depending on me.

Oh, the garage door day. Embarrassment rushed up my

neck and sizzled in my ears. I swallowed hard. If Sam had cozied up to me this way then, I wouldn't be worrying about what Rip thought of Lisa Burack because I'd be much more worried about myself.

"Now isn't a good time," I told Eunice's damned-attractive, potentially-ex husband. "I've got company, and she's sleeping."

"Letty MacNair?" Sam suggested.

"Why, yes. How did you . . . Oh. You saw us come home?" Apparently she wasn't the only observant person on the block. I remembered now that Sam's drafting table faced a front window. He could be seen working there almost any day.

"Terrible what happened to her. Any idea who did it?"

"Not really."

Then I thought to ask, "Have you had any trouble? At the townwatch meeting it sounded as if everyone else on this street has."

"No, but then I'm home more than most, and we have an alarm system."

"Now I remember." The alarm system had been Sam's reason for not joining the group.

He grunted and changed the subject. "Have you seen or talked to Eunice lately?"

"No, but I notice there's no 'Sold' sign in front of your place. I guess that's good news."

He shrugged, and I saw anger rolling through the muscles in his firm, clean-shaven jaw. He stood facing his house; and as he stared at it, I thought how pervasive a disintegrating relationship was. Was there any hope of preventing more damage? Or was divorce a boulder rolling downhill?

Sam's eyes came back soft and ingratiating. They appealed to my instincts, motherly and otherwise . . .

Quite suddenly I became impatient with the Browders and their problems. I especially became impatient with them trying to use me as a pawn.

"Listen," I said. "My coffee just isn't that good. Call your wife. She probably thinks you did something, so apologize. What have you got to lose?"

I delivered the message to Sam, but it was addressed to Rip. Talk to me you, you . . . secretive male, I wanted to scream.

By the time I got home I needed to get my hands on something inanimate. Demolishing a fence with a sledgehammer would have been ideal.

When Letty woke up around 3:30 I was out in the driveway furiously hand sanding an oak end table someone had given us when we first bought our house. The reason I hadn't refinished it before was the daunting amount of manual labor involved. Today was its day—I had energy to vent. Also, all my other repair projects would have been noisy.

"What you mad at, girl?"

Letty's soft voice coming from the walkway at my back made me jump. Down in a crouch, I swiveled on my toes toward her.

Mother's jewel-blue dress was creased and shapeless now, and the matching sweater drooped from Letty's shoulders much as her own decrepit brown one would have. She'd taken off the plastic sleeping contraption, leaving a gauze patch loosely taped across her right eye. She looked like a defective granny doll.

"You mad at sumtin'. What is it?" she asked.

"My husband," I answered bluntly, almost as if I were speaking to myself or maybe a tree. Letty had been a silent fixture in the periphery of our world for so long, it seemed natural to take her presence for granted.

Yet the way she sighed quickly exposed my mistake. Not at all a fixture without feelings, it seemed that Letty had been worried that my anger was directed at her.

Also, judging by the blinking of her unbandaged eye, my honest answer had taken her by surprise. Her head tilted and her lips pursed out.

After a moment she shook her head and told me, "I guess I dunno, but it seems ta me that table ain't whut needs fixin'."

My stunned stare followed each step as she shuffled back toward the front door.

Chapter 27

Letty was sitting on the sofa looking vacant again, making me wonder whether the wisdom she conveyed had been a product of her imagination or mine.

Either way, she had been right; the end table was not what I needed to fix. My head and heart were already halfway to school for that conversation with Joanne Henry.

Yet I was torn. Would Letty be all right if I went out?

My mother's old sweater had slipped off one of her shoulders. She looked perfectly content, as if she were in her family room instead of mine.

Barney gazed sleepily from his sitting position at her knee. From experience I knew that if someone roused his suspicions—with an expression, a smell, or just a scrap of a nasty thought—even our cream puff of a dog would turn tiger.

"Letty, um, what I said out there. I didn't mean to blurt out like that, but, um, you were right. There is something I can do, but I would have to leave you alone for a while—maybe half an hour."

"So git. I be fine," Letty insisted. I sensed that she almost wanted me gone, which caused me to remember her usual solitude. The attention she received at the hospital must have been exhausting.

At the last minute I asked if she wanted the TV on.

"Don't matter," she said indifferently.

I figured she didn't know what she was missing, so I taught her how to use the remote control. Soon she was channel surfing and snickering out of the side of her mouth.

"Go on, git," she said, her newly repaired teeth revealed through her grin.

As I turned to go, Letty wiggled her backside so far into the cushions it would have taken Goliath's shoehorn to pry her out of there.

When I whispered why I wanted to see her, Joanne Henry immediately commandeered a student to mind the reception desk and the phones. Then she ushered me into an empty classroom where we were unlikely to be disturbed. I closed the door and turned a student chair to face hers. Even that late in the afternoon there were kids and teachers passing by the door every minute or so.

"What's going on, Joanne?" I asked quietly.

Joanne flicked her flinty eyes back and forth behind her designer glasses and licked her lips. She was a meticulously maintained older woman with stiff beige hair and colorful tailored dresses that flattered her middle-aged shape. For a while we both had felt territorial over Rip, until we dipped into a bottle of Chardonnay together at my first faculty party. After that, it was understood that we were both on the same side—Rip's.

In this instance I didn't know whether that meant Joanne would help me or not.

"Hasn't Rip said anything?"

I confirmed that he had not.

"Didn't want to worry you," she concluded. "I can see why."

"Why?" I asked insistently, forgetting about the ears passing by our door.

"It's been rough, Gin," she remarked.

"What has?" I asked impatiently.

Joanne flicked her eyes back and forth again, then leaned

in and looked straight at me. "Okay," she said with a deep breath. And then she told me everything.

Lisa could not control her classes, she buddied up to the students in a manner that confused the boys, she wore short skirts and tight sweaters and had garnered more parental complaints than the entire rest of the faculty.

"One father even hinted that Rip had hired her for reasons other than her teaching ability. 'Other assets,' he called them." The sneering man who had cornered Rip in the kitchen the night of the tenth-grade parent party.

"Phew," I said, sitting back when Joanne finished. "No wonder Rip kept quiet." Fighting to preserve his reputation at school was stressful enough without starting all over at home.

I looked askance at Joanne Henry. "So why did you tell me?"

"Because you obviously needed to know. I've been thinking of calling you for weeks, but . . ."

"But what?"

"I was afraid . . ." She thought I'd get insomnia again.

The admission embarrassed us both. Joanne stood and touched the stainless steel doorknob with her fingers while I remembered the anxious time to which she referred.

Regularly I reassured myself that I was stronger now, that that would not happen to me again. And I believed it was true. Furthermore, this problem involved Rip, not an unpredictable stranger.

Yet I had been grouchy and out of sorts since Saturday night's dance, and my mood had threatened to deteriorate. Despite my husband's precautions, perhaps because of them, our relationship had been affected.

Shyly, Joanne rubbed the toe of her shoe on the neutral tweed classroom carpet.

"Thank you," I said, reaching toward her hand but not quite touching her. "You're a good friend."

"I better get back to the phones," she said, soft creases marring her forehead. "David's inclined to spell names wrong and transpose numbers.'' Despite her very convincing reason to get back, her concern seemed to remain with Rip and me.

''Take care of yourself,'' she said with a backward glance.

All at once I thought of a way to do just that—only this time I wouldn't burn the cheese balls.

When I returned home, Letty had fallen asleep with the television on—her head to the left, Barney's on the floor to the right. One of them snored.

I made my call from the kitchen. As expected, Greg Burack expressed surprise and curiosity over a dinner invitation so soon after the last one, so I told him the truth. I told him Rip needed his advice on how to handle a problem.

''Friday then,'' Rip's dear friend and mentor agreed immediately.

He almost hung up, but I hurried to stall him. ''Greg,'' I said with no effort to diminish my concern. ''Greg, Rip needs to talk to you about your daughter.''

I could hear the man's breath draw in and sigh out. ''I see,'' he replied.

Neither of us needed to say more.

To celebrate Letty's release from the hospital I grilled the steak her butcher/friend Pete had provided, topped it with sautéed mushrooms, steamed some fresh green beans, warmed some packaged rolls, tore up some lettuce . . . it was elegance within my own boundaries. My efforts tended to peter out far short of perfection. At least in this instance, they were greatly appreciated by my family—even more by the guest of honor.

''Umm,'' Letty said reaching for the bowl of beans. ''Do you mind? Just like me mum used to do. Umm.''

Chelsea had been consuming more than her recent quota, in part because the dance was over and Timmy-whatsizname was history, in part—I suspected—because running regularly required fuel. With her own plate conspicuously empty she crossed her arms and stared at our bold, unmannered guest.

Garry reached for a third roll, but an oblivious Letty beat him to it. "How about that butter there, girl," she addressed Chelsea, who delivered the plate with a glare until I cleared my throat and glared back at her.

"More salt?" Chelsea asked with sweet sarcasm.

"No not a bit of it," Letty replied. "If ye ask me, yer mother cooks with too much salt."

Letty's blotchy blush was sudden. She threw me a quick look with her unpatched eye to see if I had noticed anything amiss.

Setting an example of good sportsmanship for my kids, I kept my question light and teasing, while I privately wondered how Letty knew anything whatsoever about my cooking—other than what she was consuming right then.

"Oh?" I asked. "And what exactly would you say I salt too much?"

Letty's head hovered over her plate. She looked up at me across the table like a naughty toddler who realized she had been forgiven. "That sausage stuff with the potatoes." She pursed her lips with distaste. "Filling though. I was glad for it just the same."

"You mean that Slope Soup?" No wonder there had been less than I expected for Marc Kelman the day Liz died. Letty had helped herself while it cooled on my front step.

I knew my mouth had dropped open, but I converted my surprise into a laugh. "Is my chili any better?" I asked. The other recipe I made in big batches and cooled in the pot out on the slate step.

Our guest showed off her wrinkled new grin. "Aye," she said. "Wouldn't mind a bit more onion, but 'tis good stuff that is." Her good eye crinkled into a smile.

"Cut me that last bit, would you mind, honey?" Because of Letty's broken wrist, Chelsea had been commandeered to cut her meat. Silently, much more tolerantly than a moment before, Chelsea obliged.

I leaned in with a smile of my own. "Next time I'll put in extra onions for you," I told our next-door neighbor."

Judging by their expressions, the kids had never seen anything so amazing as the fond look that passed between Letty and me. Chelsea's eyebrows rose; and Garry hurried to check Rip's response, which was to mind his dinner plate and grin to himself. After that, Garry regarded Letty as I imagined Einstein might have pondered relativity.

During dessert Rip questioned the kids about their school day, inquired about homework, related a bit about Bryn Derwyn's sports teams, in other words behaved as if Letty were part of the family. She made it through a sizeable piece of chocolate layer cake before sagging with fatigue.

"Garry," I instructed our son, "please get out pajamas and tomorrow's clothes so Letty can use your room.

"Chelsea, why don't you bring down my nightgown with the blue stripes. I'm going to do Letty's eye drops, and then I think she needs to go to bed."

Our guest was so exhausted, she hadn't listened to any of that. Rip helped her up from her seat and guided her down the hall. I went to find sofa-bed sheets for Garry.

Later when I passed by his office, Rip was busy confiding to his computer again. For the first time since he picked up the habit, I understood.

Short term, I actually approved.

Chapter 28

The phone rang early Tuesday morning while I was dressing to take Letty to the doctor's office.

''Hello?'' I said with one shoe in my hand.

''Gin. Norman Demig here. What can I do for you?'' An attorney on the clock.

''Hi,'' I said again, this time with recognition. I hopped into the shoe.

''Listen, it turns out there is some sort of trust account at First Commonwealth Bank for Letty, and a guy named Edwin Markus O'Callahan has been administering it. He's in the hospital with a stroke right now, so I spoke to his son, Kyle. He's an attorney in Bryn Mawr.'' I proceeded to explain about the MAC card and the change in the bank balance. ''The son tried to sandbag me, but I know he knows something. Can we force him to show us the records on the trust?'' I tucked the phone against my shoulder and began buttoning my blouse.

''Sure. You can order an audit; but I want you to realize if the trust was set up properly, there's very little you can do—even if the audit proves O'Callahan has been mismanaging the money.''

I grunted with frustration.

''I just want you to be forewarned. We may find out all about Miss MacNair's assets, but nothing may change.''

I couldn't reply, just clutched at my bangs, a sign that a headache was brewing.

Finally, I asked, "Will it cost much for me to hire you to order an audit?"

"Naw," the son of my mother's admirer responded. "Not for me. Maybe for the audit. But look at it this way: How else are you going to learn anything?"

"Do it," I said. I would find the money somewhere.

After hanging up, I swallowed a couple aspirin then escorted Letty to Dr. Kinderhausen's high-rise office adjacent to Bryn Mawr Hospital. Knowing that the man primarily responsible for Letty's situation—one way or another—was recuperating only a couple of walls away built a pressure in my head that aspirin did little to dissipate.

The removal of Letty's eye patch proved to be my cure.

Guiding his patient with two hands, Dr. Kinderhausen placed her on a seat facing a huge poster of colorful flowers. Forehead creased, the surgeon then reached toward Letty and gently removed the square, taped-on gauze bandage.

Letty opened her reddened, slightly puffy eye. The doctor's lips quivered. His freshly shaven face wanted to beam.

I had been administering the antibiotic eye drops, so Letty's appearance was no surprise to me. Removing the patch actually made her look nearly good as new since the only other evidence of her head wound and fall were a row of stitches, some fading bruises, and the wrist brace.

Soon her blinking subsided, and she glanced around the room. A beautiful smile transformed the collection of wrinkles that were her face. She reached for the doctor's hand and brought it to her lips. Tears dripped from both eyes, and a nurse quickly offered a tissue.

" 'S wonderful," Letty said.

"Clear?" Kinderhausen asked with professional interest. He proceeded to determine with an examination and questions that no, her vision was not quite perfect, but it was vastly improved.

"It will probably get better throughout this week," he advised Letty. "Then when you're completely healed in a month or so, we'll see about glasses to give you even better vision. And, of course, we'll be doing that other eye when it's ready."

He patted Letty's hand between his and allowed his own gratification to show. This is what I'm all about, said his glowing face.

When thanks had been delivered and modestly accepted, Letty and I ventured out into the April sunshine. She wore boxy, wraparound sunglasses and an awestruck expression. Mother's donated dress-of-the-day was a pale rose that hung nearly to Letty's shoes. Its high, round neckline drooped below its wearer's loose, wrinkled neck. The white socks and worn black shoes confirmed that yes, this was an impoverished woman in borrowed clothes. Yet she held the sleeve of my yellow shirt like a debutante on the arm of a beau.

"May I take you out to lunch?" I asked. "To celebrate?"

A worried expression shadowed Letty's awe. "I dunno." She wagged her head.

I knew that restaurant dining might be so unfamiliar to Letty that the idea might frighten more than please her, so I intended to do whatever her response suggested.

"Think about it," I said. "We have time to kill. How about shopping for some new shoes?" Her energy was quite good today, and I thought she could manage a store or two.

When her expression remained doubtful, I added that I had obtained some money from her trustee.

Letty's receptors skipped past the trustee part—I purposely did not elaborate—and went straight to the part about new shoes.

"Like yours?" she asked, perking up.

"Whatever you want."

That's how Letty and I "did" a limited corner of the mall, she strolling along on my arm wearing a rose dress and sunglasses, me guiding her as if she were the Queen Mother.

Salespeople took their cues from me, imagining perhaps that she was my daft old relative in need of athletic shoes. For sneakers were what Letty had in mind, and sneakers happened to be what fit her bunioned, mistreated feet. A wide, jazzy black, white and magenta pair with reflective panels and treads like tires proved to be the most comfortable, so they were the ones we bought. Fortunately, they didn't cost what Chelsea's running shoes did, but damned near.

I used Letty's grocery cash, worrying once again that I might be taking food out of her mouth. However, Norman Demig was working on that problem, so I put it out of my mind.

"Now about that lunch," I said, and Letty shrank down into the dress. "I think I know the perfect place. How about it?"

"I dunno."

"If you don't like it, we'll leave."

Letty cast me a worried glance behind the sunglasses, and followed me out of the mall like a child.

My first intention was to make her feel special, but the more I thought about my restaurant idea the more I liked it. When Rip and I went out, we found ourselves transformed into a couple whose main responsibility, temporarily, was to enjoy each other's company. We spoke more freely, and perhaps more personally, than we usually did at home.

I began to hope that a face-to-face lunch with Letty surrounded by the babble of strangers would help open her up. Maybe I would learn more about who might have attacked her—and why. Maybe she even knew more than she realized about Liz.

The Clifton Hotel was tucked away among brick office buildings, a court of pricey specialty shops, and a Victorian-style railroad station presently used as an art gallery. The Hotel's wraparound porch had been glassed in and lined with bright white tables for two or four diners. The shadowy bar inside was quiet at noon, full of young professionals every night.

I thought Letty would like not only the privacy of the porch, but also the colorful view of shoppers and the hyacinths, daffodils, and forsythia decorating the brick walkways outside. Best of all, the Clifton's biggest draw was a luncheon buffet of fresh bread, homemade soups, an extensive salad bar, and several hot items no matter what time of year. Letty wouldn't need to read a menu or worry about the price.

With a slightly trembling hand, she allowed me to lead her to a table with a busy view. Every head turned to stare as we passed, but Letty held my arm and smiled shyly back at every one.

I ordered decaf from the waitress and told her we both wanted the buffet. Letty interrupted to tell us she preferred tea. Then her cheeks brightened at her own temerity; so after the waitress had gone, I leaned forward and patted her arm.

"You're doing great," I assured her. "Want me to show you how to get your food?"

The sunglasses temporarily removed, Letty's forehead creased with concern.

"It's easy," I said. "See what those people are doing? You just walk over and take what you want." My guest's face displayed disbelief, so I raised my eyebrows and nodded. "Honest. That's what we're supposed to do."

I slung my purse across my chest to free up my hands. Letty left hers under her chair. "You can come back as many times as you like," I explained. "So you don't have to carry everything you want now."

The expressions of the other diners revealed their attitudes toward us: indifference, amusement, or distaste.

"Soup smells good, doesn't it, Mum?" I remarked loudly over my shoulder. Letty's bark of laughter turned a few extra heads, but I was pleased to see that she relaxed enough to pick up a bowl. She filled it with corn chowder and put bread and the last slice of crusty peach pie on a second plate. Then she glanced at me to see whether I disapproved.

"Quite right," I said leaning down to whisper in her ear. "It might not be there when you get back."

"Aye," she agreed with a proud grin. She bustled back to our table while I made myself a salad with lots of mushrooms and chickpeas and Chinese noodles.

Settled across from each other, we alternately ate and glanced around at the busy surroundings. Letty's face reminded me of Chelsea's when the two of us had gone on a special outing to the Philadelphia Art Museum—one of those parental gambles, since I had had no idea whether our then eight-year-old daughter would enjoy the exhibits or hate them.

Our eyes had been drawn into the museum by a disorderly red metal sculpture about five feet high and six feet wide called "Clearing." Once inside, we had followed Chelsea's inner guide for an hour and a half, laughing together when we came upon a painting of a big toe complete with red nail polish or a man ascending wooden stairs that extended out from the bottom of the canvas.

"Oh, there's 'Clearing,' " Chelsea had exclaimed when we returned to the lobby, and I had realized that my daughter's mental lens had been filming every detail of our day. If I asked her about the lobby sculpture years later, she would describe it perfectly, even down to its name.

Letty wore that camera-lens look right now. I would never be further in her confidence. Yet as much as I needed the answers, I dreaded asking the questions.

Sun glinted off my fork. My eyes strayed outside to its source, a warm strip of gold streaming between cotton-wisp clouds that illuminated the fresh green grass, the purple and yellow flowers. Everything looked perfect; but just as on Beech Tree Lane, precious little was as perfect as it seemed.

"Letty," I began. "Now that you've had some time to recover, do you remember anything more about the man who came into your house?"

She dipped some pumpernickel rye into her chowder. "Nope. Nary a thing."

"Any idea what he wanted?"

"Nuk unh."

"What about the guy in the hospital—the one wearing doctor's clothes?"

Letty wagged her head and disposed of the bread. "Too dark. I told ye."

A memory teased the back of my mind. Leave it alone. Come back to it.

After I poked at my salad another moment, I said, "Do you think Marc Kelman could have been seeing another woman—you know, other than his wife?"

Letty blinked at me before spooning a mouthful of soup. It was entirely possible that no one had ever solicited her opinion on such a matter, yet she responded exactly as any confidante might: She glanced around at the other diners before giving her hushed answer. "Oooh no. Not 'im. What give you that idear?"

I sighed thoughtfully, plunged ahead. "A woman at the funeral—a young woman—talked to Marc for a long time. I just wondered . . ."

"Pretty gal?"

"You've seen her?"

"Sorta. A few times. Thought at first she was Miss Lizzie."

My hopes rose. "Yes," I replied, "except she has medium-length brown hair. Do you know who she is?"

"Heard her in their yard back awhile. Kept callin' Miss Lizzie 'auntie sumtin.' Think they was planning a weddin'. Kept talking 'bout this table'd go here, dancin' over there

. . . stuff like that. Had me hopes up, they did. Guess I won't see it now."

Eureka. And wasn't I the complete fool? Letty's reading of the relationship between Marc and the young woman seemed much more likely to be true than my own. The Liz look-alike probably *was* a niece; she certainly possessed enough family resemblance. Also, if she had been Marc's lover, he surely wouldn't have spoken to her so openly in front of Liz's friends and family. Furthermore, if a wedding reception was planned, Liz's death could have made the prospective bride frantic enough to talk to Marc about it at the funeral. I might have myself.

Letty stood with the intention of going for more food, and I rose to join her. "Don't worry about the plates," I informed her. "We're supposed to take new ones." Letty grunted with approval and rolled along in her new sneakers toward the buffet.

We were back with our loaded entrée platters before I had the opportunity to finish my thoughts about Marc.

"So if you're right about the young woman, Marc probably didn't have any reason to kill his wife," I said, glancing up from my food to gauge Letty's reaction.

"Police say it 'twere a burglar." Both her reddened eye and her cloudy one challenged me.

Really, reading into Letty's shorthand way of speaking wasn't that different from "hearing" what my mother intended to say—but never said. At the moment, Letty wanted to know why I disagreed with the police regarding Liz's death. It was a good question, which I considered with my cheek resting on my propped-up fist.

"I looked around the Kelmans' house right after her death," I finally answered, "and I talked to another woman who was attacked by an intruder a few days before Liz. Everything about the two crimes seemed different to me."

Letty waited for me to say more. I picked up my fork and poked at some broccoli. "Then there's all the rest that's been happening on our street—almost as if somebody is getting his ideas from the newspaper. And, of course, you were attacked but not exactly robbed. Although somebody did search your house—probably twice."

Suddenly the elusive thought bobbed to the surface. Letty's intruder had spoken to her—both times. The first time, he had asked where "it" was.

"What did that guy in the hospital say again?"

"Give it to 'im, 'twere 'is."

The Money Access Card. That had to be it after all. It was the only desirable thing in Letty's possession, also the only thing I knew about that might be described as not hers.

Inwardly I beamed with self-congratulation, but I tried not to show Letty a thing. Explaining now would at best confuse her, at the worst, raise unwarranted hopes.

Yet my mind raced ahead with conclusions. If the MAC card was the desired item, naturally the intruder had to be Kyle O'Callahan; his father was the only other one with an interest in it, and he had been incapacitated for weeks.

Why bother? Kyle probably thought that disposing of the card before someone like me came along would allow his father—or him—to continue doing whatever they were doing with Letty's assets a while longer. Perhaps forever.

Not forever. Letty's death would bring scrutiny to the trust. So why didn't I feel better?

Because O'Callahan's desperate actions meant something worthwhile was at stake.

Letty caught me glowering at my broccoli.

"What's sumatta? Ain't you gonna eat that?"

I focused on the food—a broad selection that had appealed to me only moments before—and reminded myself this was supposed to be a celebration, a treat for Letty. Here I was ruining it with murderous thoughts about Kyle O'Callahan.

I reminded myself that we more-evolved beings had attorneys and courts to mete out retribution to the full extent of the law. Personally, I intended to make sure Norman

Demig made Edwin Markus O'Callahan's barbaric son very sorry indeed.

My appetite back in force, I managed to polish off a quantity of food that would have challenged Garry.

Chapter 29

Back on Beech Tree Lane I decided to eliminate at least one worry.

"You want to see your house?" I asked Letty. Even though I'd put her things back where I found them, removing the filth had resulted in a dramatic change. I was afraid the actual resident would feel I had done too much.

With her sunglasses back on, I couldn't read her face. Yet she told me, "Aye," so I stopped the car at the curb between our two houses.

With Letty's still-uncertain vision and broken wrist in mind, I escorted her up her lumpy driveway. Our slow progress allowed me to appreciate the crabapple blooming pale pink inside the walled-in former kitchen garden and some lacy white trees in the yard beyond. The daffodils in the front had faded and sagged, but the trees overhead promised to unclench their leaves with the first softening rain.

To avoid the tricky lock and the rain-rotted entrance hall, we entered Letty's the usual way—through the back. By then I was so jittery I nearly dropped the key.

Two steps inside the kitchen Letty removed the sunglasses and stood staring. Her head swiveled up and down and back and forth slowly like a marionette operated by a novice.

Somebody had to say something, so I said, "I took the trash out."

"Where's me food?" Letty asked.

"Mice got it," I answered.

She threw me a glance, then rolled on her new sneakers through the pantry and into the adjacent living area. Without the drapes the room was far brighter than before, and Letty hastily replaced her sunglasses. Then her lips fell back to a parted position, somewhere between moderate disbelief and speechlessness on the emotional gauge.

"Did I get the furniture back in the right places?"

"Hassock goes here," she said, indicating the foot of a chair. She sank onto it as soon as I set it down and continued to run her eyes around the room.

"Whut'd you do to the windows?" she asked.

"Washed them?" I asked to determine whether that was what she meant.

"That all?"

"Oh. I was going to clean the drapes, but they fell apart. I have some old ones in my garage I was going to put up instead, but I haven't had time, and I wasn't sure you'd like them . . ."

"Mrs. Doland's drapes. That's it." They were gone. That was the difference she cared about.

Although the doctor told me Letty's sight had been poor, that simple observation impressed upon me just how impaired her vision had been. Now I understood why she kept her living area so free of obstacles—so she could shuffle around without tripping.

At night all her movements around the neighborhood must have been by feel and familiarity. Even in daylight any similarities she discerned between Liz and her niece must have been a simple comparison of what she saw. Neighbors were probably recognized by body shape, movements, and voice. No wonder she had asked about Sam in running clothes stretching by his mailbox.

"Smells better," Letty remarked.

"The toilet's fixed."

She looked at me, and even through the sunglasses I could see her amazement. And what else? Displeasure? Could she be reacting just as I had feared?

She stood, and with minced steps returned to the kitchen.

"Letty, I'm sorry." I followed after her. "I guess I got carried away. I'm really sorry."

At the kitchen's worktable she stopped, turned, and looked up at me. "Jus' don't do it ag'in," she said with an impish grin. Her new sneakers squeaked on the clean linoleum as she walked to the door.

Before I joined her outside I glanced around myself. Excluding the relatively new Shop-vac forgotten in the corner, Letty's kitchen and its owner matched now more than ever. Both showed wear, yet both promised to endure a while longer. I found it unimaginable that anyone had invaded this sanctuary and done harm to its elderly owner.

Of course not just anyone had done it. My fresh indignation over Kyle O'Callahan prompted another line of thought.

Naively, I supposed Kriebel's team had collected some physical evidence from Letty's to match with an eventual suspect. When I had begun to clean up Liz Kelman's house for the funeral guests, most of the dirt had been caused by experts doing just that. Now I realized Letty's mess had simply been—Letty's mess.

So apparently the official views of the crimes had been vastly different. At the Kelmans' the police had correctly anticipated a homicide investigation. Letty's attack had been treated as a dead end.

And if I now realized that the possibility of the police having forensic evidence from Letty's was futile, I also realized how far-fetched my accusation became without it. "Yes, Sergeant/Detective, I believe Kyle O'Callahan was desperate to retrieve a MAC card that belonged to his father." Kriebel would laugh me right out of the stationhouse.

I surveyed the results of my diligent work once more. The place was cleaner than it had been in years—not a fingerprint or hair follicle anywhere in sight. "Good work, Gin," I congratulated myself with a wag of my head.

The audit appeared to be the only possible way to support my reasoning, and Demig—attorney that he was—had warned me that an audit might not help. If that were the case, I had no idea what I would do.

To my surprise, Letty was nowhere in sight when I stepped outside.

"Over here," she called, and finally I noticed a path of trampled mayflowers leading to a hole in the shrubbery between our properties.

"Why not?" I thought as I made use of my neighbor's shortcut across my front lawn.

After dinner, Rip went off with the newspaper, the kids retreated to their respective desks to do homework, and Letty settled in front of the TV. Not quite finished in the kitchen, I paused to watch the last of the twilight fade into night.

Rip called to me from the family room, so I dried my hands on a dishtowel and met him in the middle of the downstairs hall.

"Look," he said, handing me the local paper folded to reveal a front-page headline:

ROBBERY SUSPECT CAPTURED OUTSIDE ATLANTA.

Wide-eyed, I began to ask, "Is this . . . ?"

"Just keep reading," my husband suggested.

> "James Rutherford, 39, wanted in connection with several local robberies, was apprehended just outside Atlanta, Georgia, where he was allegedly attempting yet another burglary.
>
> His surreptitious behavior caught the attention of a

> resident who had stepped outside to close her car windows. Police arrived in time to see Rutherford climbing over a picket fence behind the home of Mr. and Mrs. Dale Santa Maria.
>
> 'Lucky Jim,' as he is known to local authorities, might have escaped had his athletic shoe not become wedged between the slats of the fence. Before he could free his foot, one officer was able to detain him at gunpoint. A second law enforcement officer successfully vaulted the fence and sealed off any possibility of escape. . . .
>
> Once in custody Rutherford began to boast about his numerous exploits. . . .
>
> Although he has not yet admitted to the robbery in Bryn Mawr in which Mrs. Corinne Novak was injured, the MacNair break-in on Beech Tree Lane, or the nearby Kelman robbery resulting in the death of Mrs. Elizabeth Kelman, police are hopeful that physical evidence will link Rutherford to these local crimes."

The article mentioned that Rutherford earned three to five thousand dollars a week stealing Rolex watches, electronic equipment, jewelry, furs, even fine Scotch and expensive colognes. He attributed his sporadic career success—the present run extended back as far as 1993—to careful research and the aforementioned luck. Although he refused to reveal his method, he claimed to know how to disable burglar alarms with ease. However, he avoided dogs, "because of their unpredictability." No mention was made of Rutherford ever placing a toothpick in anyone's lock.

"You don't seem relieved," Rip observed. The way he pressed his lips together told me he had hoped for a more positive reaction.

"I still don't believe they have Liz's killer. So no, I'm

not relieved.'' I spoke softly so the kids wouldn't hear me in their nearby rooms.

Rip caught on and steered me back toward the kitchen.

''Because of that toothpick thing?'' he then asked, the left corner of his mouth raised with scorn.

''Why don't you hear me out before you start with the attitude,'' I suggested.

Rip folded his arms across his chest and leaned back against the refrigerator. He looked about as pliant as his backrest.

In response I folded my arms and stuck out my chin.

''The toothpick trick means that Liz came face-to-face with her attacker the day before. That's different from all the other crimes, Rip.

''Plus the Novaks' and Kelmans' houses weren't left in the same condition. Also,'' I hastened to add, ''I think I know who has been harassing Letty, and it can't possibly be this Rutherford character—especially if he was just caught in Atlanta.''

''Why?''

''Because Atlanta's too far from Letty's hospital room.''

''Gin-ger,'' Rip intoned in a warning voice. ''What happened in Letty's hospital room?''

I told him.

''Last Wednesday night? Today's Tuesday, Gin. Rutherford could have walked to Atlanta by now.''

I considered saying *but he didn't*, and settled for, ''Rutherford goes for Rolexes, not MAC cards.''

My husband wagged his head and muttered, ''Typical redhead.''

''I am not a redhead,'' I shouted. ''My hair is cinnamon brown.''

Rip snorted. I huffed. We glared at each other until we started to laugh. Then Rip gathered me in and kissed my slightly, but only slightly, reddish hair.

''You're a piece of work, you know that?'' he said.

* * *

When we parted, an unnecessary but very pleasant three minutes later, Rip tossed a remark over his shoulder as he headed for his office. "Oh, Gin," he said. "Jacob needs the school's Shop-vac tomorrow. Do you still have it?"

I groaned. "Guilty." Damn. I would have to brave Letty's house tonight. Thank goodness I had put at least one lamp on a timer. I didn't relish entering that place in total darkness.

Having grabbed a flashlight from a kitchen drawer, I put on a nylon windbreaker and trudged out the door. The dewy grass dampened my sneakers immediately, but now that I knew Letty's shortcut it seemed pointless to go the long way.

Outdoors, the amplified night noises that always comforted me inside my own home seemed to chase me through their domain. It was too early in the year for the locust and frog symphony of summer, but tree branches rustled and traffic on distant highways hummed. There were thumps and snaps and dog barks. For all I knew I could hear radon fans whirring and cats creeping. My solution was to tramp heavily enough to make my own noise.

Crash bang boom, I stomped up to Letty's back stoop. After loudly wrestling with the sticky old door, I forcefully yanked it open.

A potent smell enveloped me. Natural gas may be odorless, but the people who provide it for our stoves and clothes driers add a distinctive smell, and that was the stink that hit me full force when I opened Letty's kitchen door.

Pilot light's out, I thought.

Yet the odor was so strong I wondered whether either Letty or I had inadvertently bumped a burner switch that afternoon when we were there. With everything closed up, the heavy gas would have settled low in the house until someone came along and released it—one way or another.

When I propped the back door open, the sleeve of my nylon jacket swished against its side panel. It was just ordinary friction, but I remembered something about a spray can and spontaneous combustion sparked by static electricity, so I quickly stepped off the stoop to remove the jacket. I was a bit vague on the details of the article, and I didn't especially want to experiment with my life. Yet I really needed to turn off that stove.

As I cautiously stepped inside the doorway and shone my light around the kitchen, it occurred to me that the timer I put on the living room lamp had not yet switched on—puzzling because I had set the device to activate at 7:30, just before nightfall.

Of course the timers were fairly imprecise, and I may not have set it correctly. I would check later—after I dealt with the more urgent problem.

Fresh air from the doorway had begun to dissipate much of the gas, but I hurried to open a window over the sink anyway. Setting my flashlight on the drain-board, I then lifted the cooktop and saw that the center pilot light was indeed out.

A burner knob was also askew. I twisted it to the off position with a trembling hand. Certainly the knob could have been bumped, but neither Letty nor I had ventured very near the stove that day. Also, I had pulled the kitchen door tight every day for over a week, and the pilot light had not once blown out. Separately, either problem might have been accidental, but the odds of both happening on the same day pushed probability a bit too far.

While the sensation of someone else in the house told me to run, reason held me there. No one would hazard his own hide by lingering in such a booby trap. If I kept my head, I was safe enough for the moment.

I knew turning on electrical current always caused a spark (I'd seen the flash a few times when I'd flipped on an uncovered switch), but the air seemed clear enough now to turn on a light. Psychologically, the brightness was quite a relief. I even felt ready to brave Letty's living room.

Even though the connecting doors between the small pantry and the living area had been open, either by accident or design, the gas smell was milder there. Using the spill of kitchen light, I hurried to open the two windows, letting one of my fears back in with the cool night air—the one about a criminal with a localized agenda. If the burglar who had been working our area actually was in jail, he certainly hadn't turned on Letty's gas.

The floor lamp became my objective now, the one I had attached to the timer. To get a better look at the outlet where the timer was plugged in, I moved Letty's overstuffed chair away from the pantry wall. When I stooped down to read the timer's dial, I noticed the "on" arrow pointed to 11:00 PM—much later than I had set it.

Prickles of concern raced up the back of my neck. Without touching anything I swiveled on the balls of my feet toward the cord lying on the floor between the timer and the base of the lamp.

About twenty-four inches from the outlet was a break in the cord's plastic insulation. Someone had exposed about an inch of the two electrical wires, probably with scissors or a knife. If the timer arrived at the on position, the wires would have arced. Any gas collected in the room would have exploded.

Or maybe not. I still wasn't too sure how easy or difficult it was to get natural gas to explode, but I thought the odds were in favor of a disaster.

My hands were slick with sweat. So was my entire body now that I noticed. But my hands were the problem. I wiped them on my jeans and looked around for something to use in place of gloves.

I settled for a couple of tissues from the box I had placed in Letty's powder room. Being careful to hold only parts nobody would ordinarily grasp, I lifted the lamp out from behind the chair, then kicked the timer and plugged-in cord loose with my foot. Pinching the timer prongs between my fingers so I could lift the whole apparatus chest-high, I carried it out to the stoop.

Only then did I go back to the kitchen for the Shop-vac,

which I placed outside under a bush to get later. Then I closed and relocked the windows, finally—carefully—closing the door behind me.

Not wishing to be seen—if I hadn't been already—I proceeded to take the lamp home via the shortcut. God forbid the perpetrator should sneak back and steal the evidence.

"Rip," I whispered loudly, when I reached our front hall. "Rip, come here. I need you."

He emerged from his lair blinking. "What's that?" he asked.

"A possible murder weapon. How'd you like to phone the police for me? Sergeant/Detective Kriebel would probably be best." Much as I hated to admit it.

"Gin," Rip complained with the tone of his voice. *Not again*, he implied.

"I'm not being an alarmist," I told him emphatically. "Letty's house was filled with gas, and this thing was set to blow it up at exactly eleven PM."

That was when I noticed Letty standing six feet away in the shadows of the hallway. She looked stricken. She looked eighty. She looked bewildered and frightened and sick.

"How'd you like to meet my mother?" I asked brightly.

Chapter 30

As we drove through the dark toward my mother's apartment, Letty watched the lights streak by with childlike awe. I wondered whether this was the first time she had ever ridden in a car at night, or the first time she had ventured so far from home. Maybe sightseeing was much more pleasant than dwelling on her fears.

To me, it seemed that this latest threat to her welfare differed from what had happened to Liz and even from what previously had happened to Letty herself. Whether the gas bomb was meant to do her fatal harm or merely to frighten her, or whether the intention was to set fire to an empty house, it was no spontaneous act of self-preservation. Premeditated and sneaky, it revealed the perpetrator's growing frustration. I felt certain any future effort would be much less subtle and far more effective.

Who and why were the questions tormenting me now.

"Let's start back at the beginning," I suggested to my passenger.

As if she had very little confidence left, she hunched down inside an old coat of mine that smelled of warm wool and Charlie perfume. "I dunno," she said, wagging her head woefully. "I just dunno."

Over the years I've met a variety of women incapacitated by fear—one too insecure to choose a lipstick without help, one so terrified of disease she was unable to use a public toilet. Another's distrust of strangers—even police—caused her to wander for hours rather than ask for directions. Some fears had been learned at their mother's knee. Others developed over time. For some especially unfortunate souls all it took was one trauma to populate the rest of a life with imaginary monsters.

Letty MacNair desperately needed her confidence back.

"We're going to get to the bottom of this," I told the woman by my side. "*You're* going to get to the bottom of this."

"Me? Oh no." She wagged her head harder.

I turned off Germantown Pike onto a two-lane street that meandered a couple of miles further toward Ludwig and my mother's apartment. At that hour, a few minutes past nine, there was no other traffic to rush me, so I slowed the car's speed to match my cautious thoughts.

"You're the key, Letty," I insisted. "So let's go over what we know. Tell me again about the Crouthamel boys."

I had started with a question Letty could easily answer, and her relief was palpable. "Nice boys. Lovely boys."

"Because they give you food."

"Aye, and clothes sometimes."

I mentally crossed Beech Tree Lane to the Grogans' house. "What about Camilla and Neil?"

"Who?"

"The professors who live at the end of the street."

"Quiet 'uns. Hubby's never around."

I had to agree. The person who slit Letty's lamp cord and turned on the gas had known quite a lot about what was happening on Beech Tree Lane. Neil Grogan scarcely seemed to realize he had a wife.

"What about Johnny Raymond?" I asked.

"What about 'im?"

"You ever have any dealings with him?" I stopped at an intersection, looked both ways.

"No," Letty replied.

Of course, even if Johnny dear thought driving Letty out of the neighborhood would force his parents into a retirement home, Letty would be unaware of those intentions. Anyway, that scenario didn't explain tonight's attempt on her life—if that was what the bomb scare had actually been.

The Vickers and the Shannahans both wished Letty would move—the Vickers because they were having such difficulty selling their house; the Shannahans, as far as I knew, for social and aesthetic reasons.

I was hard pressed to imagine anyone resorting to violence for either reason; but when segregation was rampant, African-Americans regularly contended with such unimaginable treatment. And there *was* that computer-generated threat.

However, until I knew whether a Vickers or a Shannahan was responsible for tonight, I preferred to shield Letty from that particular piece of nastiness. While I might never be able to cure either couple of their snobbery, I was fairly sure I could shut them up.

My next turn brought us onto a four-lane thoroughfare with strip malls left and right. Beneath some dim security lights, commerce was in repose.

Which made me think of Richard Diamond and the mysterious items he brought home. Since the couple was new to the area, I didn't know firsthand whether Richard had been a highly placed executive with G.E. or not. I accepted that he was currently between positions because nobody lies about that, and Bonnie had once mentioned that he was off on an interview.

But what if Richard were a thief? What if he had robbed the Kelmans? If Liz had recognized him when she came home, he might have murdered her to protect himself. He could have taken the TV out of his wife's station wagon to fence it before she tried to return it to the rightful owners—or to deflect suspicions by appearing to join the neighborhood victims' club. Stealing Garry's bike—child's play for a next-door neighbor. The smashed mailboxes, the hang-up calls might have been exactly what they had always seemed—teenager's pranks.

Then there was Letty. Kyle O'Callahan was still my choice for her mugging and the subsequent break-ins—except for tonight's. Tonight's incident turned everything upside down.

Thinking out loud, I said, "If Marc Kelman really didn't have a lover . . ." My mind stopped at that particular dead end.

"Oh no, not 'im. 'Twas 'er." I had forgotten that Letty was listening.

"What?" I asked.

"Not 'im—'er."

I inadvertently hit the brakes and made the car jump. "Are you saying what I think you're saying?"

"Just whut I knows, and whut I knows is Miss Lizzie had herself a fancy man."

I coasted up to a red light and stopped. "Of course. Liz had a fancy man," I said as I hit my palm against my forehead.

The last time I spoke to Liz she had behaved quite differently—so out of character, in fact, that I had wondered about a new love interest. At the time I thought the change was too new to indicate a fully developed affair, but the potential had definitely existed.

"Son of a gun." I shook my head with astonishment. The traffic signal turned green.

"Yup. Saw 'im meself." Letty's chin dipped into the wool collar of my coat.

My hands began to tremble. There was a closed gas station on the right, and I just managed to pull into the front of its lot before my body went limp.

"You saw Liz's fancy man?" I asked just to be sure.

"Aye." There was a hint of the troll's sparkle in her smug expression.

"What did he look like? Do you know who it was?"

"Oh I couldn't say much about that. Me eyes, you know. And I wouldn't want to be tellin' tales."

"But you saw a man—other than Marc—at her house?"

"Aye. He be leavin' out the back."

The back door—the door with the lock somebody disabled with a toothpick!

"When did you see this, Letty? Think hard. It's important."

Even in the semidarkness of the car's interior I could see her face scrunch up with concentration. "I dunno."

"Was it the week before the robbery?" Immediately, I knew that my impatience had overwhelmed my judgment. Suggesting a time had been irresponsible and just plain stupid. What if I led Letty's thoughts to a wrong conclusion? To remind me to use better control, I crossed two fingers and tucked them under my leg.

After a moment, Letty said, "Naw, not so long before . . ." She shook her head with regret. She meant not so long before Liz died.

My sat-upon fingers were pins and needles before Letty spoke again.

" 'Twas that day you gimme those sticky buns," she exclaimed. "I be walkin' back from me trip out when I saw 'im. Still lickin' me fingers, I was. Messy things, those buns." She shook her head again.

I could scarcely breathe. "Liz died the next day." My throat was so tight I didn't recognize my own voice.

"Aye," Letty agreed. "That she did, poor soul."

I grasped Letty's arm with both hands. "One more question. Just one more."

"Aye," she nodded.

"This fancy man. Could he have seen you?"

Letty lifted her non-eyebrows, tilted her head. "Mebbe. Mebbe. I ain't invisible."

While my empty lungs automatically dragged in a huge breath, my head flopped back until it bounced off my headrest.

"Whut?" Letty asked with an edge of panic.

A glance at her eyes told me I had to tell her. I didn't want to frighten her further, but she needed to know.

I grabbed her hand and brought it to my lap. Then I lifted it and stroked it before I could look into her worried face.

"You didn't just see Liz's fancy man," I said. "You also saw her killer."

Chapter 31

"But me eyes," Letty lamented.

"I know. I know," I commiserated. "Trouble is, nobody on the street had any idea you were losing your sight. The doctor had to tell me."

I shook my head again. "We don't know who killed Liz—or why—but if it was one of our neighbors, and he thinks you might recognize him one day . . ."

Letty's expression told me there was no need to elaborate; she had absorbed the implied threat into her core.

I lifted my chin as I put the car into gear. "He's going to get caught. I promise you. You won't have to be afraid."

About then I had no idea how I would accomplish that feat, but it had just become a necessity. To a Struve that meant it would get done. Somehow, someway.

Soon the graceful hemlocks and dignified oaks that shaded the two-story brick apartment buildings of my mother's complex became visible in the spill of the Suburu's headlights. Colonial-style lamps like oversized candles illuminated the rest of the beautifully maintained grounds. For a predominantly unplanned, overgrown small town like Ludwig there were few respites from tacky commercialism, but this was one of them. Somebody with foresight had built the low-lying spread with the very young and the nearly old in mind.

Mother's apartment was on the first floor of Building A, which faced the street but had a view of the adjacent woods from her side patio. I drove around back and parked. Then I helped Letty out of the car and escorted her up to my mother's kitchen door.

The formidable flake who was my nemesis, my mother, and my best friend answered the first knock in a nanosecond. Standing five-foot-three in her beige Hush Puppies, she squinted out from the bright white kitchen light through the yellow bug light on her back stoop.

"Mother," I said. "This is Letty MacNair. Letty, this is my mother, Cynthia Struve."

After a moment of staring Letty said, "Pleased to meetcha."

I realized that in her borrowed coat with her stringy hair, stitched temple, and still slightly reddened eye, Letty still looked very much like a bag lady, a refugee, or—putting her in a good light—maybe an elderly gypsy.

Mother blinked behind her large pastel-edged glasses and scanned her databank for the perfect response, an uncanny talent of hers. If she hadn't been of the present century, the townsmen might have burned her for a witch.

"Come right on in, Letitia," she decided. "You must be hungry. Everybody knows Gin can't cook worth a fig."

Mother's hand guided Letty toward a round oak table and plaid-padded chairs. I was left literally on the doorstep.

"Yoo-hoo," I said.

Mother glanced out at me. "Tsk. Close the door, Ginger. You're letting in moths.

"Now tell me the truth," she addressed Letty. "What has Gin been feeding you?"

"Salty sausage," Letty sneered from her air.

"Yuck. The worst. How about some cornflakes and bananas, or maybe a bagel?" My mother can't cook either; but she had chosen her approach, and she was determined to run with it.

Beneath her brow wrinkles, Letty's eyes had taken on a

gleam. "Got any strawberry jam?" she asked.

I eased myself out the door. "I'll call you," I told my mother. " 'Bye Letty."

" 'Bye," they replied in unison.

The drive back from Mother's made me sleepy, but Rip's description of his encounter with Sgt./Det. Kriebel woke me up.

"He said what?" I ranted as I paced around our bedroom.

"You heard me," Rip said, waving his toothbrush in a circle. He wore nothing but pajama bottoms. The children were already in bed.

"I know. I know," I complained. "Kriebel thinks I ran over the cord with a vacuum cleaner. He thinks the pilot blew out when I shut the door. But what about the burner that was partly on? What about the fact that the timer wasn't the same way I set it?"

Rip wagged his head. "Either you or Letty bumped the burner switch, and you didn't set the timer the way you thought you did."

"That's pure bullshit, Rip, and you know it."

Rip winced. He doesn't think women should swear; I've never understood why.

"That well may be," he conceded, "but that's what the man thinks, and that's what's going into his report."

"Did he at least take the lamp to the lab?"

Rip nodded. "He did. After I talked him into it." The meaningful gaze that accompanied that statement suggested a moment of male bonding at my expense, perhaps a mutual consensus that taking the lamp to the lab was the quickest way to shut me up.

"Well, thanks for that," I said sincerely.

"Don't mention it."

I finally stood still, and Rip and I met each other's eyes for a long moment. Lately, what with his close-to-the-vest handling of his delicate school problem and my various involvements, we had not exactly been operating as partners. True, tonight's events had required a cooperative effort, but the gap between us still felt further than four or five feet of bedroom carpet.

"Are you all right?" I asked.

Rip snorted softly. "Yeah, sure." His tone said he'd been better. "You?" he asked.

"I miss us."

"Summer's coming."

"Used to be I got you on weekends." I sat down beside him on the bed, and he drew me in with an arm. "Look at the bright side," he said. "Time feels faster when you're older."

"You charmer, you."

He was right, though. Morning was there about a second after I shut my eyes.

Wednesday, April 19. Rested, wide awake, I saw my family off, sorted a mountain of laundry, and started the washer. I also stuck a chicken in a pot of cold water to thaw, then I poured a cup of coffee and sat sideways on the living room sofa, staring into our backyard.

A wire hanger seemed to secure my shoulders in place. My back braced rigidly against the armrest. My legs, which were stretched along the length of the sofa, curled at my ankles and toes.

"You've got to do something," I advised myself. "Before you pop a spring."

Through the window I saw a chickadee hop urgently in and out of an azalea bush. Up above the greening trees the sky was a field of mares' tails blown by a brisk breeze.

Twitching, I sat admiring the view about four minutes before I bolted upstairs as if I were being chased. After I replaced my jeans and sneaks with actual shoes, presentable slacks, and a short-sleeved sweater, I snatched my keys out of my purse and leaned down to reassure Barney.

"I'm going to Cabrini to talk to Camilla Grogan," I

explained as if he understood. "After that, I don't know what I'm going to do, but I won't be too long." Of course, I had no idea how long I'd be, but there was no sense in leaving the dog tied up in knots. "You be good," I said while patting him on the head. *Guard the house* was not the sort of thing he needed to hear.

Founded by nuns in 1957, named after the first American saint, Cabrini College was not unexpectedly a Catholic, coeducational liberal arts institution that advertised a "warm, friendly atmosphere." I once picked up their brochure from Bryn Derwyn's guidance counselor's desk and had read enough to know the enrollment was roughly two thousand (including grad students), half commuters from the Delaware Valley; and although about thirty-four majors were offered, Education and English Communications were the runaway favorites.

What I didn't realize was that the place was gorgeous. I'd driven by each of the three entrances a hundred times and never saw much of anything but an iron fence and dense towering trees. For my official first visit I accidentally chose the back driveway, but it didn't matter. After a tiny stone gatehouse, a graceful road ushered me through a wood filled with thousands of daffodils—finished now, but I could still imagine their impact. Overhead, gigantic oaks had just begun to leaf. I swear I didn't notice one neglected tree, not even a dead branch.

Dorms reposed to the left at the edge of the woods. Then classroom buildings dotted lawns kelly green with fresh spring grass, and suddenly I was facing a mansion of yellowish stucco latticed with dark brown boards. The foundation was stone, the roof red shingles. Not your conventional *Better Homes and Gardens*, just solid old elegance.

The drive diverted me around a newer administrative building that matched the mansion almost exactly. I parked in a lot to the right, then walked over to "Grace Hall."

A few paces inside the spacious interior a computer allowed you to check your tuition balance without the embarrassment of bothering a real human. Across from that sat an information desk.

"Any idea where I'll find Professor Grogan about now?" I asked the wholesome-looking black coed who manned the desk. There were only two or three other people in sight. I assumed everyone else was in class.

"She went that way," the girl said pointing toward the back door. "About sixty seconds ago." Her forehead puckered while she considered whether I was putting her on.

I hastily thanked her and hurried toward the exit she had indicated on the far side of the atrium. Overhead three gigantic skylights spilled sunlight on several sitting areas and a cluster of chairs set up for a lecture.

Outside the driveway led back to the mansion a hundred yards straight ahead. At about eighty yards I saw the back of a woman of roughly Camilla's age and shape, so I trotted to catch up. A blond girl with running shorts and a ponytail jogged by going the other way.

"Camilla?" I shouted when I came near, but a red jeep with open sides was driving by playing loud rock music. Only after the driver found a parking spot in the lot did the campus return to serenity.

"Camilla?" I called again.

She whirled to face me, surprise spreading her features into an instant face-lift. "Gin," she said. "What brings you here?"

"There's something I'd like to talk about if you have a couple minutes. Liz's murder, to be exact." We had stopped for our exchange, and I was able to catch my breath.

At the mention of Liz's death my neighbor's face darkened. Once again she became a fragile-looking woman in her late fifties wearing a pinkish-rose wool sweater and skirt with brown oxford shoes. Her hair was a chin-length bob of silver-gray clipped off her forehead with a brown barrette. I noticed the hand clutching a manilla folder to her thin chest was marred with liver spots.

"I've got to drop this off in the mansion," she said. "Then I have office hours, but nobody's scheduled. We can talk then. Follow me."

We continued past some cars parked in a stone courtyard and entered the mansion itself. "Have a seat anywhere," Camilla instructed. "I'll be right back."

She left me staring at a huge room of dark paneling. Straight ahead a fresh bouquet graced a round table centered on a red Oriental carpet. Two fireplaces were tucked in opposite corners with sitting areas in front of each. There were pink chairs, blue, deep red, and patterned wing-backed chairs clustered here and there. I sat near a window and admired the antique opulence—the small-paned leaded glass windows, the carved oak railings with tower-shaped newels that led upstairs to a square balcony. Camilla had gone up those stairs and through double doors into an office area, which was why my attention had been drawn to an especially huge chandelier.

"There's where the blood spot comes up," a voice told me.

"What?" I turned to confront an elfin man wearing a tan cotton jacket and brown slacks. I couldn't tell who he was or what he did, but he apparently had the leisure to frighten strange women at ten o'clock in the morning.

"Right over there." He pointed to an area now covered by carpet.

"What blood spot?"

The man faced me now, and I could see his waxy face and the gleam emanating from his pale blue eyes. "From where she died," he answered, waving his head back and forth. "Sad, don't you think?"

"Yes," I said. It was all I could manage.

"We used to have October dances in here, but one time it coincided with the anniversary of her death . . ." He shook his head.

"What happened?"

"Oh, we rolled up the carpet like always, but that night the bloodstains came right up through the wood. Don't have October dances here anymore."

"No," I agreed. Certainly not.

The man shuffled off, and I spent five minutes squirming and thinking about the bloodstains in Liz's foyer.

Camilla returned, and I was finally able to leave the beautiful room with its baby grand piano and fan window and its spooky/sad story. When we were once again outside on the driveway walking back toward Grace Hall, I felt comfortable enough to ask more about the tragic death.

"Oh, our legend," she said with an ironic smile. "This was a wealthy family's estate, obviously. Lonely in those days. Isolated if you can imagine it back then. The daughter of the family fell in love with the stablehand. Her father found out about her pregnancy, of course, and set off to confront her lover. Unfortunately, the young man hung himself in the tower back there before the father got to him. Some say the girl jumped off the balcony and her unborn child died with her. Others say the child was stillborn and the girl buried it in the snow out by the apple orchard."

I'm sure my face was contorted with both empathy and distaste, but Professor Grogan persisted with her lecture, perhaps amusing herself a bit at my expense.

"Now and then she goes into the dorms looking for her child," Camilla said, casting a devilish look my way. "The father walks this driveway, too," she added, waving her arm. "First year I was here a parent thought he hit somebody with his car. Turned out it was just the ghost."

"Chilling story," I remarked, relieved that it finally was over.

"Yes, but it's ours." Her smile suggested many depths within that deceptively shy facade. I realized now that I had witnessed the professor onstage, captivating and informing me whether I wanted to sit still for it or not.

Back inside Grace Hall we proceeded past the information desk and beyond the entrances to a theater and what Camilla explained was a student-run cabaret. I then followed her up a stuffy-smelling staircase to the second floor.

As we walked down a narrow, blond-paneled hallway of closed faculty offices, Camilla gossiped about her coworkers. ''This one hangs out in the Wigwam 'gathering area' with the students,'' she said gesturing toward a white door. ''I don't think he has a home. This one runs the ever-popular prelaw club. This one's away for the semester—lucky duck.'' She flicked the padlock on his office door.

She opened the door to her own cubicle only long enough to write a note on a yellow Post-it telling any student who happened by where she was. My quick glimpse inside explained why we were meeting elsewhere. It looked like my eleven-year-old's closet.

In the faculty lounge at the end of the hall the music history professor offered coffee, which I declined. She proceeded to pour herself some from the two-burner coffeemaker by the windows, then flopped into one of the two comfy-looking chairs covered in a flowered print of green, maroon, and rose. I took the other, which faced the four tall, narrow windows overlooking a parking lot and a stand of trees.

I glanced around appreciatively. Empty except for us, the room was bright with fresh paint and new furniture. A couple plants flourished on the broad white windowsill. There was a round table with four purple-gray armchairs, a clothes tree.

''This is nice,'' I told Camilla. ''You must like working here.''

She leaned forward to rest her elbows on her thighs, the styrofoam cup between her knees warming both hands. ''It isn't Villanova,'' she said suggestively.

My surprise manifested itself in a laugh; I had referred only to the faculty lounge, not the whole institution. Had the woman anticipated some snobbish comparison on my part? Ridiculous. Considering Rip's business, I had reason to know that schools had distinctive personalities just as obviously as the people who attended them. One Size does not Fit All, not even Most.

Anyhow, why would anybody denigrate Cabrini? I'd only been there half an hour, but the pride shown in every immaculate detail of the place told me they were serious about their "Why sit on the bench when you can be a star," pitch.

Then I remembered that Camilla's husband taught at Villanova, the large, prominent university about four miles away.

Looking into her cowed-puppy eyes, I'd have bet a year's tuition that was the problem. Neil's scholarly ego perpetually browbeat Camilla's timid one into a dusty corner. Mental macho. Lord how I hated that sort of posturing.

"Where did the president of the United States go to college?" I asked.

Camilla's chin jerked and her eyes opened into a stare. "I don't know."

"Nixon? Carter? George Bush? Ronald Reagan?"

"I think Ford went to Iowa. Didn't he wear that letter sweater?"

"Michigan, but he was showing off his muscles, not his brains."

Educator that she was, she was pleased by my point, which was that a student gets out of any institution about what he or she puts into it.

Camilla swiveled her head a bit to the side and smiled slyly.

"What did you come here to ask me?" she said.

"Tell me about Richard Diamond."

Her expression went defensive again. "Why do you think I know anything about him?"

"You're friends with Bonnie, aren't you? I saw you leaving their house."

Camilla set her coffee on the windowsill behind her and sighed into the cushions of the chair. "He lost a very powerful, well-paying job about six, seven months ago. Did you know?''

"I wasn't sure."

She sat forward and shook her head. "Losing his job devastated him. Bonnie was the one who had to put their previous house on the market, find a cheaper one, pack, move, settle the kids into the new school. Richard functions, but most of the time he's busy deluding himself. Still, some days he's good. Dresses the part. Goes to the interviews. Other days he pretends they've got money." She looked at me to see if I had caught on. I hadn't.

"What does he do?"

Camilla sighed sadly. "He buys things. Expensive things."

"TV's, stereos . . . ?"

"That's right."

Now I got it. "And as soon as he leaves the house, Bonnie takes them back."

"Also correct."

My disappointment probably showed. "So Richard's just another ordinary messed-up soul." Not a thief and a murderer. I had stood as I said that, and Camilla rose also.

"Yep," she agreed. "We almost have him talked into going to my therapist."

"Your . . . ?"

This time the woman's smile was straightforward, for her, almost brave. I gave her my broadest grin.

"Thanks for your help," I said.

"Don't mention it." Just as many of her other remarks had, this one suggested nuances aside from the obvious. I suspected she was a very good music history teacher.

Chapter 32

The Main Line is disinclined to have telephone kiosks. Some areas don't even have telephone poles. Considering that I did not yet own a cellular phone, I went home to make my call. Gail Vickers's car had been in their drive. When she answered her phone, I asked if I might come over and speak to her.

"In a rush, Gin," the honey-blonde replied briskly. "Another time maybe." Her tone suggested that purple snow was equally as probable.

I asked where she was going.

A stunned silence followed by an audible exhale told me I'd called her out. "The realtor's bringing someone over. I thought I'd go to the Farmer's Market for a while."

"Perfect," I announced. "I'm out of lettuce."

"Gin," my fashionable neighbor began with that motherly impatience we all love, "Gin, what the hell is it you want?"

Ah. Scratched through to the real Gail Vickers in less than five minutes. I was getting good.

"I need to ask about some of the neighbors you know better than I do. I think Liz might have been murdered by one of them."

"That's crazy. That's absolutely crazy. Besides, the police already caught the guy, that robber."

"I don't think he did it."

"Why not?"

"I thought you were in a hurry."

"Oh, shit. I am. Meet me outside. You drive."

A couple minutes later we were winding our way toward a low, tan brick building in Wayne where a Farmer's Market occurs every Wednesday, Friday, and Saturday. There you will find the fattest, yellowest chickens, tomatoes so round and red they could be used for Christmas ornaments, handmade candies, beautiful pastries from recipes so complicated that no homemaker in her right mind would bother, country this and that, and bunches of flowers—everything fresh, everything perfect, and all of it priced accordingly. I frequent the place as often as I do a museum, and then only to admire the size of the grapefruits.

Gail had no qualms about grabbing what she wanted, and it occurred to me not to worry so much about her and Don carrying the cost of two houses. After selecting and paying for mushrooms and some fresh dill, she seemed more prepared to deal with me.

"I can't believe you're involving yourself in Liz's death," she said as she hustled me down the first aisle toward the flowers and fish. I had to strain to keep her honey-blonde head in sight. Luckily she paused, finger to cheek, to admire some cheeses.

Suddenly she spun and pressed forward, asking me over her shoulder, "Don't you have enough to do?"

I grabbed her arm to make her hold still while I looked her in the eye. "Letty MacNair probably saw the killer leaving Liz's house."

"What?"

"Can we sit down for some coffee? Isn't there at least one place?" Trying to search across the aisles, I stood on tiptoe to peer over the heads of two Amish women selling noodles and pies. All I could see were tables, shoulder-high refrigerated food cases and makeshift back walls hung with kitchen implements or dried flower wreaths. I could maybe afford to love this place—if I won the Irish sweepstakes or discovered the cure for a major disease.

"This way," Gail said like the regular customer she was. "Back in the corner. It's probably late enough to get seats."

It turned out to be the inner right-hand corner where a cluster of tall stools and tables had been provided for eating some of the plentiful goodies. For the moment, we were the only customers.

I bought the Brew of the Day and an almond pastry. Gail opted for coffee and a croissant. I was pretty sure she would pick the croissant apart with her fingers, a prissy little habit I hate—and messy, too—but I would simply have to endure.

"You were saying that Letty saw the murderer?" Gail prompted, pinching a bit of croissant as predicted. I hid my wince behind my coffee mug, then I set it down.

"Actually, before her first cataract operation, Letty didn't see well enough to be sure about anything. However, the murderer doesn't know that." To help Gail appreciate the urgency I felt about getting at the truth, I briefly explained about the gas-bomb incident.

"What do you know about Max Crouthamel?" I asked. Of the men on the block, so far I had ruled out only Richard Diamond and, because of his age, Sol Raymond.

"Max is huge."

"How huge? I've never seen him."

Gail pulled a face. "Have you seen Patsy?"

I was embarrassed to have asked, but to my mind the information did rule Max out. Letty certainly would have told me if Liz's "fancy man" had been inordinately large.

"How about Marc Kelman?" I asked.

"Liz's husband? Surely you don't think . . ."

I raised my eyebrows, and Gail shrugged. "I guess you're right. It could have been him. He's cute enough to cause trouble. But that's all I know—except that he's a walking cliché."

"Traveling salesman?" I assumed she meant, and she nodded that was it indeed. Food for thought. Clichés exist because they're so often true.

"Sam?"

"He's too busy trying to get his wife back, wouldn't you say?"

My turn to nod.

"Johnny Raymond?"

Gail squirmed on her stool and wrinkled her nose. "He and I had it out when he parked in front of my mailbox, but other than that . . ."

"You yelled at him for that?"

Gail blinked with surprise. "Of course. The mailman writes nasty notes if he can't get to your box. Haven't you ever received one?"

"No-o-o."

My coffee companion sniffed. "Well, I've received a few, and I'm not about to get another. Which is exactly what I told Mr. Johnny-mind-your-own-business Raymond. Twerp."

"Okay, so you don't like him. Can you see him systematically terrorizing a whole block?"

"Maybe. But why would he do it?"

I sipped my coffee. "To convince his parents to move so that he can have their house."

"I don't know, Gin. You're reasoning is sound enough, I suppose, what with Sol being so sick and all. It's logical for even a creep like Johnny to want his parents where they'll get good care. But commit crimes—even murder? I don't think so."

"Sol's sick?"

"Cancer. Didn't you know?"

I shook my head. The possibilities were beginning to whirl around in my mind.

After a minute, I said, "I have to ask about one more thing. It's a little touchy."

"Pray, don't stop now." The sarcasm was only half

friendly, and I was reminded of her earlier purple-snow attitude.

In response I gave her my best head-on stare. ''Somebody wrote Letty a threatening letter suggesting that she move,'' I said. ''Did you or Don have anything to do with that?''

Gail flushed to her hairline and glared at me. ''You've got a lot of nerve . . .''

I held her gaze until she had to speak. ''Okay. It's true we'd love the old bat to clean up her yard. And to be honest, we don't think she belongs on Beech Tree Lane or anywhere within ten miles of the Main Line, but threaten her? Why bother? What good would it do?''

''You are having trouble selling. Are you absolutely certain Don didn't write the note?''

Gail huffed. ''That's pretty insulting, wouldn't you say?''

I kept quiet, and eventually she relented.

''Okay, yes, we're having trouble selling. So are lots of homeowners with houses in our price range. And yes, it's killing us financially.''

I inadvertently glanced around at the selection of pricey delicacies, and to my surprise Gail began to cry, big wet sniffles she fought hard to suppress. I handed her my paper napkin.

''This place is my treat to myself, okay? My personal vice. And thank you very much for spoiling it.''

''I'm really sorry, Gail. I didn't mean to pry, but Liz's death never sat right with me, and now Letty's in grave danger. I can't let her go back to her house until I'm positive that it's safe.''

''Somebody really threatened her?'' she asked, dabbing at her eyes.

''Yes—and sabotaged her house.''

''Was the note a computer printout?''

''Yes,'' I answered with a rush of anticipation.

''Nelson Shannahan,'' Gail pronounced like a jury sentence.

''Why him?'' The urgency in my voice was apparent. Gail sat up straighter, sensing that I was onto something.

''He writes scathing messages to anybody and everybody. Considers himself the troubadour of good taste.''

''I thought that was Wendy,'' I said, referring, of course, to her penchant for holiday decorations.

''Opposites don't always attract. Anyway, she told me about some of the notes Nelson's sent. To the mayor of Philadelphia, the coach of the Eagles. Once to the owner of a store who put up a particularly garish window display near Nelson's office. He's a pompous prick. Bet you anything he wrote Letty and thought he was being clever as hell.''

I believed her. Trouble was I wasn't sure note-writing translated into violence. Then again, I never understood violence.

''Thanks,'' I told Gail. ''You've been a big help.''

''Let's get out of here before I buy anything else.'' Her resentment hurt me, as she probably knew it would.

I took what I deserved in silence.

Back home I let my fingers do the walking. If I was going to dislike myself for spoiling Gail's respite from financial agony, why not make a morning of it and find out where Johnny Raymond was Tuesday afternoon when the gas bomb had been rigged. The hard way, by worrying his mother.

''Margaret,'' I began very tentatively, as if I were reluctant to go on, which I actually was.

''Yes? Has something else happened?'' Good guess, Margaret.

''No,'' I lied. ''I just wanted to ask you something about Johnny.'' Mainly because he wisely refused to speak to me and I was not acquainted with his fiancée.

''Margaret, I know Johnny's engaged . . .''

''Yes . . . ?''

"But, but does he have another female friend? I mean a woman he might . . . spend time with?"

"I don't understand."

I sighed heavily. "I saw this man and woman yesterday afternoon. They looked . . . very friendly. I was afraid the man was Johnny."

"You're sure he wasn't with Diane?"

"Quite sure," I replied with confidence. As far as I knew, he wasn't with anybody.

"Where was this?"

"At the Wayne Hotel," a posh restaurant, and needless to say—hotel.

"And when did you say this, this meeting took place?"

I roughly calculated the time Letty and I finished looking at her house. The gas bomb would have been rigged sometime between then and approximately 7:00 PM when I went over to get the Shop-vac. If I figured in a few hours to allow the gas to accumulate, that meant the perpetrator broke into Letty's somewhere between 2:30 and 4:00.

"After 2:30," I told Margaret. "I had just finished a late lunch when they arrived."

"Johnny should have been at work," Margaret mused. I could sense her concern, and I longed to dissipate it.

"Maybe they were planning a shower for Diane?"

"Maybe . . ." She sounded doubtful.

"Maybe it was somebody else."

"Maybe."

"Is there any way to find out without, you know, upsetting anyone?"

"I suppose he knows what he's doing, but . . ." But she knew her son and didn't entirely trust his ethics.

"If you find out, would it be asking too much for you to call me? I'd feel so much better knowing I was wrong."

"You probably are wrong."

"Of course." And yet. "You'll call me?"

"Yes. All right. I owe you that for letting me know."

"It's probably nothing."

This time she didn't answer.

Margaret phoned back at 3:45. Before that, I managed to give myself indigestion by eating a hot dog for lunch. My frantic housecleaning and laundry folding drove Barney under a bed.

After her call, I became the most tranquil I had been in the two and a half weeks since Liz's murder. I hung up the kitchen phone and stared out the window at the delicate spring leaves, savoring their beauty while considering the implications of my internal change.

Such an inner calm could only mean that I was secure in my assessment of what had been happening.

Speaking to Camilla, Gail, and now Margaret had provided most of the answers I required. Completing the process would be much more difficult.

And not nearly so safe.

Chapter 33

"Where did you get those ridiculous balloons?" Rip boomed at me as soon as he got home. He referred to a handful of Mylar monstrosities I had attached to Letty's mailbox right after lunch. "Is she home already?"

"The Party Nook," I replied with very little volume. "And no, she's not home yet. Come in here, and I'll explain."

I led my husband to the space in front of our living room's walk-in fireplace, the broadest pacing area available and furthest from where the kids were doing their homework in anticipation of dinner.

Because of the danger, telling Rip my plan was essential. I might need his help, but I didn't want his interference. That's why I chose my words very carefully.

My husband's initial astonishment transformed into stubborn opposition in about half a blink.

"Let me run through this again," he said, green eyes flashing. "You put those ridiculous Mylar 'Welcome Home' balloons on Letty's mailbox to trick the neighborhood psychopath into thinking that Letty went home today."

Reluctantly, I admitted that was pretty much the idea. I wasn't entirely comfortable with the psychopath description, but I prudently allowed Rip to make his point.

"And for some reason you think this loony person you believe jerry-rigged that lamp and turned on the gas is going to revisit Letty's house tonight?"

"Well, maybe," I said. When he put it like that, it sounded a bit far-fetched.

Rip made use of the pacing space. "You realize, of course, that Kriebel doesn't think anybody did anything to that lamp."

"I know. And the gas got turned on by accident." Exactly the reasons I yearned to catch the despicable bastard in the act and serve him up to Kriebel on a platter. Or, pardon me, alert Kriebel and let him catch the despicable bastard.

"And if nothing happens?" Rip asked.

I'd been stationary while Rip whirled and flailed to vent his agitation. Now we were both still, facing each other like the boy and girl on a fancy cuckoo clock—wooden, programmed to reveal ourselves only periodically, destined to touch only twice a day.

I said, "If nothing happens, then I guess Letty can really go home."

Rip blinked with surprise. He hadn't envisioned any practical purpose to my plan. Now he suddenly saw countless evenings with Letty parked in front of our television coming to an end.

"Oh," he said, and I felt his attitude downshift from exasperation to amused tolerance.

Hands on hips, he wagged his attractive shoulders. "Okay, so what's the rest," he teased. "I hide behind a door with a baseball bat, or what?"

Since I needed his cooperation, I pressed ahead. "No. All I think we should do is watch the house and try to identify the culprit. After we spot him, we call the police." Townwatch rules. Neither of us had any business trying to physically apprehend a man who had assaulted two women.

"We wait inside the house, or what?"

''I thought we'd hide outside in the bushes.''

''All night?''

Yes, all night. Of course all night. But I couldn't say it aloud, especially since Rip's interest was visibly slipping away.

He shook his head. ''The odds of this scenario you've described happening at all are pretty remote.''

I sighed. He wasn't going to do this for me.

''Maybe.''

I thought the chances were pretty good, but Rip didn't know that the murderer thought Letty could identify him; and if I used that particular argument, Rip might not cooperate at all.

My husband's fists rested on his hips. He stared at the middle distance while he considered his options.

''Sorry, Gin,'' he concluded. ''I'm with Kriebel on this one.'' I wanted to mention Liz, perhaps say something that would remind him that he hadn't married a dunce, but no words would come. ''Sorry. I'm not sleeping outside on a lawn chair for a theory I just don't buy. Tomorrow's a school day, remember?''

Ah, there was the rub. We only humor our wife's silly notions on weekends. My ears swelled with the rush of pressure from my pulse.

''Mind if I do it without you?''

Rip gave my face a quick glance and shrugged. ''You can do whatever you want.''

Thank you ever so . . .

''You'll call the police if I need you to?'' I asked.

''Sure,'' said my husband. ''Of course.''

My chest hurt so much I wanted to cry. That snide, ''alarmist'' remark Rip made to Greg Burack hadn't just been the wine talking—my husband really seemed to believe my solving the flower-show murder had been a fluke.

Soon he breathed audibly and his hands slid down his corduroy pantlegs. He started to speak once but stopped.

Finally he looked up from the floor and gave me half a smile. "Go get 'em, tiger," he said.

After that, he went straight into his office and turned on the computer. Maybe he confided to his journal that he was worried about my sanity. Probably he just griped about the school.

I proceeded to inconspicuously gather my equipment. The lump in my throat soon went away. The ache in my chest would take a bit longer.

Garry's old toy walkie-talkies required fresh batteries. Even then my words echoed into the hall closet like boots on gravel. Yet if I needed help, the initial squawking of the call button would be enough to awaken Rip. He hadn't slept soundly since he took the job at Bryn Derwyn—why should tonight be any different?

Outside, twilight was coming fast. With Barney on a leash, I made a noisy show of walking up Letty's driveway—ostensibly to visit. Meanwhile, I scouted out a spot to hide in the thicket between our property and Letty's. Barney was kind enough to provide an excuse to rummage around in the bushes.

Next I stood on Letty's back stoop and called hello into the empty house. Then letting myself in with a key, I unhitched Barney and allowed him to perform the usual canine routine. Like a regular night watchman he secured the kitchen visually and aurally before stepping inside, sniffing for intruders, locating the exits.

Since it was still just light enough to move around freely, I made my own way into Letty's parlor and turned on a table lamp, making the house appear the same as on any previous night before anything had happened. The floor lamp and timer, of course, were at the police lab.

Although I should have been accustomed to the creaks and groans of the old house, tonight they set off my imagination. Surely, that squeak was the sole of a shoe, that rustling sound—a man preparing to attack.

Yet Barney remained calm, so I tried to emulate him. He

even flopped down on the one small kitchen rug as if he expected to stay awhile.

When I was almost ready to go, it occurred to me that it really was a good idea for the dog to remain behind. If my culprit knew how to gain access to the house other than through the kitchen door, Barney's barking would certainly alert me to his presence.

"Yes," I congratulated myself. "Great idea!" Maybe, just maybe, this foolish notion of mine would work.

"Good boy. Stay," I told our family pet. I filled one of Letty's thick glass mixing bowls with water and set it on the floor. The remaining daylight was so dim the yellow bowl appeared to be gray.

"I'll be right outside," I said. "You have permission to bark your ass off if anybody comes in here. And believe me, I'm not kidding."

Barney panted in his smug, wise way. Had I forgotten that his instincts were better than mine? Why did I always have to belabor the obvious?

"Good," I said, making a show of being in charge. "See you later."

Back home I performed the motherly goodnight routine with the kids, but I didn't mention my evening plans. Informing Rip had been difficult enough.

The man himself waited for me in the doorway of his office. Not knowing when—or whether—the neighborhood nemesis would show up, I had to force myself to give Rip my whole attention.

He ignored my twitchy eagerness to begin my watch and gathered me into his arms. "Sometimes I don't understand you at all," he said.

"A lot of that going around," I observed with a sigh.

He breathed into my hair. "Maybe we need to get away this weekend. Your mom available?" To be with the kids.

I thought of the secret dinner I had planned with Gregory Burack and lied into Rip's shirt. "She's busy," I said. "But you're right. We need time for us—real soon."

I wanted my husband to learn to trust my judgment again, whether he understood what I was into or not. I needed to reassure him that he could share all his problems with me, even the ones that threatened to hurt us as a couple—especially those. We did need time for us. I would make that my top priority—first thing in the morning.

I handed Rip one of Garry's black plastic walkie-talkies. "Put this on the nightstand right by your head," I advised.

Rip pushed the button, and the toy crackled like a wet log on fire. "Jeez, it's loud." He smiled and shook his head. "You're crazy, you know that?"

"How about 'unconventional'?" I suggested.

"That too," he agreed.

Soon I was huddled on a dusty beach chair under a bushy yew, hidden by rhododendrons on our property's side and weeds on Letty's. I trusted that the low sand chair and I were practically unnoticeable in the shadows.

Luckily, the spot I chose—four feet back from Letty's shortcut—allowed me to watch the decrepit back stoop at a distance of about twenty-five yards. The stone wall of the kitchen garden began further to my left, and the formerly decorative stone wall in the front was no factor at all.

Binoculars were out because they pinpointed my view too narrowly. So it was naked eyes and the one cup of strong coffee I had after dinner to take me though the night.

The temperature was a decent sixty degrees; but after an hour of holding still, my circulation needed movement to keep me feeling warm.

Boredom was not yet a factor. I mused about my relationship with Rip, past and present. I listed symptoms of trouble, signs of hope. Curiously, I did not think much about whether the murderer I expected to show would show. Suppression, probably. Cowardice of the mind.

I imagined Barney breathing the slow breaths of sleep, maybe twitching like he did when he had dog dreams of pursuit and capture. I wished he could be back in Garry's bed snuggling with my son instead of doing perhaps the most important job of his life.

Around 10:30 I crept back into my house, skulking along the bushes and in through our back door for a rest stop and a quilt. The whole effort took about six minutes, most of that time spent tiptoeing along the edge of my yard. Arranging myself back in the chair caused the most noise; but Barney had remained silent, so I knew I hadn't missed anything.

Around 11:30 keeping awake became a concern. I entertained myself trying to remember the birthdays of my friends and relatives—a dismal failure as either a memory test or entertainment. So instead I began making up dates I thought suited the person. April Fool's Day for Didi. Halloween for the woman who lived next door when I was six, whose anger had initiated a spanking—my one and only—for picking all her tulips.

I had just begun to contemplate a birth date for Letty's butcher friend, Pete, when I noticed a ghostlike shadow moving inside the old mansion's parlor. It was exactly what I had expected, only different. Something felt very wrong, terrifyingly wrong—Barney had not barked.

"Rip," I shouted into the walkie-talkie. "Rip, I need you."

Waddling in a duckwalk, I made my way to the shortcut path, then slowly rose to my feet. My circulation painfully filled in tucks and folds long pinched by sitting. My hands were slick with sweat, as was my whole body. What should I do? Stay quiet? Run?

Our front porch light flicked on and suddenly Rip burst outside. Wearing a warm-up suit and work boots he bounded across our yard until he stood panting beside me.

The sight of him spiked my mood by fifteen degrees. He had slept with clothes on—*in case he was wrong and I was right.*

Letty's kitchen door swung outward and hit the wall with

a resounding thump. The man who had been inside sprinted toward the street.

Rip took off after him, his heavy boots crunching underbrush into kindling.

By cutting the angle across Letty's lumpy driveway Rip soon caught up with the intruder and took him down with a dive-tackle. The two men grappled, untangled, rose and ran again toward the Browders' driveway where a streetlight illuminated their struggle. I moved along behind, unable to help, unable to leave.

Rip kicked at the man's leg with his boot. The man grunted and swung. Rip grabbed the swung arm and pulled. Then they were down again and rolling, stopped at the left edge of the drive by some rocks edging a small garden.

My own breath came in frantic gasps. My hands opened and clenched, opened and clenched as I rocked back and forth on my feet. Desperately, I scanned the area for something unattached I could use to help, a piece of wood, a rope, anything. Nothing useful came to light. Not even a trash can lid.

At least Rip seemed to be winning the wrestling match. Straddling the man's chest, he clutched the front of his opponent's black sweatshirt, lifted him by the shoulders then heavily dropped his torso on the macadam. Sam Browder's horrified face flicked in and out of Rip's shadow. My guess had been right.

"Police, Gin. Call . . . the . . . police."

I stifled a groan. Rip hadn't stopped for 911, just rushed to my rescue. Sweet. Crazy.

Big problem. What if Sam suddenly prevailed? What if he broke away? My body wouldn't move.

The rocks at the edge of the garden were of various sizes. I picked up the smallest I could find, one slightly larger than a softball.

Sam had caught his breath and had begun to fight harder. I considered slamming the rock into the top of his head, the only place I could reach without risking Rip or myself unnecessarily.

I couldn't do it. Liz had died from a blow like that.

So I stood and watched Sam push Rip's jaw away, watched Rip bite his finger to get free. They rolled some more. Sam's shoulder got loose. Rip slammed it down. Sam punched Rip's stomach, up from underneath. Rip flopped his whole body onto Sam's and stunned him momentarily. When Sam recovered, Rip was positioned above him, his weight on Sam's thighs, left arm pressing Sam's shoulder to the ground, Rip's right arm fisted and ready to punch Sam out.

"Why Letty?" Rip demanded to know as Sam cowered beneath him. "Why her?"

Even in the eerie evening shadows, I could see Sam's crazed glare radiate hate.

"He killed Liz," I alerted Rip. "He thinks Letty can identify him."

Rip flicked a glance at me for confirmation.

Then he growled like a neanderthal and slammed his fist into Sam's face, knocking him unconscious.

I became aware of the heavy rock in my hand.

So that my throw wouldn't fall short, I walked a few paces toward the Browders' house. Then I winged the rock through their bay window into Eunice's yellow drapes. An obnoxiously nasal-sounding burglar alarm ruined the dampened night silence and set off bedroom lights all up and down Beech Tree Lane.

"Let Kriebel respond to that," I said, dusting hunks of rock and mud off my hands.

Rip remained astride a motionless Sam Browder, too exhausted to move, so I told him I'd be right back, that I wanted to check on Barney.

Trotting across Letty's front weeds, I then picked my way among the potholes until I arrived at the broken back door. After I flipped on the kitchen light, I saw that our dog was not in the kitchen. Likewise the parlor and the downstairs bathroom.

I headed for the front hall, and that's where he was.

Because of all the leaks, the overhead light fixture no longer worked. All I could see was Barney's prone form lying by the difficult-to-open front door.

A damp draft blew in through an ancient mail slot, which had probably been pried open to feed Barney something in a piece of meat. Disused for decades, the mail slot had stuck in the open position. Our optimistic dog had waited beside it hoping for another treat.

I touched him.

When he did not respond, a monstrous hate welled up in me. Sam Browder was no longer a pathetic man desperately attempting to get back his wife. He was a killer of one lonely woman, nearly the killer of a harmless old recluse, and now he had harmed a sweet old dog who had never done anything to anyone.

The hateful monster took charge of me. I flew from the house, ran to where Rip kept Sam Browder subdued. Whoever I was just then shoved my husband off balance and onto the driveway and replaced him on the unconscious killer's chest.

I took two fists full of black sweatshirt and hefted Sam's deadweight shoulders up off the ground then slammed them down.

"You . . ." up, ". . . killed . . ." down, ". . . our . . ." up, ". . . dog . . ." down with a vengeance.

Sam's eyelids flickered. "You . . . killed . . . our . . . dog."

"Gin!" somebody said. Up . . . down. The monster refused to be diverted.

"Tranquil . . . izer," gasped the man on the ground. "I . . . gave . . . him . . . tranquilizers."

"Gin, stop it. You're going to . . . Gin, stop it."

I wouldn't though. Not until the police wailed up to the curb.

When Kriebel arrived, summoned by the sector cop, Rip still had me in a sort of bear hug from behind, making sure I wouldn't break free and kick Sam Browder in the kidney. After relating the essentials to the sergeant/detective, Rip explained that I also thought Sam killed our dog.

Miraculously, Kriebel seemed to understand. Somehow he managed to pressure Sam, I don't know how, to tell him what he fed Barney, which was about eight five-milligram Valiums. Kriebel even helped us phone our vet from the squad car.

By the time Rip and I got back to Barney, the dog had already started to come around. Apparently, even a dose that large doesn't last too long, part of the reason Sam hadn't waited longer to break into Letty's far-side window. Between Rip and me we guided the staggering animal home to sleep it off per the vet's instructions.

A bit later the emergency room doctor who was setting Rip's broken hand told us Sam Browder had sustained a fractured jaw from Rip's punch and a cracked rib from wrestling on the ground.

I took credit for the concussion.

''Mom?'' I said into the phone about 1:30 the next afternoon.

''Yes, dear?'' Cynthia replied as if the outcome of her day depended on my call.

''Letty can come home now. The police arrested the guy who was after her.''

''That's wonderful, dear. But would you mind terribly if Letty stayed a few more days?''

Rip tapped my shoulder with his good left hand and wiggled his fingers good-bye. He had roused and dressed himself to open Bryn Derwyn's school day with the traditional morning assembly, then he had driven himself back home (automatic shift) and slept for six more hours. We had just finished lunch.

''Bye,'' I mouthed over my shoulder.

"Now, Mother, about Letty staying. What's going on?"

"She's trying to remember how to make osterfladen."

"What's that, Mom?"

"I'm not sure, dear, but it smells awfully good."

I had a flash-image of our next dinner at Mother's, replete with generous portions of this mysterious osterfladen.

"Could you please put Letty on the line? I'm sure she'd like to hear what happened."

There were mutters I couldn't make out while Mother covered the mouthpiece with her palm.

"Letty isn't fond of the telephone, dear. Why don't you just tell me."

Oh? "Okay. Money must be pretty tight for the Browders these days, considering what they both do and how they've been behaving. But Sam wasn't taking any chances. He thought if the neighborhood seemed unsafe enough their house wouldn't sell and his wife wouldn't be able to afford an apartment, let alone a divorce. She would have to come back to him—at least long enough to give him another chance. You with me so far, Mom?" I thought I felt her paying more attention to the osterfladen than to me.

"Go on."

"So he started duplicating the kinds of crimes that were happening in other parts of the county. You there?"

"Yes . . ."

"Except his first big robbery went sour when Liz came home. He had flirted her up so he could stick a toothpick in her back door lock."

"A toothpick? How strange. What did he do that for?" So she was listening, sort of.

"So the door wouldn't really close, Mom. So he could rob the Kelmans when Liz went out the next morning. Except she came back. And because she saw him, he hit her a little too hard. Maybe on purpose. Maybe not. That probably only matters to the jury. Maybe not even to them. Anyway, Letty was outside and saw Sam leaving Liz's by the back door. She couldn't see well enough to testify that it was him, but he didn't know that. And the more he worried about it, the more he didn't want to risk her telling the police anything.

"So you'll tell Letty?"

"Tell her what, dear? That switch over there." The latter was addressed to her houseguest. I heard the garbage disposal noise immediately thereafter.

"Never mind. Would you like to hear about Barney's adventure?"

"Barney? Of course." Now I had her. Barney she knew and loved. Sam Browder was nobody to her.

"Sam . . ." Check that. ". . . *Somebody* fed him tranquilizers in a piece of meat last night. I thought he was dead."

"Oh dear! Had he been barking?"

"No, Mom."

"Is he all right?"

"Yes, Mom. Back to normal."

I still felt embarrassed at my irrational response to what appeared to be our dog's death. However, Rip assured me repeatedly that Barney had represented my last straw, that I had not really felt more emotion over an animal than a person, no matter how it looked. He was right, of course. Now and then he was right, too.

My arm was a bit stiff today, so I switched the receiver into my other hand. "I'll pick Letty up Saturday," after Friday night's surprise dinner for Greg and Rip.

"How about Monday, dear?"

Four more days? Oh. Cynthia Struve had taken on another cause, the assimilation of Letty MacNair. An interesting prospect. By Monday either Letty would have eyebrows or my mother would know how to use the word "methinks" in a sentence.

"About ten?" I asked. Norman Demig had promised the results of the audit by Monday morning.

"Perfect," Cynthia replied.

Chapter 34

The screeching tires and *ratta-tat-tat* of the gangster movie Garry and Dave were absorbing like paper towels became a sheltering background noise before it reached our living room. Fortunately for her ears, Chelsea was out earning more honest money—babysitting next door while the Diamonds were out celebrating Richard's new job.

''When I lost Carol, I thought there would never be another woman in my life,'' Greg Burack earnestly told Rip and me. ''Then wouldn't you know, the very first one I met showed me that you never say never. Pat . . . Pat simply saved my life. And Lisa—Lisa was a miracle.''

Pat had literally been the grief counselor Greg consulted after his first wife died. Lisa was their only child, the much-indulged marvel of Greg's middle age, doted on by her older siblings, her father and her mother, too, until Pat's own untimely death.

Our guest recited this personal litany to us in a tone of marvel, coffee cup aloft, left hand waving, eyes misted with bittersweet memories. Although we knew the story well, we respected his need to ease into the discomfort that was to come. There are times when a man needs to heft the weight of his blessings.

I watched the men from my seat at the end of our plank table and listened to their thoughts, louder to me by far than the riot of television fiction in the far room. When Greg finally lowered his cup to its saucer, I held my breath, releasing it only when Greg sighed and folded his hands on the cleared place mat.

He addressed Rip directly. "She's not right for teaching, is she?"

The question had not invited denial, but Rip said, "Maybe with a little more maturity . . ."

The older man shook his head and sighed. "No," he stated in a way that was both sympathetic and final.

During the ensuing silence, Rip's torn emotions played across his face. One of them was the temptation to lie.

"Don't," Rip's mentor quickly interceded with a raised palm. "Don't try to spare an old man's feelings. You're in the business of telling the truth. Remember that."

Rip's shoulders sank forward. His head nodded heavily. "All right," he agreed.

"When will you tell her?" Gregory Burack asked.

Rip murmured, "Monday, I suppose," referring to the first opportunity he would have to speak to Lisa face-to-face.

Her father glanced toward me and shook his head. "No," he said again. "This has gone on long enough. Call her tonight."

Rip met his mentor's gaze.

After a moment he rose, dropping his napkin behind him. He walked into his office and closed the door.

Chapter 35

After an emotional meeting in Norman Demig's office Monday morning and a Burger King lunch, I took Letty to visit Edwin Markus O'Callahan in his Bryn Mawr Hospital room. I thought seeing the man's condition might help with the difficult confrontation yet to come.

Unfortunately, visiting hours had not quite begun.

"It's really complicated," I explained to the nurses at the nearby station. "He's her trustee, and she just needs to look at him." Two pairs of eyes stared at me blankly. "For reassurance," I added. "It'll only take a minute."

The shorter nurse shrugged, which I took for assent. I spun Letty on her sneakers so fast that she nearly tripped.

As soon as we stepped inside his room, O'Callahan rolled vacant eyes toward us. His face was almost fleshless, his mouth slack.

Letty strode forward, kicked his bed frame, and yelled, "You sneaking, lying, sonova no good . . ." and other assorted high-volume epithets that brought the two nurses and a strong orderly running.

In short order we were out on the curb. Our three escorts waited with folded arms until we were half a block away.

It seemed prudent to leave the car where it was and walk the few blocks to O'Callahan's law office. Letty needed the time to cool down; and, all things considered, I felt a review of Norman Demig's recommended game plan had become essential.

"Don't make any accusations you can't prove," the counselor had emphasized. "He may be recording your meeting. Don't give him any legal weapons."

"But, but, but," I had objected.

Norman had raised a bushy black eyebrow. "You'd lose," he stated flatly.

While Letty and I rested briefly at the bench area dedicated to Philip Giagnacova "for his tireless effort to the betterment and beautification of Bryn Mawr 1994," I delivered my spiel. Unfortunately, Letty seemed to pay much more attention to a sparrow pecking at the dirt than to my admonitions, causing me to carry quite a bit of trepidation with me into our 2:00 PM appointment with O'Callahan.

"You may go, Ms. Hollyfield," the Lincolnesque son told his secretary after she escorted us into his father's disused office.

The blonde woman I had followed from the post office that day threw me a confrontational glare before flouncing through the fake cherry door.

"Please be seated," the attorney addressed us. He chose to remain standing off to our left behind the huge antique cherry desk.

I settled into one of the facing velvet-seated armchairs, but Letty wandered over to finger the ancient typewriter on the stand in front of the broad window.

Against the background of law books and beige drapes she made quite a contrast—a shrunken, wrinkled woman temporarily wearing large, black-framed glasses, gaudy sneakers and my mother's favorite pale aqua suit. Unfortunately, the suit's color made Letty look like a vampire's victim.

The younger O'Callahan—speaking relatively, for the man was at least sixty—could easily have been the vampire.

"I'm busy, Mrs. Barnes," he said. "Let's get to the

point.'' The creases on his scowling face were nearly black, and the dark eyes he aimed at me were bright with anger.

''You really should be speaking to Ms. MacNair,'' I told him, nonchalantly setting my purse on the floor and clasping my knee with both hands.

''The point, Mrs. Barnes.''

I glanced at Letty, who appeared to be mildly absorbed with the pleasant view of the adjoining yard.

''As you know,'' I began, ''we had an audit done of Ms. MacNair's trustee account.''

''Yes.'' The lawyer's expression suggested that his stomach had begun to turn.

Behind me the rickety typewriter stand wobbled and nearly fell. If my peripheral vision served, Letty had swung into it with a hip. O'Callahan glared in her direction a moment, then returned his attention to me.

I placed my feet side by side and leaned forward. ''There was quite a bit of questionable activity,'' I reproved lightly before allowing my voice to become hard. ''. . . about forty years' worth.''

O'Callahan's narrow nose tightened, and his frame went stiff.

''My father handled her account with the utmost care,'' he proclaimed. His hands were joined behind his back and his chin jutted forward.

''I'm sure.'' *''Extortionate fees . . . ,''* Norman Demig had told Letty and me earlier that morning. *''. . . seemed to consider her account his personal retirement fund.''*

I wiped my damp hands down my thighs. ''Yes, we know the kind of care he took, Mr. O'Callahan, and I believe it is his great good fortune that Ms. MacNair has chosen not to press criminal charges.''

Behind my back a thick law volume dropped to the floor. I could sense Letty's movement as she stepped away.

''You're supposed to be a menace—not a poltergeist!'' I wanted to remind my next-door neighbor. But maybe she didn't know the difference.

I shifted on my seat and tried to secure her attention. She had drifted over to an ashtray stand next to a reading chair.

Kyle O'Callahan spoke. ''My father did nothing illegal,'' the son maintained from a lofty height.

''Oh?'' I said sarcastically. ''Is that why he preferred to deal with Letty anonymously?''

The ashtray went over with a crash.

''Stop that,'' O'Callahan scolded.

Then he spoke in a nasty hush as if Letty were no longer present. ''The woman can't read,'' he told me. ''That's not Father's fault. He dealt with Ms. MacNair in a manner he thought she could understand.''

I jutted my chin right back at him. ''He dealt with her as if she were a child.''

''When Ms. MacNair inherited, she *was* a child.''

''Not quite.''

''She was not competent to make her own decisions.''

''And how about when she became older? Your father changed nothing. He kept her just as uninformed and impoverished as before. That's unconscionable.'' If it weren't for the old man's battleship of a desk, I would have kicked his shifty son right in *his* bed frame.

''Father paid all her other expenses automatically.''

''He's a crook.''

''My father is an officer of the court. He knows what is within the law.''

Yes, I thought, and that's why Norman Demig informed Letty as tactfully as possible that there was no way to recoup the hundreds of thousands of dollars that her legal trustee had bilked from her account.

''How much before?'' Letty had asked. When Demig told her the original amount of the inheritance, she wobbled and looked away.

''What about now?'' I asked while she recovered her breath.

''In terms of income?''

''Sure.''

"Enough for Ms. MacNair to live comfortably—but not extravagantly—for the rest of her life."

Naturally, Letty and I had launched into some giddy giggling and dancing, but Demig's sobering face soon settled us down. The only viable course, he informed us, fell well between the lines, a dilemma that clearly distressed him greatly.

After a prolonged internal struggle, he exacted a pledge of silence from both Letty and me. Then, when he was at last satisfied with our sincerity, he threw legal caution to the wind and told us exactly what to do and how to do it.

Now that the time for her part of the performance had arrived, Letty stood staring at Edwin Markus O'Callahan's shelved law books as if she could read their spines—or maybe as if she couldn't.

I took a diver's breath and leaped ahead.

"Letty?" I prompted. "Tell the man what you want."

She turned gracefully and stepped up to O'Callahan Senior's desk. "I wants . . . want . . . a new trustee," she informed O'Callahan, the younger.

The man immediately shook his head. "I'm afraid Mrs. Doland's will is quite explicit . . ."

"I *want* a new trustee. Not your dad. Not you. One o' me own." Letty rocked on the bulky gym shoes, her hands clasped behind her back like a schoolgirl. She glanced at me for approval, and I gave her my proudest smile.

"Out of the question," Kyle O'Callahan intoned in a very judicial, very bullying voice.

Letty's non-eyebrows raised to ask me if it was time for Phase Two. I nodded.

She stepped closer to the cherry desk and looked up at the attorney's chin. "I know what you did, young man," she said. "All o' it. And I want me own trustee. *Or else.*"

O'Callahan's mouth opened, most likely with the intention of expressing some intimidating reply, but Letty's pursed lips and unwavering glare caught him up short. I could only see her profile, but I would have detoured out of my way to avoid that glare.

"You . . ." O'Callahan began.

"Or else." She lifted her hair away from her temple to reveal the scar from the injury Kyle O'Callahan had personally inflicted.

The man's coloring disappeared. He looked at me with a slack mouth and stunned eyes. If the police hadn't connected him to Letty's break-in and attack, the search through her trash, or the threatening hospital visit, how was it possible that a couple of mere women had?

His incredulous eyes switched from me to Letty and back. Despite the audit, he had expected to continue his father's profitable setup until Letty MacNair's death, to retain the inheritance from her mother's dear friend and employer as the O'Callahans' private golden goose.

And now the incomprehensible had happened. He couldn't quite cope.

"Find a way," I said. "You're a lawyer. You'll come up with something."

The man lowered himself into the large black desk chair as if his joints ached. "My father was a blood relative, a second cousin to Eleanor Doland. He should have inherited, not . . . not her." He shot a resentful glance in Letty's direction.

Letty narrowed her eyes like a gypsy administering a curse.

"Make it happen," I interceded. "Unless you'd like to go to jail."

O'Callahan gawked at the open air between us.

"Your choice," I pressed.

I realized the man had crumbled inside his clothes. Only a shred of habitual arrogance kept his spine from folding altogether.

"Yes?" I urged.

His eyes had gone puffy. Gravity tugged at his creased

and narrow face, making it appear pressed in from both sides.

"The stroke," he said quietly. "I have power of attorney. I shall resign on my father's behalf."

I stood, feeling no mercy. "Do it today," I said. "In writing. You know the address."

Before Letty followed me out of the room, she ran her hand along the edge of the desktop, sweeping a pen set and a pair of framed photographs to the floor.

Chapter 36

Unintentionally, I closed the cereal cabinet with a slam. "Sam Browder must have taken my eighty dollars!" I exclaimed to Rip, who stood behind me in the kitchen finishing his coffee.

It was a sunny Saturday morning in May, about three weeks after Kyle O'Callahan had resigned his father as trustee of Letty's assets. Chelsea and Rip planned another lengthy run around Valley Forge Park, reminding me once again about Chelsea's running shoe purchase—which I had not yet found a way to address. And now Sam Browder had just occurred to me as the perfect scapegoat.

"He was standing right over there by my purse when I came out of the bathroom." I gestured toward the other side of the plank table.

"You're saying Sam Browder was in our house? When?" Rip asked with a scowl.

"You were at that conference in Baltimore. I came home and found the garage door open, so I asked Sam to check the house for me." I wagged my head. "What a laugh he must have had." Particularly since he had lifted the garage door opener from my car and stolen Garry's bike himself. "I guess my wallet was too tempting to resist." I shook my head again. "And all this time I was worried that Chelsea took the money for those damned sneakers."

"Running shoes," Rip corrected me, but I noticed that he looked acutely uncomfortable when he said it.

"What?" I prompted. Then I realized why he was squirming.

"You?" I said. "You snitched the eighty bucks?"

"Guilty," Rip admitted. "I forgot to get petty cash from Joanne before I left. Sorry. Next time I promise to leave an I.O.U."

"You better," I said with a crooked smile. "You have no idea how many times I almost accused our daughter."

Yet relieved as I was, I still didn't know how Chelsea could have afforded the shoes.

Rip responded to my puzzlement. "I thought she said she earned it baby-sitting."

"That is what she said. But I can't remember her having any jobs that big."

Rip crossed his arms and stared at the refrigerator. "Didn't she stay overnight at the Rogers' when they went down to Annapolis for sailing school?"

"You're right," I said gleefully, grabbing his arms. "I completely forgot. Thank you."

"Anything to make you happy," he replied with a devilish smile. "Say, why don't you come along with us this morning? Garry's using the new bike, but I'm sure he'll let you use the old one."

"No thanks," I declined with a shudder. Rip knew that ever since the police had found the stolen bike in Sam Browder's basement, I couldn't stand the sight of it. My ad to sell the thing was scheduled to appear in the local paper that week.

"Okay," he conceded with mock regret, "but the next time you lecture me on family unity I'm going to remember this."

I spread some marmalade on a last scrap of English muffin. "When I exert myself," I said, "I want something to show for it." I put the bite of muffin in my mouth.

"Pragmatist."

"Masochist."

Rip patted me on the rump and followed after the children, who had just thundered past us out the front door. "Have fun planting your flowers."

"How did you . . . ?" I wondered aloud after Rip was gone. Then I realized I was wearing my oldest sneakers, my most derelict pair of jeans and one of Rip's T-shirts that had shrunk. Gardening clothes.

An hour and a half later I looked up from planting my forty-eighth and final white impatiens to notice a colorful blur through the trees. Letty was on her way to the lawn chairs in her kitchen garden. I straightened up from my crouched position, jiggled my muscles back into place and wandered over. Recently Garry had been seeing more of Letty than I.

Of course there was a reason for that, which I had learned only a few days before.

"You smuggling cookies next door, or what?" I asked my son as he started for Letty's with a loaded backpack for the third time that week. I had taken our neighbor grocery shopping twice since her financial status had improved, so I knew she hadn't completely broken the junk food habit.

Addressing my motherly stare, Garry sighed and temporarily swung his heavy backpack to the floor. "Promise you won't say anything. It's a secret," he said, a secret he yearned to share. His face was getting older, wiser, and more devious every day; but despite his many sessions with Letty, he still wasn't very good at poker.

"I promise. What's going on?"

Garry's lips compressed in a phoney you're-forcing-this-out-of-me reprimand. "I'm teaching her to read. Okay?"

My mouth dropped open. Words failed me. Leave it to an ingenuous eleven-year-old to break through the pride, the years of deflection and self-doubt and just plain get the job done.

Lamely, I asked if they still played poker, too.

"Of course."

To his amazement I handed him a new box of chocolate cupcakes to take along. He was growing again; there was no way they would spoil his dinner.

"This Garry's chair?" I asked Letty when I got to her yard.

"Not a bit o' it. 'Tis all your'n."

Except for the rubbish pile and its inhabitants, which were gone, the kitchen garden was the same—waist-high weeds, new and old, fallen branches, a path leading through the crumbled stone arch toward the butcher shop.

"Beautiful, i'n' it?" its owner remarked with a contented smile.

Letty still wore the black-rimmed glasses with the temporary prescription, and one of the jellybean-colored sweat suits she bought at KMart that were probably giving Wendy and Nelson Shannahan hives. Today's choice was an incredible flamingo pink.

"Lovely," I agreed, thinking more of the weather than the view.

"Did you like Norman's financial planner?" I asked after a silence. At our request, Demig had recommended a firm with impeccable credentials for managing Letty's money. Then he, not I, had accompanied her to the initial meeting. With each new decision Letty regained more and more of her old confidence. Soon she would use buses to get around, or maybe even taxis. We would say "hi" at the mailbox, visit each other at holidays.

"Nice and quiet," I remarked, having realized that the contractor who was shoring up the front of Letty's house and replacing the roof was done hammering for the weekend.

"Aye. That's how come I'm visitin' wid me friends."

Since I had just arrived alone and uninvited, she didn't mean me. "Who are these friends?" I finally asked. "Why don't I ever see them?"

"Mebbe you never look," Letty said with a twinkle in her eye. "There's one over there."

"What? Where?"

"There," Letty whispered, pointing to a spot under a bush fifteen feet away. "There's me friend Tony."

"Tony who?" I asked.

"Mum called them towhees, but when I was little I called 'em Tonys."

"What are you talking about—the bird?"

"Aye. Me little friend."

I sat up straighter and squinted into the shadows under the distant bush. A mostly black bird two-thirds the size of a robin, but with some robin red as well as bright white on its chest hopped forward and back in one single raking motion.

"That's how you tell 'im. That little scratch 'e does."

I nodded silently, not wanting to frighten the bird away. He was exquisite, and the singular behavior suggested a personality quite his own.

"I like the little wrens best," Letty said. "Wicked tempers when you gets near a nest. Sets off quite a racket for all 'er size. But a right bonny tilt to 'er tail."

"They're your friends," I remarked incredulously.

"Aye," Letty agreed. "Pure pleasure. Nice 'n honest, too. Not like some I could mention." She tilted her head more or less in the direction of the rest of the neighborhood and crinkled her nose.

Wait a minute. Had she also included me in that sweeping condemnation?

Letty shrugged her answer.

"No! Not me," I protested.

"No?" Letty's wrinkled lips pushed out in a pucker. "What about yer mum tellin' me *her* mum never knew Missus Doland?"

"So?"

Oh dear. So Letty knew I had fibbed about why I had

visited her in the hospital and brushed her hair and all the rest.

"What can I say, Letty?"

She sucked her teeth and patted my knee. "I forgive ye," she said. "Jus' don't be doin' it ag'in."